THE LONG ROAD FROM
SEQUEL TO RAGE IN PARIS

Critical Acclaim for *RAGE IN PARIS*

"A love of Paris and its people, including the poor and the crooked, comes through...as does a passion for jazz. A finely wrought story that depicts the violence of an era with a solid noir touch." -Publishers Weekly

"An intricate tale of romance, mystery and class struggle...the action unfolds at a dizzying pace...Those interested in a fast-moving account of the volatile issues in 1930s Europe will enjoy the book." - Foreword Reviews

"A raucous exercise in...historical fiction with some hard-boiled action blended...into this slam-bang vaudeville revue of mayhem, murder and cross-racial mischief "- Kirkus Reviews

"A stunning debut novel resplendent with history, jazz, mystery and flat-out farce. This novel is perfect for fans of Nathanael West, Dashiell Hammett and of the "Lost Generation" of American writers in Paris such as Ernest Hemingway and F. Scott Fitzgerald."- Bill Henderson, Pushcart Press

THE LONG ROAD FROM PARIS IS THE SEQUEL TO RAGE IN PARIS

Critical Acclaim for *RAGE IN PARIS*

THE LONG ROAD FROM PARIS

a novel

KIRBY WILLIAMS

ISBN 978-1-888889-94-9

Published by Pushcart Press
P.O. Box 380
Wainscott, New York 11975

Distributed by W.W. Norton Co.
500 Fifth Avenue
New York, New York 10110

This is a work of fiction comprising historically factual events, as well as historical events which have been fictionalized. All names, characters, institutions, places and incidents mentioned in this novel either are the product of the author's imagination or are used for the purposes of creating a work of fiction. Any resemblance to actual persons, living or dead, or to events, institutions or locales is entirely coincidental.

PRINTED IN THE UNITED STATES OF AMERICA

Note to the Reader

The novel includes a number of terms relating to African-American ethnicity which were in wide use in the period (from 1895-1946) in which the novel is set, but may be unfamiliar to today's reader. For example, the term "African-American" had not yet been conceived. "Colored" was considered a polite term for referring to African-Americans and did not bear the derogatory connotations associated with it by some today.

Similarly, a number of terms for ethnicity used in the context of the novel's time period may be unfamiliar to the present day reader. These include:

"mulatto"(for a person of half-African and half[white]European ancestry);

"quadroon"(for a person of one-fourth African and three quarters[white]European ancestry); and

"octoroon" (for a person of one-eighth African and seven-eighths [white]European ancestry).

Note to the Reader

To Liz

"There's a man going 'round taking names
There's a man going 'round taking names
He's been taking my father's name
an' he left my heart in vain
there's a man going 'round taking names

There's a man going 'round taking names
There's a man going 'round taking names
He's been taking my mother's name
an' he left my heart in vain
there's a man going 'round taking names

There's a man going 'round taking names
There's a man going 'round taking names
He's been taking my sister's name
an' he left my heart in vain
there's a man going 'round taking names

There's a man going 'round taking names
There's a man going 'round taking names
He's been taking my brother's name
an' he left my heart in vain
there's a man going 'round taking names"

Negro Spiritual

Part I

PART 1

Chapter 1

<u>Mardi Gras Day, New Orleans, Louisiana, February 28, 1911</u>

I don't know if it was because Mardi Gras fell on the last day of February and the weather was so warm that people were talking about a topsy-turvy city on the verge of Summer before we even had a Spring. Maybe the heat deranged my brain and made me do what I wanted to do more than anything in the world: play clarinet in one of the street bands, marching with the colored carnival Krewes gallivanting around in their flashy Indian outfits.

So I decided to disobey the Eleventh Commandment that Father Gohegan, the head of the Saint Vincent's Colored Waifs' Home for Boys, had ordered us to follow on pain of expulsion: NO COLORED WAIFS SHALL LEAVE THE HOME DURING MARDI GRAS. He added that commandment because there was always trouble waiting to come down on us during Mardi Gras. Bands of drunken white toughs were out prowling the streets, spoiling for a fight. If any white folks made up a story that we'd beaten or robbed them, gangs of armed vigilantes and police would vent their rage on as many of us as they could, with whippings, lynchings, and church burnings. It was worse than The Slavery, some old folks told us. Father Gohegan came down really hard on waifs like me or Louis "Strawberry" Armstrong, who were lead musicians in the famous Waifs' Home Marching and Ragtime Band.

I didn't make a habit of disobeying Father Gohegan be-cause I owed everything I was to him. He'd found me on the front steps of the Waifs' Home in a Moses basket when I was a few hours old, on July 4, 1895. He'd told me that, because I was a newborn baby, he should have turned me over to the authorities. Instead, he'd decided to keep me and call on a succession of devout Catholic colored women to add caring for me to their housekeeping duties in the Home. They mostly took charge of me until I was five years old and he'd taken me in tow himself after that. When I first started questioning him about my parents, he'd said that I was the product of the mating of a quadroon woman named Josephine Dubois and a white Frenchman.

Father Gohegan later told me he'd named me Urby Brown be-cause it was similar to the Frenchman's name. The man had scuttled back to France when he learned that I was inside Josephine's belly. I kept asking Father Gohegan what the Frenchman's name was, but he'd never give it to me. What he did tell me, when I was older, was that my mother was a sinful woman, a prostitute from that "den of vice and iniquity" called the District and later, Storyville.

On July 4, 1913, the day of my eighteenth birthday and the next to last day of Father Gohegan's life, he revealed more of my story to me:

Josephine Dubois had committed suicide about a week after I was born because Father Gohegan had turned down her re-peated pleas to write to the Frenchman asking him to take me to Paris and raise me. Tears streaming down his face, Father Gohegan told me he'd refused because of his own prejudices. Her suicide changed all of that for him and he sent a heap of letters to the Frenchman begging him to come for me, he said. He never received a reply.

I was fifteen going on sixteen when I disobeyed Father Gohegan's Eleventh Commandment. Like Strawberry Armstrong and a few others in the Waifs' Home band, I wanted to get out into the world and make some fast money on the riverboats plying the Mississippi River and Lake Pontchartrain. When we'd stashed away enough money, we dreamed of buying our own instruments and high-tailing it out of the Home. We wanted to try our luck with the new "jass" thing, later called jazz, because we were tired of playing the Waifs' Home Band's old-fashioned marching and ragtime music.

Everyone knew that if we left the Home before Father Gohegan decided we were ready to go, he'd throw us out. He warned us that he had no choice because politicians kept rabble-rousing about the Home being a refuge for black scum from the Battlefield, the most dangerous neighborhood in New Orleans. The only thing it was training us for was to play jungle music in the bordellos of New Orleans, they jeered. The New Orleans bigwigs wanted us to be shipped back to the Battlefield, uneducated for anything, to face a future of drugs, crime and violent death. They wanted the police or the National Guard to keep us fenced in there or somewhere like Angola, the Louisiana State Penitentiary. The dignitaries licked their lips at the thought of us breaking rocks with sledgehammers in the baking sun, instead of playing music in fancy bordellos where we might "glimpse the naked flesh of white women."

⅄

Strawberry Armstrong and I crept out of the Waifs' Home right after morning roll call. We ate a breakfast of yesterday's hominy grits smothered in blackstrap molasses under the watchful eye of Father Gohegan who sat at the head of the long pecan wood "eating table." When the Father rang his handbell to signal that all thirty waifs could rise and file out, Strawberry and I figured we could make it back to our cells before lunchtime roll call. We knew that we could outsmart Buster Thigpen, Father Gohegan's slow-witted quadroon "whip boy" to make our getaway. His brain only fired up when he was working out the drum rudiments he was fixing to diddle and paradiddle on Sunday with the Marching and Ragtime band. Slow-brained though he was, everyone agreed that he was the best drummer in the Home. Give old Buster two drumsticks and he could set a zombie to high-stepping and juking just by rapping out rhythms on his wooden bunk. Our bunks, like his, were covered with arrow-pierced hearts and messages of love, hate and faith carved out by the white convicts who'd occupied them until the faubourg prison became Saint Vincent's Colored Waifs' Home in the 1880s. On full moon nights, some waifs swore they could hear the ghosts of those white inmates talking in strange tongues.

Strawberry and I were wearing our shirts with "Saint Vincent's Colored Waifs' Home" printed on the back when we stepped up into a streetcar to ride to the French Quarter. I told Strawberry that we should turn our shirts inside out, so nobody would report to Father Gohegan that two of his waifs were lollygagging around in the Mardi Gras parade. But Strawberry told me that if we didn't have our color branded on our backs, I'd look like the rest of the white folks and he, only ten years old, feared that he'd be left to face them alone.

We were lounging in the colored section at the rear of the streetcar on its wooden benches. The colored section was defined by seats on either side of the aisle with a race card on the back which read "For Colored Patrons ONLY." The race cards could be removed and placed on seats further back if white folks needed more room.

Strawberry and I saw an old white man with long grey hair falling to his shoulders from his fancy straw hat. He was puffing on a corncob pipe and reading the "Picayune." We snuck quick glances at white womenfolk gliding along the streets in their finery, twirling brightly colored parasols to protect their pale skins from even the faintest darkening.

A lot of the white folks in the streetcar were fanning themselves. The colored folks just sweated inside their starchy clothes, their hands in their laps, trying to look cool so as not to let the whites know how much they too were suffering from the heat.

Some of the colored passengers were looking askance at me, as if they thought that I was a lazy white boy, pretending to be colored to take up some of the limited seating space available to them in public transportation. That space had been shrinking ever since New Orleans brought in Jim Crow laws on the street-cars about ten years ago, people told me.

Strawberry and I played a game whenever we had time and idle hands. We fingered invisible keys of the horns we played in the Waifs' Home band. Knowing what sounds our fingerings would make, we duelled in silence, trying to fake each other out with tricky chord changes.

We saw two spiffy mulatto girls carrying spanking new musical instruments. They were pretending to ignore our mummery. The other colored passengers were feigning that we were invisible too. I reckoned they were afraid that the white passengers, some now turning their heads to eye us, would think that they were crazy too.

One of the girls, who was about Strawberry's age, had wiry red hair, buck teeth and freckles all over her face. She was holding a gleaming cornet. The other was a beautiful pale-skinned girl of sixteen or so with straight black hair like Pocahontas cascading down the back of her yellow dress. It matched the color of her cat-like eyes. She was cradling a brand new shiny clarinet in her arms and I wanted it. I jabbed Strawberry in the ribs and whispered,

"I take clarinet girl's bone, you take red's cornet." He looked at the younger girl and whispered back, angrily,

"I ain't wastin' no time on that buck-tooth girl even for no cornet."

"She's got your horn, ain't she?" I asked. Nodding my head toward the other girl, I whispered, "I'd tear that pretty one limb from limb to get at her clarinet." He sighed like a lost soul and stepped over to the redhead, who wasn't studying him. He bowed deeply to her and to her beautiful companion like a tuxedoed beau at a cotillion. In a mincing voice he asked,

"Would y'all lend me and my friend them fine horns? For a few minutes?" The redhead looked dubiously at her companion who was sizing me up out of the corner of her eyes.

"Cousin Monique?" the redhead asked. Monique nodded regally, and said,

"I suppose it's all right, Daphné. After all, they can't run off with our instruments in a moving streetcar." That got them giggling behind their lace-gloved hands.

As soon as we had their horns, I stood up and started stomping my right foot, firing up to the downbeat. Some white passengers turned around to look at us and then sat bolt upright when Strawberry and I went striding out in a duet on the gospel song "Deep River." We toyed with the music, improvising on it as we played. The mulatto girls' mouths swung open like picket fences. I reckoned they'd never heard musicians play like us before. What they were all listening to was jazz and it was making strange sounds in their horns.

A few of the colored passengers bobbed and swayed when they recognized a gospel song before Strawberry and I turned it inside out. Most of the others looked worried that the mood of the white passengers could turn to anger at the sounds they heard.

I saw the old white man with the "Picayune" knock tobacco from his pipe onto the floor and fold his newspaper. He reached into his pocket for his wallet. He pulled some folding money and a white card out of it, got up and made his way to the back to the colored section. He made a little bow and solemnly handed Strawberry and me a dollar each. He passed me the white card, carefully avoiding touching me.

"Have somebody read out that address to you, boy. Be there at 3 p.m. There may be a lot more money for you if you can keep up with the men." He bent down and whispered to me, nodding towards Strawberry, "Don't bring that tar baby with you."

He returned to his seat, unfolded his newspaper, and resumed reading. Strawberry and I pocketed our dollars. I waved off Strawberry's questions about the card and put it in my pants pocket to read when I was alone.

Strawberry and I gave the girls their horns and bowed and scraped thanking them. The colored passengers shrank away from us and started getting off at the next stops, which did not look like places they came from or should be going to. I looked through the rear window and saw that most of them were standing at the streetcar stop, waiting for the next one.

The two mulatto girls signalled for the conductor to stop and headed toward the exit. They both stuck their chins in the air, pretending they'd been unmoved by our music, but the beautiful Monique dropped her pose for an instant to eye me again. I smiled at her and said,

"Thank you, Cousin Monique." She didn't smile back at me.

When we got down from the streetcar, we followed the blaring music leading us toward Jackson Square and the Mississippi River. People flowed by us, some staring at the words on our shirts. Others had their foreheads scrunched up as they deciphered what was written on our backs. The faces of most of the white people we passed went red with anger at seeing us. They thought they were seeing a young white man with his arm draped over a "nigger's" shoulders, I reckoned. Maybe they were thinking I was a "traitor to the white race" like the hated Abraham Lincoln.

A group of five tough-looking white boys in ragamuffin duds with sharpened sticks in their hands started closing in on us. I nudged Strawberry.

"We was wrong to leave the Home. Let's get back fast," I said.

A small white boy picked up a rock and hurled it at us, just missing my head. Then his older companions picked up rocks and one of them said,

"Let's stone 'em and strip 'em buck naked. Leave Whitey to me!"

We took off like greyhounds and kept sprinting hard until they fell far behind and gave up. We jogged through back alleys until we found our streetcar stop and stepped up into one heading back to Gentilly and the Home. We would be there well before roll call. And we had some silent money to add to our stashes.

ᴧ

Printed on the card which the streetcar passenger had passed me were the words "Colonel Rexford J. de Lancy, Colonel, C.S.A. (Retired)." He'd written "Come to Madame Lala's Mahogany House at 3 p.m." with fine penmanship. I knew that Madame Lala's was a bordello in Storyville, a place that I'd best not go near. But the Mahogany House was legendary because the greatest jazz musicians passed through it. Even gates who'd left New Orleans for Chicago or Harlem came back to play there, because its ragtime and jazz music were non pareil.

I knew I was tempting fate when I asked Strawberry to cover for me when I snuck off after lunch. Despite his bitter words and reproaches, I refused to tell him where I was going.

ᴧ

I had a feeling that the fates had more twists in store for me on that Mardi Gras day in 1911. I'd already met Colonel de Lancy who'd given me a card inviting me to play the clarinet at the Mahogany House for a chance at some serious money. What was next? I wondered as I ran to Madame Lala's to arrive there at 3 p.m. sharp. I walked up the steps. They fronted a fairy tale castle. There were angels and cupids carved into the white stucco surrounding the door. A high yellow woman with a mouth full of gold teeth opened up for me. I'll never forget the aromas that exploded from inside; I was in a paradise garden, its air thick with the remembered scent of magnolias and roses. The woman turned me around and ran her hands over me like I was a prize-winning show horse.

"Who are you, sir?" she asked in a flutelike voice. Before I could answer she said, " Come on ladies, take a look at this young sprout pretendin' to Madame Lala he be a sportin' man."

I heard the hissing of cloth and then a group of girls gathered behind her, their skin colors varying from pale white to the milky café au lait hue of quadroon girls I reckoned she passed off as octoroons. They were wearing light dresses so open at the front that I could feast my eyes on their naked breasts and thighs and woman parts. Seeing my wide-eyed stares, Madame Lala's face burst into a grin which gaped open her dark red-painted lips to reveal tiny gold ingots. The girls crowding behind her tittered and fixed their eyes on my crotch. Madame Lala was giving me a thorough inspection, her eyes searching me to make sure that I was "alright," meaning "white."

"My name's Urby Brown," I said, my voice breaking. I draped a hand over my hardening Johnson to shield it from their staring, calculating eyes. That really set Madame Lala and her girls to laughing and slapping their thighs. I must have blushed, making me more of a laughing stock. I cocked my ears when I heard a

piano playing inside the maison. I heard the same music with its sashaying style wailing from player pianos in bars I passed on Rampart Street. Was it a player piano or Jelly Roll Morton himself playing his "King Porter Stomp?"

Suddenly a gigantic white dog appeared from behind Madame Lala's silky pink gown. The canine stared at me like I was nothing but a future meal then stalked over to sniff at my clothes and my hand and my crotch. Nothing scared me more than dogs, especially ones the size of the albino monster staring me down. His chops yawned open to expose yellowed fangs and a scaly pink tongue. Then he licked my hand and panted, his blood-shot eyes still fixed on mine. When he wagged his tail slowly, Madame Lala loosened her grip on his studded collar.

"Ease up, Alonzo," Madame Lala said, casting a friendly look my way. She smiled and extended a bejewelled hand as if expecting me to kiss my way through all the rings and shiny geegaws on it.

"Mr. Urby Brown, I'm Madame Laurence Thigpen de Lavallade and this dwelling is Mahogany House. Entrez!" The girls yanked me into Madame Lala's parlor, rubbing their nipples against my arm and licking their lips as they passed me along from one to the other like I was a warm, sweet yam.

"Don't do that," I said to a pretty, baby-faced white girl. She wasn't more than fourteen years old, but she'd landed a knowing hand right on top of old Johnson.

"Stop that Blanche," Madame Lala scolded her. "If Mr. Urby Brown want you, you'll have plenty of time to play with him later." The girl child plumped down on a plush sofa, sucking her thumb and swinging her thin pink legs.

"What brings you here, Mr. Urby Brown? You kind of young to be a sportin' man. Lala expect you be the son of some wealthy folk come here to sow you some wild oats? You do got cash money sir?"

"No m'am," I said. "I come here to make me some cash money." Madame Lala looked at me as if she hadn't heard right.

"Whazat?" She sputtered. "You don't look like no pimp, and if you is I'm gone sic Alonzo on you." When the dog's ears fetched up the tone of her voice, it roared at me, baring all its teeth.

"Where you from you ain't got no money?" she shouted, loosening her grip on Alonzo.

"I'm from here and there," I answered, my legs turning to jelly.

"'Here and there' ain't no place in New Orleans I knows of. Where you live at, sir?" I made up an address in the Battlefield. She touched my hand and when I didn't flinch she whispered in my ear,

"You colored?" I nodded Yes. Suddenly frightened, her whisper went quieter.

"Lord have mercy, boy, you better get yo' ass gone real quick. You tryin' to get me lynched?" Alonzo started barking furiously, his eyes flaming up like coals in a fiery furnace. It took all of Madame Lala's heft and strength to keep him from pouncing on me for a killer bite to the throat. All of Madame Lala's girls shrank back as if I was a leper or something worse. The piano music stopped.

"Y'all don't come through the front door of Madame Lala's house!" she rasped in a whisper only I could hear. "You git or I'm really gone let Alonzo sink his teeths into you." She and Alonzo backed me toward the front door.

I took out Colonel de Lancy's card and managed to pass it to her a split second before Alonzo could gnaw my hand to the bone. Madame Lala fetched up pince-nez eye lenses from her cleavage and twisted the card this way and that to catch a ray of light. She read it, turned to the frightened girls huddling together and called out,

"Old Colonel de Lancy done sent him." I could hear sighs of relief.

"You must be good, Urby Brown, if the Colonel carded you. What you play, boy?"

"Clarinet," I answered.

The piano started up again. When I'd been in the parlor, I'd noticed that it was a gilded upright, but I couldn't see the piano player. If it was Jelly Roll Morton cuddling those 88s, I'd recognize him from the portraits of him I'd seen on posters. Madame Lala frowned at my best Waifs' Home Band Sunday duds and said,

"You go round to the back door and Isabelle gone let you in. That be for colored musicians and delivery folk to come into Mahogany House. Isabelle!" Hearing her name, a tiny, near-white girl joined us at the door. Madame Lala put on a baby-talk voice to tell her,

"Sweetie pie, you make sure Urby Brown dress up nice." She turned to me and, as if giving me orders, barked out,

"You pick yourself a clarinet from the music room! There gone be lots of notables here to start on their Mardi Gras so you got to sharpen up!" When Madame Lala had marched off, I asked Isabelle,

"You an octoroon like me?" She nodded Yes and then led me down a long hallway. Her pink silk negligée split open in back from time to time as she glided along, flashing her pale, naked behind. She opened the door of a room filled with men's clothing.

"Take what you need," she said. I'd never worn a suit or jacket before or a fancy shirt or tie. Isabelle saw my confusion and asked, happily,

"Y'all don't know how to dress like a real man got money? I'll do it, I like dressin' mens up, me." Isabelle started stripping me down and then rested her hand on my waist and said,

14

"You skittish, boy. You want me to calm you down? Don't worry, Madame Lala need know nothin' about it. This be for free."

She started unbuttoning my fly and I stopped her.

"Let's you and me do that later, girl. Help me put on these here duds now." Little Isabelle dressed me, pressing her soft body against me all the while and she felt so good that I didn't want to leave her. But Colonel de Lancy had said that I could make me a heap of cash money in this place and I needed that more than anything Isabelle could give me.

"How come your Madame Lala got that albino dog Alonzo runnin' around? He here to protect y'all?" Isabelle laughed.

"He here to protect us from niggers. Madame Lala trained him up as a 'Jim Crow dog' and he only bite colored mens. That way the white mens come in here knows this be a clean house. They won't close us down and likely stretch Madame Lala's neck. Most time, old Alonzo can sniff him out a nigger from a mile away, but you sure fooled him."

"Don't keep saying 'nigger!'" I shouted, enraged at hearing those words coming from the mouth of this sweet-looking girl. "Ain't you got no race pride?"

"Thems be Madame Lala words, not mines."

She was close to tears. I kissed her and she smiled, my anger forgotten.

Isabelle led me up the backstairs into the darkened living room, which was beginning to fill up with white men. In the roped off section where the musicians played, I saw a dapper caramel brown-skinned man over by the piano, making a cricket laugh in his throat as he talked to the pianist. He was holding a gold-colored clarinet and sporting an all white suit and gleaming black and white two tone shoes set off by white spats. I recognized the man as Stanley Bontemps from posters I'd seen.

I reckoned that most colored and white folks in New Orleans knew who Stanley Bontemps was. He was the best clarinetist in town. Piano rolls of his ragtime music and marches sold like hotcakes all over the city. A cornet player strode up to Stanley Bontemps and shook his hand. He was the great King Oliver.

Madame Lala spotted me and came bustling toward us, followed by her laughing girls. They'd changed into fancy gowns in gaudy colors and put on carnival makeup. Madame Lala looked me up and down, nodding her approval.

"Urby Brown, I want y'all to meet the musicianers you be playin' with when the city council come in. Y'all gots to make do with just you four. The white folks don't want to hear no drummers or kazoo or paper and comb players in here, 'cause they says that ain't civilized instrumentation." King Oliver stabbed out a laugh and hissed lingeringly, Sheeeeeeiiiittt."

My legs turned to jelly again as I shook hands with Stanley Bontemps. He stared at me hard and then smiled and said,

"Hello, son." His voice dripped honey. It sounded like his clarinet.

He kept eyeing me and then whispered something to Madame Lala who looked surprised and then nodded Yes. I held out my hand to the King, who slapped my palm angrily and went back to blowing spit out of his cornet's mouthpiece. He was a hard man you wouldn't want to mess with. He smeared some salve on his lips and then started warming up. Finally, I turned the corner of the upright and saw Jelly Roll Morton smiling at me. He stopped playing the "King Porter Stomp" and pumped my hand with his ring-covered fingers.

"Stanley, this be the boy old Colonel de Lancy say you best keep your eyes on. He say this youngster can blow him up a storm on the clair'net." Stanley took his eyes off my face to look

at the battered horn that I'd picked out from the instruments in Madame Lala's music room. It was the best-looking horn there but it had seen better days. Stanley chuckled, saying,

"You ain't gone play that raggedy bone, yo' first time in the Mahogany. Give it to me, son. You play my clarinet. She all clean and ready to rip. All you gots to do is blow."

Just like that, Stanley handed me his horn. I ran my hands over it. I'd never held anything as beautiful. Stanley laughed.

"Just do like this, son," he said. He held Madame Lala's battered clarinet up to his lips and mimed playing it.

The white bigwigs were filing in and Madame Lala was greeting them with a curtsey and handing out carnival masks. I recognized the mayor and the police chief, before they donned their masks. I'd played gigs before them with the band from the same Waifs' Home they were clamoring to shut down.

The girls were bringing up armchairs and setting them in rows in front of the cordoned-off area where we players were. Alonzo the Jim Crow dog was stationed next to our cordon, his leash tied tightly to a black lawn jockey. The King was the darkest-skinned man in the room. Alonzo kept barking at him so loudly that Madame Lala finally muzzled the beast. The politicians were slipping their hands inside the girls' gowns and laughing when the frails swatted them away, giggling invitingly. The men guffawed and grabbed at tits and jammed the girls' hands onto their Peters.

"Rub it, cher, it won't bite you," I heard the Mayor say to Isabelle.

King Oliver was blowing mean riffs, improvising on the "King Porter Stomp." He and Stanley and Jelly Roll were making new music out of stiff old rags. Jelly Roll was striding through it with elaborate runs and rills. Stanley was working magic with Madame Lala's battered clarinet, wagging it at me to get me playing. Finally, I put Stanley's clarinet to my lips and almost stopped at once, surprised by the beauty of the sound coming out of it. I'd never played any clarinet like it before.

I knew every note of Jelly Roll Morton's "King Porter Stomp," but with Stanley's clarinet in my hands, I started reshaping the music by throwing in riffs that I didn't know I had inside me. I closed my eyes and I could see colors and pictures and lights exploding inside my head like Mardi Gras fireworks and my ears shut out the racket that the white men and the girls were making. I could hear only Jelly Roll, the King and Stanley. We were breaking off the shackles of ragtime and grooving into jazz playing behind Jelly Roll. All we needed was a hot drummer and we'd turn Madame Lala's into mahogany toothpicks.

We were all wailing through King Porter and the big shots had settled back to puff on their cigars and listen. Jelly Roll and the King stopped playing to hear Stanley and me go at it. We started improvising, "bucking," in a clarinet battle, feinting at each other like colored bare-knuckle fighters trying to land haymakers in a battle royal. There were rebel yells and applause as Stanley and I raced through chorus after chorus, flinging every trick we had up our sleeves at each other. I heard coins bouncing near our feet and ricocheting off the piano. Somebody shouted,

"Gents, I'm goin' to wager fifty dollars on the light-skinned boy beatin' out old Stanley."

"Cover that and raise you fifty," another man called out. I could hear the swish swish of paper money coming out of pockets and looked up to see Madame Lala's girls flouncing around, fetching the bettors' stakes.

Stanley and I were really going at it hammer and tongs and I was beginning to feel groggy. I was running out of ammunition. I snuck a look at him; he was just getting warmed up. King Oliver had sat down next to Jelly Roll Morton and they were wagering too, cracking up at what they were whispering to each other. Stanley kept smiling at me, urging me to go on. But I was tuckered out and beaten and I started lagging behind Stanley as he kept up a torrent of riffs and runs on King Porter. That's when I heard change jingling and Jelly Roll's barking laugh. I looked up to see him collecting money from King Oliver, who looked at me, the whites of his eyes bloody, then snatched his cornet from the top of the piano to join in the final crescendo.

There was loud clapping and whistling and then the masked men started trooping off to the rooms with the girls they'd chosen. One of the men came over to me and patted me daintily on my clothed arm, as if he wished he had gloves on to provide another layer of protection. He slipped me a five dollar bill and, pointing to the money around Jelly Roll's piano, said,

"I told you you'd make yourself money you come here. You're good with that clarinet, boy. Real good. Stay out of trouble and you'll go a long way." I recognized the man's voice as Colonel de Lancy's.

Madame Lala and Jelly Roll kept beady eyes on the girls picking up the money that had landed around us. After they carried it to Madame Lala, she counted it and then announced,

"One hundred and fifty dollars and seventy-five cents. Y'all split it up any which way you likes." Turning to Jelly Roll, she said,

"Professor, be generous to Urby Brown. He done put up a good fight, but Stanley still the boss. Urby, you come by my office next the music room before you steps out." She handed the money over to Jelly Roll, unmuzzled Alonzo and headed up the stairs, leaving the hound, still hitched to Jocko, to keep his burning eyes on us. Jelly Roll riffled off a bunch of banknotes and said,

"I done compose King Porter, so I reckon I gets the lion's share. Y'all fine with that?" Stanley and the King nodded and Jelly Roll pocketed a bunch of dollar bills.

"That leaves ninety dollars and change for y'all to split. Me, I'm goin' to go do me some sportin' in this town." He handed the rest of the money to Stanley and swaggered towards the back door without looking back. Stanley patted the King on the shoulder and said,

"You take forty, King, you deservin' of it." The King frowned and grabbed the dollars. From the rumors I'd heard, he wasn't likely to be spending the money on a woman these days. He was too busy inventing new music on his cornet. King Oliver, with a hate-filled backward glance at Alonzo, left me alone with Stanley.

With the King's share gone, there were just fifty dollars and change left in the pot. Stanley held five tens in his hand. He handed two of them to me and took three of them and the change for himself. I was amazed, expecting five dollars at most.

"That's a fair split, son. I just edged you out," he said. "But you Claudette's boy and..." That came crashing down on me like a tidal wave.

"My mama named Josephine Dubois. Who be Claudette?"

Stanley looked nervous as he said,

"She were a fine Yankee lady, real name be Mary somethin' and her luck done ran out in this town. She play the piano and read music and all. Can you read music, son?"

"Yes, Father Gohegan taught me to."

"Well, whenever I be at Mahogany with Jelly Roll or King Oliver or whoever, Mary sit me down at that there piano and try drummin' that music readin' upside my head. But I ain't got the gift of readin' nothin' 'cept numbers. Madame Lala, she done shoo that Claudette away from me, 'cause she be scared her white girls gossip to the big shots that colored mens be sittin' next to white womens in here." He peered at my face, as if seeing something else in it. Then he said, "I known your mama Josephine Dubois 'cause she work here the same time as Claudette and I sometime mixes them up inside my head. I must be gettin' old." He looked relieved when I said,

"That happen to everybody sooner or later, I reckon." He went on,

"Your mama deservin' of better than what life done thrown her way. She and Claudette was so much like sisters your mama even started puttin' on airs like she be a white girl from up North like Claudette though she be from our own Battlefield. They was so tight they give birth on the same day. You was born right here in the Mahogany House." That rocked me back on my heels. I knew my mother was a fancy woman, but I never knew where I was born.

"Did you ever get any jelly roll off of my mama? I mean out in town." It was Stanley's turn to look shocked.

"Shame on you, son! Don't you never talk about your mama like that, it ain't righteous. They was hard times for our people back then, even harder than now. Josephine tell me she only be with one man before comin' to Mahogany, that no account brother of Madame Lala. After he bring her to Mahogany she stick to white mens. She done her best to stay alive, you better believe it." I still felt he was leaving something out of his story, but just said,

"Thank you for letting me play your clarinet, sir."

"You call me Stanley from now on, not 'sir' or 'Mister,' hear?" he said. "You so good I reckon you can call me Stanley any time you likes. If you in for it, I show you a few tricks 'bout jass which be fixin' to kill off the ragtime. But there ain't much I can teach you, 'cause the Good Lord done gifted you, like He done me. I'm gone give you my clarinet, soon's I feel I can't blow it good as you." I knew that I had to snap up Stanley's offer before he changed his mind.

"I'd sure love you to show me them clarinet tricks, Stanley."

"That's what I wants to hear you say. Still, I must be crazy as a hoot owl, son. I'm gone use this money we just make here to buy me a soprano sax in case I gots to give you my clarinet real soon."

We arranged to meet two days later at the riverboat dock on Lake Pontchartrain for the first lesson. I told him I could get away after roll call at around two in the afternoon and we shook on it.

"I'm gone like a cool breeze," he said, getting ready to leave. "I got me some playin' to do for the colored carnival Krewes. Then I got me a date on a riverboat the Gov'nor of Louisiana done rent for a party that be bound to last all night. I'm gone rake me in some big cash money today. King size money. You soon be makin' you some heavy change too. Somethin' tell me we gone be tight, maybe partnerin' up some day."

I couldn't believe what Stanley Bontemps was saying to me. I wasn't sixteen years old yet, I was nothing and nobody, and he was famous. He was talking about being my friend, even my partner. About me making big money and him giving me his clarinet when I outplayed him. I stammered thank you and then Stanley took his clarinet back from me, placed it carefully in a plain leather case and left, escorted out of the back door by Madame Lala herself.

She came back to me, untied Alonzo and grasped his collar with all her might. She led me to her office in the basement and sat down behind a desk covered with little statues of the Virgin Mary alone or with Baby Jesus copping a little slumber in her arms. She tied Alonzo to her desk on a short leash.

"You one fine-lookin' buck and you sure knows how to blow that bone," she said. "But, no musician never be great, les'n he know somethin' about womenfolk. You ever been with a girl, Urby Brown?" I blushed all over and she said,

"I can't let you sport with any of my octoroon girls 'cause they reserved for the white mens come here. But I give you the address of my cousin, Charlotte, live over by South Rampart and Perdido." She wrote on a piece of paper and then handed it to me.

"My Charlotte gone treat you right. I used to sneak her into the Mahogany for gents with special tastes for dark-skinned girls. I done blackmail them to keep they mouth shut about bein' with her. But she such a little bitty thing she like to split like a wishbone she got so many white mens jumpin' on her. You ain't got nothin' against a dark-skinned girl, has you?" I shook my head No and said,

"We all colored ain't we?"

"You ain't wrong, but some of us be darker than others, honey. It's hard to be part white like you and me 'cause both races hates us deep down. Now a dark-skinned girl like Charlotte don't trouble her head with none of that business. She just get down and pleasure you."

I paid a visit to Charlotte who lived alone in a wooden shack. After I read Madame Lala's note to her, she just took my hand and led me to a pallet laid out on a floor covered with rushes and corncobs and we went to it until we were both screaming like banshees. When I finally peeled her off me, I was a man. I had more cash in my pocket than I'd ever had before. My future was staring me straight in the face because Stanley promised to teach me to jazz.

At Madame Lala's I'd worn the Colored Waifs' Home band's black Sunday-go-to-meeting shirt turned inside out so nobody could read "Colored Waifs' Home" painted in white letters on the back. I felt bad about doing that, because there was always a voice in my ear tempting me to "pass for white" and pretend to be something that I wasn't, just another ghost wandering the streets of New Orleans. Then I'd hear Stanley's music in my head and it would set me straight and make me proud to be colored.

Ashamed of myself, I still didn't turn my shirt the right way around when I left Charlotte's shed. I didn't want my happiness spoiled by rednecks with rocks, as it had been in the morning.

I was melting into the swarms of white revelers, floating above them, watching the parade from the sky. Near Jackson Square and the Cabildo, I descended to earth and watched the spectacle while I sat on a bench.

Day turned to night and the air was filled with music and laughter and the smell of frying fish and chicken and beignets and sweat and tobacco. I walked to the Mississippi to stare at the lights blazing on the riverboats. I could hear their music floating across the water. A paddle-wheel steamer as big as Jonah's whale flared like a giant torch fixing to set the Mississippi on fire. Ragtime music blasted from it. A clarinet's sound came cakewalking across the river. I reckoned that was Stanley blowing on the Governor's boat.

The sounds of revelry and the lapping of the river drifted away and then it grew quiet and my eyelids closed. The next thing I knew, someone was shaking me awake. Morning had broken and it was already heating up. I jumped to my feet, saw a uniform and shot to attention with my thumbs digging into my thighs. Because I was wearing my Waifs' Home shirt inside out, I wasn't so afraid that the policeman would wallop me with his club the way they usually did to colored people straying outside our neighborhoods. I eased up when I saw that the policeman was Patrick Doyle. Father Gohegan had sent him out to fetch me back to the Home a bunch of times. He just nodded to me and we got into his police wagon and he took me back to the Waifs' Home. I knew he'd hand me over to Father Gohegan. I was dreading the Father's anger at me breaking his Commandment after everything he'd done for me.

Patrick knocked on the door and waited with his head bowed respectfully. I did the same, my legs trembling so badly I thought I'd fall.

"Come in!" Father Gohegan shouted. When we walked in he was standing behind his desk in his black cassock, all smiles at the policeman, but ignoring me. I stared at the worn wooden floor. I was ready for Father Gohegan to yell at me to leave the Home and never come back. When I finally raised my head, he was looking at me as if he didn't know who I was. The policeman said,

"Good morning, Father. I found him."

"Usual place?" Father Gohegan asked.

"Yes, Father. Sitting on the same bench, looking at the same riverboats. Been sitting there all night he said."

"How's the family Patrick?"

"Fine. We miss you at mass, though. They're wasting you here, Father, if you don't mind..."

"I'm doing the Lord's work, Patrick. But sometimes it sure is hard to fathom what He has in mind." They both chuckled. Father Gohegan made the sign of the cross and the policeman crossed himself and left. I kept my head down, staring at the floor. Father Gohegan went to the door and shouted,

"Buster!" I heard the sound of bare feet slapping on the floor of the corridor and then Buster Thigpen came into the office, a smile of anticipation on his face. Father Gohegan took a leather whip out of his top drawer. Buster grabbed it eagerly, flicking it against his palm.

"Five, Buster and mind that you only whip his left hand." Buster sneered at this command and, yanking my right arm, marched me into a small room adjoining the office where punishments were meted out.

"Hold her steady, boy," Buster said. I held out my left hand and watched Buster brace himself as if he was going to swing at a fastball. He brought the whip down hard three times. He wanted to keep going, but Father Gohegan had a change of heart and he rushed into the room and pulled the whip out of Buster's hand. Buster looked surprised and then said,

"Father, if you too easy on him, he just gone run away again."

"Three's enough for now," Father Gohegan said, irritated that Buster was challenging his orders. Then he shouted,

"Go! Both of you. Urby, you run away again and I'm going to take Buster's advice." I was shocked that a whipping was the only punishment I was going to get for stepping out during Mardi Gras. Even worse, I'd spent a whole night away from the Home. Despite breaking the rules big time, I was going to stay there after all.

Buster shoved me along the corridor into the small passageway leading toward our cells. I was catching up to him in height and muscle, having put on a spurt of growth over the last few months. I felt that the time had come to put an end to Buster's bullying. I was going to kick his butt once and for all, while we were inside the Home. He wouldn't be able to call on his friends from the Battlefield to gang up on me when I stepped outdoors.

"Why you hit me so hard?" I asked, my words fanning my rage.

"Hard?" Buster asked. "Me, I got worst when I run away. I caught ten. On this here right hand, my bestest drummin' hand and on my hind parts too. Father G hisself whupped me and you got to believe that hurt. But 'cause you the Clarinet Man, he ease you up.

"You better ease me up next time, boy." He was so amazed at me talking back to him that he went silent. Then he stuck his face into mine, his yellow-green eyes full of menace.

"Me ease you up? Next time, you dead, Whitey. What you gone do then, sic yo' mama on me?" I looked away, bowed my head as if giving up, then quickly spun around and headbutted him on his breastbone so hard that he was propelled backwards and his head rebounded off the floor. He tried to stand up, then sprawled face down, unconscious, his arms and legs flopping spread eagle.

"Don't never mouth me again. I'm gone kill you, you call me Whitey again, you hear?" I screamed as I stood over him. Then I brought my foot down hard on Buster's right leg. I kept stomping on his leg until Strawberry Armstrong heard the ruckus and came racing out of his cell to drag me off him.

I remember shouting at Buster...

CHAPTER 2

"...*C all me Urby Brown, you hear!*"

"You here, Urby?" I heard Hannah ask as she opened the door while I sat at the piano scoring arrangements. She kissed me, pressing her cheek against mine.

"You're freezing," I protested, pulling her on top of me and kissing her. She stood up and doffed the funny-looking red wool cloche hat with ear flaps that she'd knitted. She took off her gloves and rubbed her hands together to warm them. Finally, she unwound her blue woollen scarf and unbundled herself from her grey tweed overcoat, revealing the sunburst of the yellow and blue floral print dress which she'd made from a pattern and fabric she'd bought for herself at the nearby Marché Saint Pierre.

"April in Paris...." she sang, mocking the lyrics as we always did.

"I'm definitely buying you fur-lined gloves for Christmas," I said.

" I sure could use some. I'll do the buying." She kissed me on the cheek and then rummaged around in the scores and sheet music on top of the piano and fished out her violin and bow. She closed her eyes for a few seconds to concentrate and then launched into Chopin's Nocturne in E flat.

It was the piece that she'd played from her window as I stood with Strawberry Armstrong and her father, Abe, the man Father Gohegan hired us out to. We were up to our ankles in the rusted machinery and scrap metal littering the Korngold's back yard in New Orleans on my eighteenth birthday, July 4, 1913.

"Chopin's Nocturne in E flat," she'd called down.

Her long black hair framed her pale, oval-shaped face as she played in the stifling heat, staring straight at me. I held her gaze an instant then looked away. Father Gohegan had warned us Colored Waifs never to hold a white person's gaze, especially a white woman's. It could get you beaten up or even lynched in New Orleans. But, from that first glance at her, hearing the beautiful music she made on an instrument I'd never listened to before, I'd fallen in love with Abe's daughter Hannah. Today, twenty-five years later, every sight and sound from that moment and the sudden love for her that flooded my heart was as present as the lingering chill from her cheek.

I remember that Hannah suddenly switched from Chopin's nocturne to "Happy Birthday to You." Abe Korngold unwrapped a gleaming clarinet from some oily rags, handed it to me and said, "Happy Birthday, Urby. Now you got your own horn, you can duet with Strawberry." Abe had given Strawberry Armstrong a cornet on his eleventh birthday, a year before. I stammered out a Thank You and Abe said,

"Stay out of trouble and you'll go a long way with that clarinet." People were always telling me that I'd go a long way if I "stayed out of trouble." But trouble had a way of finding me, whether I stayed out of its way or not. Then Abe said,

"Let's sort out this scrap boys." We all got to work flinging scrap metal, raggedy remnants of clothing and beaten up bric-à-brac into bins.

Hannah resumed playing her violin at the window and then stopped and called out,

"Bye for now. Urby, next time you come, I'd sure like to hear you play that clarinet." I loved listening to the sound of her low-pitched, teasing voice. Just hearing it made me want to pick up a clarinet and blow. Abe stared at me. I didn't look up. When I did, she was gone.

⚓

Hannah braved her family's threat that she'd be dead for them if she left America to live with me in Paris. Her mother called it "sitting shivah," Hannah said. I didn't know what that meant, but it sounded like a serious curse on Hannah. She moved in with me late in 1921. Having Hannah by my side brought me back to life after the four years I'd spent in the French Foreign Legion dodging bullets in the muddy red trenches in Northern France or as an airman in the Lafayette Flying Corps engaged in high speed shootouts with dead-eyed German pilots.

It was such a good time to be in love with Hannah and to be a jazz musician in Paris that I didn't bother to look for the Frenchman who was my natural father. Stanley and I and other colored musicians were raking in money hand over fist. The Parisians had started a love affair with jazz from the time they'd first heard it played by the all-colored 369th Infantry Regiment Military Band of the "Harlem Hell Fighters." They couldn't get enough of our music or of us. So many of us played in nightclubs in Montmartre near Place Pigalle that the area came to be known as "Harlem-in-Montmartre."

With my meager savings from fighting for France in the Foreign Legion and in the all-American volunteer Lafayette Flying Corps of the French Air Army, and using the serious dough I'd made from jazz after the war ended, Hannah and I opened our first Urby's Masked Ball in 1922. We hit the jackpot. Lines of patrons wound along the sidewalk all the way from Place Pigalle to enter our small, dingy nightclub. Only Chez Red Tops, which opened up a few blocks away in 1926 with help from Stanley and me, was more popular than our club. It owed that to the personality of its owner, my good friend Redtop. She was a lesbian mulatto redhead, who sported lavender fingernails and a smile like a sunny Spring day. She'd left Harlem to come to Paris with Josephine Baker and her Revue Nègre as a twenty-three year-old singer and dancer in 1925 and vowed never to return to America. She'd told me early on that she'd blow her head off with her shotgun if the French ever deported her to Jim Crow land.

She'd said that because some of us had been caught up in police dragnets and sent back. Under pressure from the French musicians' union, jealous of our success, the cops had started gradually enforcing a 1922 law limiting to ten percent the number of non-French musicians in a musical formation. Usually a well-aimed bribe would get the cops off our backs. But from time to time, some straight cop would squeal, usually tipped off by a musicians' union man, and someone would get a fifteen-day deportation notice returning them to America and Jim Crow.

After the onset of the Great Depression in 1929, things began to fall apart big time for Paris-based Americans as their dollars turned into funny money. Droves of them, even colored ones, lit out for "home" fearful for their futures. Economies crashed all over Europe. The French, who'd been at the top table carving up Germany after the Great War, started fighting among themselves, right versus left, haves against have-nots, as their economy, and our businesses, were sucked down into the whirlpool.

⟁

On a late March afternoon in 1932 as I lay in our bed at the Hôtel Royal Montmartre sleeping off a hangover, Hannah dumped a bucket full of chipped ice on my head. She'd pushed frilly pink panties into my face and yelled,

"Who do these belong to? They aren't mine, Urby. Are they yours?" I sobered up real fast. I wagged my head No and she slapped me across the face with them, knocking ice to the floor.

"Did you make it with her in our bed? Right here?" she asked, running an angry hand over the sheets on the right side where she slept. I couldn't remember. My last memory was autographing a playbill from the Moulin Rouge. One of its tall blonde cancan dancers asked me to sign it beginning "Chère Yvette..." She'd asked me if I'd ever been to her hometown of Lille and I said something about stopping off there during the war...the rest was a blank.

"This is the second time you've let me down." Hannah said, crying. Seeing her tears made me want to cry too, but I wasn't able to, just like some genteel women I knew weren't able to spit. I jumped out of bed and tried to embrace her but she pushed me away and took her suitcase out of the closet.

"You swore blind it wouldn't happen again." I tried to take her in my arms, to beg her for another chance. She pushed me away.

"Do you know what's going on in the world and in America while you pretend you're looking for work? Last week that fascist Henry Ford set the Dearborn, Michigan police and his own factory police on laid-off autoworkers at his plant in River Rouge. They opened fire and killed four workers and wounded loads more." It was all news to me. I only read bits of the newspapers that Hannah left around, usually the socialists' bible Le Populaire.

"Have you ever heard of the Scottsboro Boys?" she went on. "Nine colored boys falsely accused of raping two white girls jus because they were riding the rails and beat up some rednecks who attacked them? They're being railroaded towards a lynching in Alabama. Do you care about anything except running after fake blondes and boozing? You don't even practice clarinet anymore."

Hannah was so fired up that I reckoned she'd been spending a lot of time hanging out with her political friends in the Latin Quarter, now that business at the nightclub had tailed off. Hannah always came back like a fire-breathing dragon after talking and drinking with them in cafés and at left-wing political rallies at the Maison de la Mutualité near the Sorbonne.

She'd hit home with what she'd said about me pretending to be looking for work. Instead, I'd been sneaking off to watch movies or to drink booze and smoke Muggles reefers with out-of-work jazz musicians.

"I love you, Hannah. You're all I **can** care about now," I pleaded with her. "I'm sorry I'm not as fired up about helping my fellow man as you are. I promise, it won't happen again. I really love you." She kept packing her things, which meant we were breaking up big this time. When she'd finished, she put her violin and bow in their case and said,

"The fight's gone out of you, Urby. Maybe if I'd been through hell in the war like you, I'd see things differently. But the fascists are winning here now and I've got to do something to stop them from taking over America. I'm going back."

"To do what?"

"Anything I can to get Roosevelt, FDR, elected. President Hoover and all the bankers and bigots supporting him have to be stopped." I tore her suitcase out of her hand and pressed her against me hard.

"You're hurting me!" she cried out. I loosened my arms. Tears starting in her dark brown eyes, she said,

"It hurts so bad because I love you." She walked past me and turned at the door to nod goodbye, tears in her eyes.

I envied her the tears she left on my cheeks. I first realized that mine had dried up for good during the Battle of Arras in April 1917. I'd spotted a lone German Albatros biplane fighter below me as my squadron of the Lafayette Flying Corps hunted down strays after a dogfight near the Baie de Somme. Our squadron leader, Tex O'Toole, pointed at me and gave me the thumbs up and I revved up my SPAD's Hispano-Suiza engine and dived at the Albatros with the sun warming my back and the wind tearing at my leather flying cap and goggles. I pulled the trigger of my Vickers machine gun and it jammed. I saw the German pilot shade his eyes, then he spotted me coming out of the sun. He tried evasive action but it was too late for him. My machine gun was still blocked so I rammed the Albatros and it flipped over, burst into flames, then disintegrated. The pilot looked like a flaming torch as he fell to earth, his arms flapping like fiery wings. I saluted him then steadied my plane, trying to reach the Bay to glide to safety on its surface. But the engine stalled and I plummeted toward the water. No one had parachutes then; I knew I was a goner. In the instants before I slammed into the Bay and died, I wanted to pray and cry but only felt The Big Nothing inside. Finally, I took my hands off the useless joystick, closed my eyes and waited. Before I hit the water, I imagined myself flying into the mouth of a giant whale and spiralling down toward the dark warmth of its belly.

Witnesses later said that, just before I crashed, a sudden gust of wind righted my plane enough for it to ricochet across the Bay's surface like a skipping stone. It came to a sudden stop and started sinking. I cut myself out of the harness with my airman's knife and swam to the shore, where I lay breathing cold air into my lungs and watching my plane's tail sink into the water. When I thought about the German pilot being burned to cinders in the air, I felt sorry for him but good to be alive myself. I didn't cry tears of joy though. I'd discovered, at death's door, that I'd run out of tears. They called me a hero for ramming the Albatros when my Vickers gun failed. I'd never worn my Croix de Guerre, as a token of respect for the German pilot I'd brought down.

A

We sold our nightclub and split the proceeds fifty-fifty. Hannah had already left France, so all the financial arrangements were handled through my bank in Paris and hers in Manhattan.

Stanley made me lie about the next part of my story. The official version was that I used my share of the money to set myself up as a private eye.

Stanley never wanted anyone, not even Hannah, to know how low I sank. The real story was:

When Hannah left Paris, my music left with her. Within a year, I'd run through my dough on booze, drugs, women and betting bad tips on fixed bicycle races at the Vélodrome d'Hiver. Then I knocked around, busking outside Metro stations and bistrots and cafés that had been popular with Americans before the Depression sent them packing.

I hated the sounds coming out of my clarinet, so I finally hocked it at the *Mont de Piété* to buy *gros rouge* wine and *gnôle* moonshine and to pay my hotel bills for another few months. To save money, I'd ended up taking my empty wine and *gnôle* bottles to the *Bougnats,* wine, wood and coal merchants from Auvergne whose shops were scattered around Montmartre. They'd fill the empty bottles with cheap red rotgut and French white lightning for a few sous. I warmed up on booze for inspiration for the flood of letters and songs I mailed to Hannah's New York bank, the only address I had for her. I never got a reply.

As the beginning of Fall 1933 approached, I was down to my last thirty francs. That would buy me one more month's stay in a cheap hotel and a few dozen bottles of booze and as many baguettes and tins of sardines. Then I'd be joining the ragged army of jobless *clochards* sleeping rough in doorways or warming themselves on metro gratings as the weather grew colder.

I'd hidden from Stanley Bontemps, spending my days playing jazz on a kazoo or a waxpaper-covered comb, busking around the Champs-Elysées and the Left Bank and sneaking back to Montmartre at night. I didn't want him to know how far I'd fallen. But he had his Corsican gangster friends out looking for me. They tracked me down to my fleabag near Place Clichy and marched me to his penthouse apartment on the rue Caulaincourt. He'd treated me to a feast accompanied by his finest wines and his choicest Cuban cigars, while I told him all about my breakup with Hannah.

I had a good night's sleep in a clean bed for the first time in months. When I woke up in the morning, my underwear, shirt and socks had been laundered and pressed and my tie, jacket and pants had been dry cleaned. Stanley had bought me an overcoat, a suit, a pair of patent leather shoes and a fancy Borsalino hat. He begged me to stay with him until something turned up. I lied that I was doing fine and getting close to hitting the jackpot again. He ended up giving me one hundred francs and made me promise that I'd stay in his place once a week. Using this windfall, I moved to a flophouse on the Left Bank on the rue de Buci, hoping that Stanley's Corsicans wouldn't trace me to my hideout. I stowed my new duds away for better days. Stanley's money, my busking and my weekly stay with him kept me alive through the freezing Fall.

On Christmas day in 1933, we lounged on one of Stanley's modernistic saxophone-shaped white leather couches after our Christmas feast of roast turkey, chocolate cake and Bordeaux red wines and my favorite Domfront calvados distilled from apples and pears. We were reminiscing about New Orleans as we drank the calvados. Suddenly, he turned serious and asked me,

"Urby, you gone suicide yo'self now? After you done survive four years of war in the mud and in the air spittin' lead at them German planes and such? You tellin' me you ready to up and die **now?** Sheeiiitttt! My Corsican boys done tracked you down. They be tellin' me they seen you playin' music on a paper-and-comb sandwich at metro stations and in the streets on that Left Bank of the river. Like you was nobody. You been bummin' around for a year now. That shit gots to stop!" Stanley was furious at me for the first time since I'd known him.

"I'm not ready to die yet, Stanley, I swear," I protested, defending myself. "I want to get Hannah back. As long as she's alive, I want to live. But my music's gone. I've lost it, Stanley. It won't come back until she comes back." He glared angrily at me for a while, then hid his face in his hands as if he was having second thoughts. His shoulders started heaving. Outraged, I realized he was laughing. Finally, he gave up all pretense and laughed and slapped his thighs, tears streaming down his cheeks.

"Lord have mercy Urby," he said. "You goin' on like you was that Bible man name of Job the Lord decide to teach him the righteous gots to suffer. You done learned that already so you can take care of your own business now, son. I known you since you was a young sprout bested me on the clarinet when you was nineteen. I give you my own clarinet 'cause you bucked me down. Where that clarinet be right now by the by?"

I handed him the *Mont de Piété* receipt and he pocketed it. I knew that he'd get my horn out of hock and keep it in case I played it again some day.

"You know peoples all over this town," Stanley said. "You ever think of private eyein'? Peoples always gone need a private eye to take care of they dirty business. Just like they needs them *laveries* to wash they dirty laundry." I laughed so hard that I spilled half of my snifter of calvados on the table and had to stop myself from lapping it up like a cat. I had no skills for sleuthing, I thought, remembering Sherlock Holmes and Charlie Chan movies I'd seen.

"I can hardly find my way around Montmartre without getting lost in some back alley," I said. "How do you expect **me** to solve crimes?" He chuckled.

"Urby, private eyes don't **solve** no crimes these days. They mostly tracks missin' peoples down or takes a photo of them doin' somethin' they oughtn't to be doin.' You tracked German soldiers down with a rifle and such when you was in the Foreign Legion, didn't you? It's gone be like that, 'cept for the killin' part."

"That was war, Stanley. I was young then. I was good at tracking folks down."

"Tell you what, Urby. I'm settin' you up as a private eye and we see how she goes."

"You'd be wasting your money."

"I got lots of them francs and dollars and such, but they's only one you. 'Sides, I'm sick of you actin' like you ain't nobody or nothin' since Hannah leave town. You still loves her and I reckon she still love you. Get down to some workin', Urby. Get you some pride back. Then all your music gone come back and Hannah too." Stanley reached behind his couch and said,

"I bought you a Christmas present." He handed me a box wrapped in shiny red paper and white ribbons covered with pictures of candy canes. I felt like crying but no tears came.

"Thanks...I..."

"Ain't you openin' it?" There was a Leica camera inside with a bunch of lenses and filters. I reckoned I'd never learn how to work the thing, but I thanked Stanley, finally getting the words out. He handed me a brand new brown leather wallet with two hundred francs and a private eye's license with my photo and signature on it inside.

"How'd you get the license?" I asked, astonished. He ignored my question and handed me my residence permit, which had gone missing days ago.

"I thought I'd lost it. I was ducking the cops," I said.

"My friends borrowed it so's you be the number one private eye in Paris."

I knew he must've sprinkled some bribes around the Préfecture of Police and had his best forger put my John Hancock on a bunch of documents.

"Now you fetch them clothes I bought you a while back and get to work, Mr. Private Eye. These the keys to your office and to an apartment above it," he said, handing them to me on a miniature Michelin tire key ring with a tag reading "Détective Domino-Enquêtes."

"It's on the rue Houdon, a few blocks away," he said. "You got a big gold eyeball painted on your office door. You can't miss it."

I learned how to work the Leica Stanley had given me, but my conscience kept me from using it to get the drop on some unsuspecting soul, even if I could have made a few hundred francs of blackmail money from my photos. Instead, I scrounged a few francs from recovering runaway American youngsters and taking them back to the ritzy town houses or hotels where their parents were staying. I was sinking fast as a private eye, but Stanley kept me afloat. Finally, I refused to take any more handouts from him.

I was wondering how I was going to get through the Winter without my electricity being cut off. I had a fireplace in my small apartment where I made fires which kept me from turning into a giant icicle, thanks to a *Bougnat* who gave me a half cord of wood and a demijohn of Auvergne moonshine as payment for tracking down his German shepherd named Frisé. He needed the dog to protect him when he went to visit his Auvergne friends living on the Left Bank around the Gare Montparnasse. There were pitched battles in the area as the socialists and communists squared off with the fascists and monarchists, who'd felt the wind in their sails ever since Hitler came to power in Germany the year before.

Everything changed for me on February 6, 1934 when I was drinking a snifter of calvados on my tab at the bar at Chez Red Tops in the early evening. A man sat down next to me and asked in a Yankee accent,

"Ah you Uhby Brown? Private investigations?"

"Maybe," I answered, sipping my calvados. The man had come from America looking for me on the advice of Tex O'Toole, my old squadron leader from the Lafayette Flying Corps in the Great War. He was a Wall Street millionaire from Boston living in New Jersey named Barnet Robinson III. The fool wanted to hire me to track down his daughter, Daphne. Her last S.O.S. about being kidnapped asked him to come to Paris to pay the ransom of one hundred grand. My instincts told me not to take the job, because I sensed the man was a phony and worse, but I needed to pay off stacks of overdue bills.

What really appealed to me, though, was that tracking down his daughter sounded like real private eye work instead of the stuff I'd been doing since I'd become a shamus. I took the job when Robinson III splashed down some serious dough just to cover my immediate expenses. It was more than I'd ever dreamed of making as a private eye and he was ready to keep forking out top dollar to keep me hunting for Daphne. Because of the growing political violence, I took to toting my Colt M1911, a gift that Stanley'd given me when I opened the first Urby's Masked Ball nightclub back in 1922. The gat made me feel authentic, like the kind of serious private eyes I saw in the movies.

I learned during my investigation that Daphne had faked being kidnapped to shake down her wealthy family for enough dough to follow her crazy dream of dropping out of some place called Smith College and running away to become the bride of Adolf Hitler. She'd met my yellow-green eyed quadroon nemesis from the Colored Waifs' Home, Buster Thigpen, when he was playing drums in a Harlem nightclub. Daphne told me later that her date, the scion of an old Long Island banking family, had taken her there hoping to buy some dope for them and to get her into his bed. To the horror of Daphne's family of Wall Street titans, Buster Thigpen had become her lover. Later, Daphne confided to me that she'd planned to ditch Buster in Paris before scooting off to Berlin to seduce Adolf Hitler. But after they arrived in Paris, he'd stolen all of her money and flogged her jewelry to buy drugs to feed the Happy Dust cocaine monkey on his back.

Daphne told me that Buster had drifted into one of the fascist-monar-chist movements called "The Oriflamme du Roi" because he liked to beat up on non-white people like himself and on Jews. The leader of the movement, Count René d'Uribé-Lebrun, had taken a shine to him, Buster had bragged to Daphne. The Count had told him that Buster resembled someone he'd met in New Orleans who'd been very dear to him a long time ago. In order to raise enough funds to finance her scheme to become Hitler's bride, after Buster had filched her money and jewelry, Daphne'd concocted a story of being kid-napped by Buster, which her family fell for. Buster agreed to play the villain when she promised to give him a juicy slice of the hundred grand ransom. They disappeared and my job was to track them down.

Not knowing at the time that the kidnapping was part of a scheme set up by Daphne, I and my friend Redtop had tracked Daphne and Buster to a hiding place in a disused stable in the Bois de Boulogne. As I watched him through a hole in the wall, holding my Colt M1911 at the ready, Redtop waited outside for my command to storm the stable with her sawed off shotgun so that we could "rescue" Daphne from Buster without firing a shot. But the drug-crazed Buster got the drop on Redtop, wrestled her shotgun away from her and dragged her into the stable holding the shotgun against her head.

He was about to blow her brains out when I aimed at him through the hole and shot him in the ear, killing him instantly and saving Redtop's life. Daphne lay on the ground inside the stable, unconscious. We left her there, while Redtop and I bundled Buster's body into the trunk of her Hispano-Suiza and then raced off to Argenteuil, where the Seine reaches its widest and deepest point. I deep-sixed Buster and then we raced back to the Bois de Boulogne to recover Daphne, only to find that she'd disappeared.

When I met up with her a few days later, she seduced me in a private dining room in the Lapérouse restaurant, then slipped me a Mickey Finn and headed to Germany. Wanting to honor my contract with the Robinsons and infatuated by Daphne, I followed her to Germany and rescued her from Hitler's fat number two, Hermann Goering, who was planning to turn her into his personal sex slave. We escaped from Germany by the skin of our teeth.

I'd kept my trap shut about Daphne's shenanigans with the Nazis in Germany and got the hundred grand ransom from her grateful family to clam up about the affair. That was peanuts for the Robinsons. According to the French scandal sheets, her relatives and husband had died-by murder, suicide or natural causes-within a little over two years after she returned to America in late February 1934. She inherited the family fortune and control of its businesses, making her, at the age of twenty-three, one of the richest and most powerful women in America.

▲

Hannah told me that her bank finally contacted her and turned my letters and songs over to her when she returned to New York from a trip to Richmond, Virginia in March 1935 to demonstrate for voting rights for colored people. She said the state troopers who'd escorted her out of Virginia had handcuffed her before hurling her into the back seat of their patrol car. When they riffled through her handbag and saw her name on her driving license, they asked her if she was a Jew. When she said Yes, they started making Nazi salutes and praising Adolf Hitler for everything he was doing to chase "people like you out of Germany." When the bank turned my letters and songs over to her, she told me that she'd sat down and read every letter and hummed the music to every song I'd written. She'd cried for days, she said. She spent another year in Manhattan playing in the New York Philharmonic and collecting more of my letters and songs from her bank.

As she sat in Central Park, humming "April in Paris" to the blossoming trees and to the songbirds on an early Spring morning in April 1936, she started laughing at the falsity of the lyrics, she'd told me later. That's when she thought of me in Montmartre shivering alone in the cold rain of a real April in Paris. She read through my latest batch of letters and love songs then marched off to the Cunard office to book passage on the next liner to Le Havre, France. She cabled Stanley to tell me when she was arriving and I was there, waiting at the bottom of the gangplank waving my clarinet at her. She'd taken her violin out of its case to wave it at me. I swept her up in my arms, violin, luggage and all.

"I love you. I don't want to lose you again," I said.

"Is it over? The dyed blondes? The drugs? "

"It's over," I answered. This time, I knew I'd keep my word.

Thanks to the Robinsons, Hannah and I had enough money to live in style until we figured out how to spend the rest of our lives together. We searched around for premises to open a new night club. We put the word out three months later that we were going to get married and open a new night-club on my forty-first birthday, July 4, 1936. The news was picked up by all of the Paris dailies except the right-wing ones. But Hannah had a change of heart at the last minute. She wanted us to spend more time together before we went ahead with marriage, which was, she said, "an institution I don't believe in, Urby. We love each other. Isn't that enough?" I argued that it wasn't and I was beginning to sway her my way.

Then the Spanish Civil War broke out in mid-July and Hannah was caught up in a whirlwind of marches and demonstrations in the Latin Quarter. She tried to talk me into leaving for Spain to take up arms as a volunteer to fight for the Spanish Republic against the Nationalists led by General Franco. I told her I'd made a vow never to kill again, without explaining why. That was the last time she asked me to go to Spain to fight. I knew I'd let her down again, but this time she stayed with me.

Chapter 3

Our apartment was three flights up from my second Mardi Gras-themed "Urby's Masked Ball" nightclub, which reopened on July 4, 1938, the day of my forty-third birthday. I inherited the whole shebang, with its nightclub premises on the ground floor level (formerly "Chez Red Tops") as well as a vintage black Hispano-Suiza automobile from Redtop following her suspicious suicide nearly six months ago.

My unexpected inheritance was my second big windfall after the Robinson family bonanza. Fortunately, all the dough from the Robinsons and Redtop's inheritance and, above all, the new feeling of love and purpose in my life after Hannah's return to France, resurrected me as a clarinetist playing New Orleans jazz and the new swing music.

Hannah had gone into the Latin Quarter to meet up with her left-wing pals. These days they were marching and giving the socialist clenched-fist salute in demonstrations to protest France's neutrality in the Spanish Civil War. Meanwhile, General Franco and his German and Italian fascist allies continued to bring the sledgehammer down on the Spanish Republican forces.

Hannah and her buddies were also protesting a possible sellout of Czechoslovakia to Hitler and Mussolini by England's Prime Minister Chamberlain and France's Premier Edouard Daladier at the Munich negotiations.

Meanwhile the French government was preparing for the worst. There was talk in Le Populaire about plans to evacuate a million people from Paris if things went haywire in Munich. The newspaper also reported on trucks being commandeered to remove the art treasures of the Louvre Museum and take them to secret hideaways all over France.

Hannah read me articles that got me scared that another Great War would break out after tomorrow night's Big Four meeting in Munich. I had time on my hands before rehearsals for tonight's two sets at the nightclub, so I figured I'd cool down by watching a movie until I could wail with my quartet again.

I took the metro to the Rue Montmartre stop and then walked to my favorite movie house, the Cinéma Max Linder on Boulevard Poissonnière, to catch the 3p.m. showing of the tear-jerker "Camille." Hannah had told me it was based on a book by the French octoroon, Alexandre Dumas *fils*. All I cared about was that it starred Greta Garbo. With her blonde hair and chiselled features, she reminded me of Daphne, who was even more beautiful than La Garbo. I'd already seen "Camille" twice. I reckoned that my eyes were the only dry ones in the Cinéma Max Linder.

The Pathé newsreel preceding the film had been made over a week ago. Hitler was menacing Czechoslovakia with the full weight of German might if it didn't meet his ultimatum of handing him a region called the Sudetenland by October 1, 1938, which was in two days' time. There were shots of Hitler, iron-faced like a Roman Emperor, flicking the Nazi salute at endless lines of tanks and goose-stepping, helmeted soldiers, while his fighter planes thundered overhead. Then the next newsreel segment came on.

This one showed clips from the last big street riots in Paris a week ago. The narrator said that fascist student supporters of Hitler and Mussolini and their socialist and communist opponents were slugging it out toe-to-toe, with brass knuckles and bicycle chains, near the Sorbonne University. The combat was all about whether France should intervene in the Spanish Civil war now that the Republican government had its back to the wall, with Madrid on the verge of surrendering to General Franco. Spearheading and supporting the fascist students was

"...The war-hero and former Aide-de-Camp of Marshal Philippe Pétain, General Count René d'Uribé-Lebrun, leader of the Oriflamme du Roi movement. His uniformed militia, which is fighting side by side with the extreme right-wing student groups, has long been active in opposing France's intervention in the conflict on the Iberian peninsula."

The screen showed a close-up of a handsome, aristocratic-looking elderly white man wearing an eyepatch over his right eye. He screamed into a lollypop microphone like a madman, "Les Communistes et leurs commanditaires juifs ne passeront pas! La France aux français! ("The Communists and their Jewish bankrollers will not win! France for the French!).

I knew this man and his face as well as I knew my own. General Count René d'Uribé-Lebrun, was my father. Except for the eyepatch and the grey hair, he was my physical twin in looks, although, at sixty-six, he was twenty-three years older than me. I learned from him that he'd been dogging my steps ever since I was discovered, a few hours old, in a Moses basket on the front porch of the Saint Vincent Colored Waifs' home in Gentilly, New Orleans by its head, Father Gohegan. The Father had refused to tell me the name of the man who'd sired me, because my mother, Josephine Dubois, had uttered it in the confessional. He'd only say that the moniker "Urby Brown" that he'd given me was similar to my father's name. When I learned of our connection later, I found out that I was "Urby" because it's close to "Uribé" and "Lebrun" means "Brown" in English.

Father Gohegan had died in a fire which destroyed the Saint Vincent's Colored Waifs' Home on July 5, 1913. General Count René d'Uribé-Lebrun, now spouting his hatred in the tinny sound of the newsreel, bragged to me during the Daphne Robinson case that he had given his chief stormtrooper, Pierre Lestage, the order to set the Home on fire. The Count's aim was to destroy all traces of my identity as a colored man and have Pierre Lestage drive me out of the United States towards him in France, like a wrangler herding a prize bull into his boss's corral. He was also proud of himself for pulling the strings on me like I was a marionette so that I ended up leaving Harlem for France in July 1914.

I was then the fallen nineteen-year-old "Mozart of the Creole Clarinet," an out of work alcoholic recovering from a serious cocaine habit. The Count told me later that he'd paid for the drugs and pimped some women my way. I'd hit rock bottom so hard that no nightclub owner would let my size tens into his club. Any money that came my way I spent on a near-lethal mixture of rotgut wine and bathtub gin to blot out my feeling that I'd thrown my life away before it had really begun.

Hannah had given a violin recital at Carnegie Hall, after which she took a taxi to go looking for me all over Harlem. She found me on a bench at the northern end of Central Park, next to the Harlem Meer, sleeping off another hangover from skid row booze. I repaid her, once I was up on my feet again, by cutting out to France to tour with a New Orleans Creole group. I'd headed to France because I knew that my natural father by Josephine Dubois was a Frenchman. Maybe I'd figured that I'd find him somehow. When I did, I wished I'd never come looking for him because he turned out to be the man in the newsreel.

⨂

A few weeks after I arrived in France, the Great War erupted. I did a stint in the French Foreign Legion before being assigned to the all-volunteer, all-American Lafayette Flying Corps of the French Air Army as its only colored pilot. I was itching to fight the "Boches," which I quickly learned was the derogatory French term for the Germans. I rejoined the Legion when America entered the war in 1917. The American Air Army turned me down as a pilot because of my race. I refused to fight in the all-colored Jim Crow units which President Wilson had put under French command because American officers under General "Black Jack" Pershing refused to lead us.

On February 6, 1934, the French fascists and monarchists led by my father launched street riots that turned into a violent coup d'Etat to bring down the French government and the Third French Republic. It was a co-incidence that the same night, Barnet Robinson III hired me as the family's shamus to track down Daphne Robinson. My journalist friend Jean Fletcher and I got caught up among the rioters on Boulevard Saint-Germain-des-Prés, within eyeshot of the Count. She told me to really look at him and that's how I'd found an older twin, who was my natural father.

It was during the days following the failed coup d'état that my father revealed to me that I'd never been in danger of deportation, because he intended to keep me living in France, whether I wanted to stay or not. He told me that he'd kept eyes on me all the time I'd been in the country, without ever letting me know it, while he decided what to do with me.

Already a career soldier serving as the then General Philippe Pétain's aide-de-camp before the start of the Great War in 1914, he'd had a nightmare that the coming battle with Germany would prevent him from fathering a male heir to preserve the thousand-year old d'Uribé-Lebrun lineage. He knew from Father Gohegan's many letters to him that my mother, Josephine Dubois, had given birth to his octoroon son and he'd decided in 1913 to have his henchman Pierre Lestage track me down in America again and report to him on my physical appearance. When Pierre told him of my pale complexion and my resemblance to him the Count decided that he wanted me close at hand in case his nightmare came to pass.

Later, he told me that, because of a wound to his manhood chalked up by a German sniper at Verdun, I would indeed be the sole "fruit of his loins." After keeping me under observation almost from the day I was born he finally started planning to do everything in his power to legitimize me as the heir to his lineage.

He'd lost his right eye at Verdun too, which didn't seem to bother him. The gold eye-patch covering it had become his trademark. It helped him to become the darling of the "Anciens Combattants," mostly right-wing French Army veterans of the Great War, as well as of like-minded politicians and most of the Army and Police. He led his private band of Oriflamme du Roi stormtroopers from the front in bloody street battles with "leftist agitators," as he called them.

In February 1934, I rejected his offer to join him and his stormtroopers and he went into a frenzy of hatred when I told him I was in love with the daughter of a Viennese Jewish rag-and-bone man who'd arrived in America at Ellis Island and not at Plymouth Rock on the Mayflower. I told him I planned to marry her if she forgave me and returned to France some day. He warned me that such a marriage would be fatal ...for her.

In meetings with the Count over the years since his failed coup d'Etat, he kept hammering away at me to join his movement and to ditch Hannah. Two obstacles stood in the way of his plans, he said, and he told me that he intended to eliminate both of them : first, he'd "erase" all traces of my origins as an octoroon and his bastard by a quadroon whore from Storyville; second, he'd keep " the Jewess Hannah Korngold" out of my life and marry me off to a rich woman from a suitable French noble family. I was expected to go out to stud with his chosen bride like Man o' War, mounting her often enough to keep the d'Uribé-Lebrun lineage in the running for generations to come.

Watching my father spouting hatred in flickering black and white images on the movie screen, I realized that he had as magnetic a personality as Adolf Hitler and Benito Mussolini, men he called his "dear friends." With the right breaks and with the help of his hoary mentor Marshal Pétain, I reckoned he'd end up as the Hitler of France some day. His fanatic's eye shone like the one at the top of the pyramid on the back of FDR's new one dollar bill.

Because Redtop knew so much about my origins, I was certain that the Count was responsible for her death. Within hours of learning the details of her so-called suicide, I confronted him and flat out accused him of murdering her. The Count just laughed in my face and passed me a draft of the findings of the official police investigation of her death, which some Inspector at the Quai des Orfèvres had cooked up in record time. It concluded that she'd committed suicide by slitting her wrists and bleeding to death in her bathtub. I knew it was a cock-and-bull story, because Redtop would never have slit her wrists. She had a horror of blades and kept them out of her nightclub. She'd have blown her brains out with her shotgun if she felt the need to die.

Was Hannah going to be the next target for the Count's plan to "erase" my racial origins. Or Stanley? I owed it to them and to Redtop to prove that the Count and his pet executioner, Pierre Lestage, were behind Redtop's death. My track record showed that I was no Sherlock Holmes, but I planned to uncover evidence to send them to the guillotine, or *la Veuve*, the "Widow" as the French called it. The problem was, they had stuff on me that could be twisted around to send me to the "Widow" too.

After the newsreel ended, I watched about a half hour of "Camille," feasting my eyes on Greta Garbo and thinking of how I'd fallen for Daphne Robinson, hook, line and sinker back in February 1934. I'd fallen for her, despite her lies about being kidnapped and her Mickey Finns and having to track her down into the heart of Nazi Germany to save her from her own crazy scheme to seduce Adolph Hitler and become his bride. I finally gave up watching the film because the cigarette smoke in the movie house had my eyes stinging and my lungs burning, so I headed back to Pigalle.

CHAPTER 4

Paris, September 29, 1938, Late Morning

H annah came into the living room wearing her favorite knitted red sweater and a pair of the blue overalls French workers wore. She looked so good in her outfit that I wanted to drag her off to our bedroom, but one look at the determined expression on her face told me that she meant business. She yanked a brown and white check flatcap over her ears and laced up a pair of black leather clodhoppers. She stared unhappily at my usual duds: dark grey suit, white shirt, half-Windsor knotted dark blue tie, grey Borsalino.

"You can't wear those clothes to the Maison de la Mutualité in the Latin Quarter," she said. "We're going to a meeting of the Socialiste International, for Christ's sake. Some of them are real hardliners. If they think you're a cop sent to spy on them..." She slashed her index finger across her throat. I knew she disapproved of my clothes, but I'd always dressed the same way in France, except back in the days when I wore a military uniform. Any jazzman with a following dressed sharp in Paris because that's what our fans expected.

"You look like *Gavroche* going to a masquerade," I countered, remembering the name of a character in Hugo's *"Les Misérables,"* the only book I'd read since I left America. "It's a great disguise-it must be hard for a woman as pretty as you to look like a Paris street boy." I could see parts of my compliment pleased her and she laughed. Then she turned serious again.

"Urby, you're the only person I've ever known who thinks that Inspector Javert is the hero of 'Les Misérables.' Why not Jean Valjean?" I was about to tell Hannah that it was because Javert never gave up tracking down Valjean, when she continued,

" This is the most important socialist meeting in France in a long time. All the warring factions want to agree on a unified front about tonight's Big Four meeting on Czechoslovakia."

I'd told Hannah I wanted to go with her to the socialists' meeting to find out more about the happenings in Spain and Czechoslovakia. But I intended to act as her bodyguard in case she got into hand-to-hand combat with the right-wing bully boys who'd be sure to turn up to derail the meeting.

Nowadays, I only went to the Left Bank to drink with my journalist friend, Jean Fletcher, at the La Coupole bistrot/restaurant in Montparnasse. I stayed away from the Latin Quarter altogether. There were more violent riots and street combats there now than at any time since the mid-thirties. Left-wing workers and students from the Sorbonne clashed daily with fascist and monarchist students and stormtroopers from my father's outfit the "Oriflamme du Roi" which meant "The King's Battle Standard." They fought with an arsenal of bicycle chains, sling shots and the brass knuckles they called the "coup-de-poing Américain."

"What do you want me to wear?" I asked her. "I don't have anything like your getup."

"Wear that blue and white check sweater I knitted for you. No jacket. Nail a yellow Gauloise to your lip and keep it there. I bought you this." She handed me a grey cloth cap then helped me put on my disguise.

A

As soon as we walked up the steps of the Maubert-Mutualité metro station in fifth arrondissement, a long stone's throw from the Sorbonne University, I knew we were in for big trouble. Platoons of stormtroopers from the Oriflamme du Roi, all wearing red, white, and black uniforms the colors of Hitler's swastika flag, were distributing tracts to shoppers in the street market. It stretched for blocks from the Place de la Mutualité almost to the doors of the Mutualité Hall. Tough-looking workers wearing cloth caps like mine, yellow corn paper Gauloise cigarettes glued to their lips, were shadowing the stormtroopers and grabbing the tracts from the hands of shoppers.

They'd tear them up under the bland gazes of the stormtroopers who knew they were vastly outnumbered in this stronghold of left-wing workers and students. One huge "gueules cassées" veteran of the Great War, one of thousands of men whose faces had been smashed apart by German bullets or shrapnel and had to be cobbled together again, swung his giant's arm like a battering ram, sending two members of the Oriflamme sprawling into the gutter. The "gueules cassées" giant, who had one eye and no ears, picked up the scattered tracts and flung them into the air. Carried away by the wind, they looked like a flight of geese fleeing Europe before Winter set in. I grabbed one of the tracts as it tried to flutter away. It had the usual hate-filled message from the Oriflamme about chasing the Jews, foreigners and other undesirable elements out of France so that she could join the forces of progress led by Hitler, Mussolini and General Franco.

Hannah tore the flyer out of my hand, ripped it to shreds and tossed the bits into the air like confetti. I heard a tin whistle and saw a large truck filled with stormtroopers arriving from the direction of rue Monge. Twenty or thirty Oriflamme stormtroopers jumped down from it and started running toward their comrades who were being forced back by the workers and stall owners. The shoppers fled in panic waving their string shopping *filets*, knowing that a big street brawl was coming. The Oriflamme reinforcements piling out of their truck were carrying billy clubs, sticks bristling with nails and more bicycle chains.

There was a shout of "à moi, les gars" from the direction of the Mutualité Hall as more workers piled out of cafés brandishing wine bottles, sticks and slingshots. Some of them carried buckets of the bolts that their slingshots would launch at the Oriflamme.

"Let's get the hell out of here and back to Pigalle, Hannah. This is going to get real nasty." I tried to pull her back toward the metro station but she squirmed away from me, saying,

"I'm going to the Mutualité and no fascists are going to stop me." She started running toward the Maison de la Mutualité and I followed hard on her heels. Over the Maison's door hung a giant white banner with blood red letters reading "Non à la mort de la Tchechoslovaquie à Munich. Non à Hitler et Mussolini et Franco! Le fascisme ne passera pas!" If the Mutualité Meeting went as planned, Hannah had told me, the different socialist factions would call for the workers to carry out massive demonstrations and hold a General Strike in case the English and French governments sold Czechoslovakia out to Germany and Italy.

The overwhelmed Oriflamme stormtroopers had been forced to form a defensive perimeter at the end of the market in front of the stalls of the fish merchants and the pork butchers as more and more workers streamed in from side streets and building sites. We watched them surround a group of about twenty Oriflamme. The workers were closing in for the kill. I could hear breaking glass as wine bottles thudded against the Oriflamme and shattered on the cobblestones. One of the pork butchers had wrestled an Oriflamme to the ground, knocked off his spotless peaked cap and was forcing a pig's head onto his curly blonde locks. The fish merchants and workers were hurling whole salmon, trout and trays of oysters and clams onto the tight circle of Oriflamme. The stormtroopers were flailing about them with their bicycle chains and nail-studded sticks as they hacked an escape route through their frenzied assailants.

Hannah and I walked into the Maison de la Mutualité and saw that the socialists were duplicating indoors the chaotic street scenes we'd just passed through. The Chairman, a goateed specimen wearing rimless eyeglasses, was a dead ringer for Leon Trotsky in the newsreels that were shot at the height of the Russian Revolution. He hammered his gavel on his lectern so hard that its head flew off and hit a slogan-shouting man square in the chops. He wiped the blood from his broken teeth and waved his bloody handkerchief like a Spanish matador's cape.

His faction immediately charged the Chairman who, meanwhile, had drawn what looked like a Napoleonic era cavalryman's saber from a scabbard on a chair behind him. He fended off his attackers with some fancy fencing thrusts. They, in turn, were showered with a barrage of wooden folding chairs by the Chairman's supporters. "Vous n'êtes pas des socialistes, vous êtes des fascistes!" the Chairman shouted, accusing the socialists from the opposing faction of being fascists. Suddenly, a rotten tomato knocked the eyeglasses off the Chairman's nose. He collapsed, pulling his lectern on top of himself and dropping his saber like a soldier scythed down at the Battle of the Marne. The contents of crates of tomatoes and rotten eggs and cabbages flew through the air along with folding chairs, books and even a hot water bottle. Hannah and I had crawled under a table to shield ourselves from the mayhem. I grabbed her arm and shouted to her,

"Pigalle?" She nodded Yes, then said angrily,

"This is madness! How're we going to stop the fascists when we can't stop fighting among ourselves?" Hannah let me run interference for her and I elbowed aside lunatics rushing the stage. On our way back to the metro station, we stepped gingerly over the produce and bouquets of orange and yellow flowers from overturned market stalls littering the cobblestones. They wafted their various scents through air that smelled of sweat and cigarette smoke. We heard the be-bo-be-bo of police vans as the cops finally arrived, probably tipped off by the Oriflamme. The last wounded stormtroopers were being bundled into their truck and then it pulled away from the curb heading down the rue de Pontoise toward the Seine. I reckoned they'd speed off to the Oriflamme headquarters on the Right Bank near the American Embassy and the Hôtel de Crillon. The police were inspecting the workers' papers and shoving them violently, guns drawn, into their *"panier à salade"* police vans under a hail of jeers and curses.

Same Day, September 29, 1938, Early Evening, at the Café Paname, Place Pigalle

In a half hour, at 5:30 p.m., Hannah and I would start getting the nightclub ready. At 6:30, I'd spend an hour or so with the three other members of "Urby's New Orleans Jazz Quartet," running through the numbers for the evening's two sets. We'd open the doors at 7:30 and the first regulars would sidle in to sit on barstools at the tiny bar if they were sober enough not to tumble off them onto the red carpeting. They'd be the serious drinkers, who wouldn't notice how much Hannah had spruced up the club since I'd inherited it. Red velvet fabric now covered the walls instead of the tobacco-stained yellow beeswax colored wallpaper with autographed caricatures of famous jazzmen on it that was a famous feature of Chez Red Tops. Only a few would hang around until the first set began in the expanded seating area with its classy fake Second Empire armchairs with cigarette burns dotting their red velour upholstery. All the seating was clustered around a small bandstand spangled with Mardi Gras streamers and carnival masks, some of them Venetian.

My boys and I would kick off the first set an hour later with W.C. Handy's "Beale Street Blues." Around midnight tonight, after the second set ended with Ellington's "In my Solitude," we were going to lug out Hannah's wooden radio console and rig it up on the bandstand. Everyone would listen to the news from Munich to learn Czechoslovakia's fate.

⚓

There was a chill early evening wind that swirled dirt, trash and the usual nighttime odors across Place Pigalle as the lights flickered on. We could smell smoke from coal and wood fires, from braziers toasting chestnuts and from countless thousands of caporal tobacco cigarettes. There was a lung-wrenching fug of exhaust fumes from cars and buses, their engine noises covering the clopping of the hooves of horses drawing rag-and-bone men's wagons.

The *filles de joie* sitting next to Hannah and me in the Café Paname had thrown coats over their *peignoirs* to swallow down a fast café exprès and a cheap applejack calvados before rushing back to their hourly rate hotels to provide some low-priced comfort to their clients.

Stanley Bontemps came toward us glad-handing customers and autographing proffered photos. He was the most famous, and the best, American jazz musician still living in Paris. But he wouldn't be able to play his soprano saxophone much longer. His magical fingers were being crippled by arthritis, which came and went but was getting worse.

Stanley kissed Hannah on the cheek, gave me a bear hug and sat down at our table. A waiter dashed over and planted a full tumbler of rye, straight no chaser, in front of him.

"Bonjour, mes amis, how y'all doin'?" he asked in his usual way. We three New Orleans natives were surrounded by a ragtag frenzy of shouting French drinkers sweating fear from every pore. I closed my eyes and tried to ignore the hubbub and that acrid, sweaty smell of fear I knew so well by sneaking a swig of Domfront calvados from my hip flask and breathing in its strong scent of apples and pears.

At five minutes to five Hannah and I started saying our goodbyes to Stanley and heading off to our nightclub. Stanley promised to come by later in the evening and jam with my quartet for as long as his arthritis would let him. Hannah looked around at the crowd in the Café Paname and said,

"I bet there's going to be a full house at Urby's tonight too. We could run short of booze if Hitler and Mussolini are forced to climb down."

"We've got plenty more in the cellar," I said, not optimistic at all. From the faces of the four leaders that I'd seen in the newsreels, only Hitler and Mussolini looked likely to win the high stakes poker game they were playing with England's Chamberlain and France's Daladier.

Hannah stood up, shivering. She wasn't cold; she was flat out scared, like I was. I held her in my arms, the two of us clutching each other as if we could keep the world at bay. But seeing the chaos around us and remembering the scenes at the Place Maubert market at lunchtime, I reckoned that sometime after midnight, the news from Munich was likely to change things forever. Stanley, as usual, appeared to be as cool as a cucumber. You would've thought that none of it concerned him, but I knew him well enough to know that he was plenty worried.

We shoved our way through the crowd, saying swift "Bonsoirs" to any friends we spotted through the pall of cigarette smoke and then we emerged into the chilly, pungent air of Place Pigalle and breathed it in deeply as if its funky aroma might fade away forever after midnight.

We said goodbye to Stanley and went our separate ways. The pimps near the entrance of Urby's Masked Ball were shoving each other and fist-waving to lay claim to the turf that their shivering girls would work tonight. But, for once, these sharply dressed young *macs* seemed to be carrying on half-heartedly. They probably pictured themselves marching towards their doom to defend the sacred honor of France, just as their fathers had done two decades before.

"Poor kids," I said. "How many will be alive a year from now?"

Early morning, September 30, 1938

A half hour had passed since our last set ended at midnight. The drummer, Lonny Jones, a grisly old professional hit man and ex-Baptist preacher from Natchez, Mississippi, who was about Stanley's age, as well as my two young fellow New Orleans creoles, Isidore Ardoin, piano, and Baptiste Laffont, cornet, sat beside me among the patrons. All of us were drinking fast. Isidore and Baptiste burned their way through a bunch of marijuana. I reckoned they were trying not to think of what the future held for them in America.

They'd both been summoned to the Préfecture of Police in the afternoon and notified that their residence and work permits had been cancelled. I'd paid out the usual bribes but they'd been told they had fifteen days to leave France. I reckoned that their deportation was my father's doing, his way of showing me who was boss.

I felt really sorry for Isidore and Baptiste. They faced a long freighter voyage back to America, probably in segregated steerage. They'd have a lot to worry about after crossing the Atlantic. Colored musicians who'd escaped back to France from America had warned us that our communities were being ground down by the Depression and by growing violence against us from whites. Meaning that even if Isidore and Baptiste avoided being invited to a KKK necktie party after they arrived home in New Orleans, they might not find work as musicians, or even cotton pickers.

As usual, Lonny's papers had been extended for another six months, just like Hannah's, Stanley's and mine were because of arrangements that I'd made with my father to keep him dangling until I figured out how we could escape from him. For Lonny to receive the same special treatment as us made me wonder whether he earned it by passing on to cops and to my father scuttlebutt about the doings in my nightclub and in Harlem-in-Montmartre. Another thing that made me uneasy about him was that he'd once been a first rate drummer, working in a nightclub called La Belle Princesse around the corner from Chez Red Tops in February 1934, when the Daphne Robinson case fell into my lap. He'd been a big friend of his fellow drummer and my nemesis from the Colored Waifs' Home, Buster Thigpen, who Daphne had drawn into her schemes. I wondered if he'd heard any rumors about how Buster died.

⋏

The brown wood box radio on the bandstand occasionally crackled with static and the high-pitched whine of the French announcer would pierce through to say there was no news from Munich. Lonny Johnson put down his bible. He tongued his toothpick around his mouth and said,

"I'm sick of waitin' for them folk to make up they minds. Shoot, they don't give my man Hitler nothin', he gone kill 'til he get what he want, you know that! Man's a stone killer, like me. And we be the Lord! 'Vengeance is mine, saith the Lord,' that be what the Bible say. Right here..." He jabbed his finger at the scriptures, then went on in his high-pitched preacher's voice "... and stone killers like Hitler and me and..." He backed down from adding my name to the list when he spotted my balled up fist " ... gone keep on killin' 'til we wreaks us our vengeance. You can always tell we be stone killers by that look in our eyes." He pointed two gnarled black fingers at his dark eyes and then grinned and spat out his toothpick. Baptiste, the cornetist, said to Lonny,

"You one crazy cat, you know that? You best hope Hitler don't get him no vengeance." Baptiste stubbed out his reefer and wiped Carmex lip grease from his mouth with a soiled grey handkerchief. He went on, "An African French army veteran I know tell me them Nazis hates colored folks worse than Jews. If France lose to Germany, we all best be Stateside to escape that Hitler vengeance you be mouthin' off about, old timer."

Suddenly we heard the French commentator screech,

"Ici Munich. Enfin, c'est la paix! Peace at last!"

We all jumped to our feet, clapping and hugging and swigging down our drinks and slapping each other's palms, "giving skin," as some jazzmen now said. Hannah frowned, her face gone dead white. The newsman said that Chamberlain, Daladier, Hitler and Mussolini had just signed an agreement to turn Czechoslovakia's Sudetenland region over to Germany. In exchange, Hitler had promised that he'd never demand more land in Europe.

Stanley had slipped into the room. He was watching Hannah, his soprano sax at the ready. The heaving crowd gathered around the stage. They were dancing the Lindy Hop to "When the Saints Go Marching In."

Hannah elbowed her way through the crowd and signalled to my men to stop playing. People started stomping their feet in the suddenly silent room. They whistled and shouted "Music!/Musique!" Some of them banged their fists on the tables or dinged their whiskey glasses with their switchblades. Hannah shouted over the din,

"Don't you know this peace means another war? What's happening in Czechoslovakia and Spain will soon be happening here! We should all go to Czechoslovakia and Spain to stop the fascists instead of boozing in nightclubs!"

"Say what?" A confused patron asked, his head bobbing in bewilderment. Another cried out,

"Why don't you sit yo' pretty self down, honey? I wants Urby and his gates to lay some jazz upside my head! I don't want no jive about no war in no Spain."

"We're closing up!" Hannah shouted louder, facing them all down.

I packed up my clarinet and gestured to my men to leave the bandstand. Lonny sneered at Hannah until he caught the look on my face and he turned away, humming to himself. Whenever I caught him looking at me I'd see that sneer. If I ranked him about missing beats or making the wrong sound, he'd say, in a threatening tone, that we had friends in common back in the States and he was keeping an eye on me for them. Then he'd hum the Negro spiritual "Dere's a man goin' round, takin' names" and look at me with menace in the reddened whites of his eyes. I wrote him off as a nut case who'd go too far one day and I'd kick him out. In the meantime, I kept him on because drummers were in short supply these days. Lonny wasn't a top drummer anymore but he usually kept good time. The problem was that the sounds from his drums now raged with threats and anger, like Lonny himself.

One by one, our customers filed silently past us out the door, saying their goodbyes, the colored Americans who had the groove giving skin to me and my musicians. After I'd paid my men, only Hannah, Stanley and I were left in the nightclub. Stanley held Hannah's hand.

"I'll never do that again Urby, promise," she said.

"Do whatever you need to do, baby," I said, hugging her and burying my face in her thick black hair that always smelled of French lavender shampoo.

Stanley lit one of his custom-made Cuban cigars and watched us as he blew perfect smoke rings into the air and then stabbed them out of shape.

"I don't know 'bout y'all, but I ain't ready to dance no Lindy over this here peace," he said. "Urby, I'm gone talk to our friend in Berlin on the phone, find out what he thinkin'. Stop by my place tomorrow afternoon, say around four?"

"Sure, Stanley. See you tomorrow. A demain," I said.

I knew that Stanley was going to get the lowdown on Munich from our jazz-loving friend Colonel Dieter Schulz-Horn. If anyone knew about Hitler's schemes and his cronies' dealings, it would be him. He'd hinted to me in Berlin in 1934, when he helped me escape from Germany with Daphne Robinson, that he was high up in Germany's intelligence service, the Abwehr.

"'Night, Stanley," Hannah said. She pecked him on the cheek and fussed with his lapels.

"'Night, honey," Stanley said with the shy smile he reserved for Hannah. When he walked out the door, he let in, for an instant, the sound of wildly honking horns and of thousands of voices raised in the "Marseillaise."

I held Hannah and she looked at me, her dark brown eyes full of the fear-filled questions I knew she'd be asking until the end of the night.

"Let's go home." I said.

"I want to close up first." I made noises about helping, but she wanted to be alone for a while with her fears.

"Are you awake Urby?" I heard Hannah call out when she finally returned to the apartment an hour later. I'd lain awake, worrying about her.

"Come to bed. It's been a long day," I said.

"I don't want to sleep. I want you to make love to me."

Hannah and I kept waking each other to make love, until we fell asleep as dawn was breaking.

▲

I opened Stanley Bontemps's private entrance door with my key and took the elevator up to his penthouse apartment, right around the corner from our nightclub. Stanley greeted me with his klieg-light smile as I stepped out of the elevator directly into his living room.

"Did you get the lowdown from Colonel Schulz-Horn?" I asked.

"He be somewhere in France and gone phone you at four..." he squinted at the clock. It was 4:12 p.m. I knew that he'd long ago memorized the positions of the hour numerals on clock dials but he couldn't work out the intervening minutes.

"...in three minutes, at 4:15?" I asked. He nodded Yes. We waited in silence for a while. Then Stanley said,

"Hannah be right about that Munich deal. The Colonel let on to me it ain't nothin' but a pig in a poke." The telephone rang and Stanley handed me the receiver. He listened in with the spare earpiece.

"Hello," the Colonel said. "Is that Herr Urby Brown?"

"Good afternoon, Colonel," I said. There was no static. I guessed that Colonel Schulz-Horn was using some kind of special telephone. He was still alive after over five years in a Germany under Hitler's rule because he was a very cautious and scheming man.

"I can't talk for long. I must swear you to secrecy on the details of what I am going to tell you," he said in his light German accent. "You may give the outlines to your journalist friend, but, as usual, nothing that will allow her story to be traced back to me. I prefer to stay alive as long as I can to fight the madness there."

"Don't worry," I said, knowing by "friend" he meant Jean Fletcher.

"Item one," he said. "Within the next two months, Hitler, Himmler and Goebbels are planning to move against all Jews, as defined by the Nuremberg Racial Laws of 1935. There will be much blood spilled and they will all become prisoners here until such time as they can be disposed of." Shocked, I blurted out,

"Disposed of? You mean killed?"

"Yes. Wiped out, men, women and children. Item two. By this time next year, Hitler plans to invade Poland. When France and England declare war on Germany, as they must do by their treaty obligations, we will launch 'Blitzkrieg,' that means 'Lightning War,' to conquer every country in Western Europe. The aim of our offensive is the rapid defeat of France and England."

"But America will come in, like we did the last time," I protested. "Hitler can't defeat America, France and England. Then there's the Soviets."

"Stalin and Hitler are planning to sign a non-aggression pact."

"That's impossible! Germany and the Soviet Union want to destroy each other," I said. He laughed.

"You're right. But first they want to carve Poland up like a Christmas turkey and gobble her up like an hors-d'oeuvre. As for America, Hitler, Goering and Goebbels have set forces at work to defeat your President Roosevelt in your 1940 election and replace him with one of our supporters, like the heroic Charles Lindbergh, conqueror of the Atlantic. Then, we begin the conquest of America itself. Say goodbye to Stanley for me." The Colonel hung up. Stanley took back the telephone saying,

"Hannah's gone be real upset. Real upset."

We finished our drinks then I went home to give Hannah Colonel Schulz-Horn's bad news.

CHAPTER 5

Hannah knew something was wrong the moment I sat down at our table at the Café Paname.

"Bad news, right?"

"Stanley asked Colonel Schulz-Horn to phone me at his place to give me the lowdown on Munich." I paused when Hannah squeezed my arm. I was afraid my news would be too much for her to take.

"Let's talk about it tomorrow," I said.

"Now," she said, "I can handle it."

"The Colonel said Hitler's going to move against the Jews within the next two months. It's going to be a bloodbath. And you were right about Munich. Hitler's going to flush the deal down the toilet and invade Poland within a year. Stalin's going to sit that one out."

"We haven't got much time then," she said, calmly. Her eyes were steelier than I'd ever seen them before.

"To do what, close up shop and head off to America?"

"No, to get some Jews out of Germany."

That rocked me back. I remembered what Germany was like four years ago when I went there to track down Daphne Robinson. Getting into Germany back then had been risky, despite my American passport and my looking like a respectable, "Aryan" American bearing a name that made sweet music in their ears. Even with my passport and its photograph of me in their hands, the SS border guards, wearing long black leather greatcoats, kept asking me,

"Isn't your real name Evan Shipman?"

"No, Urby Brown." They smiled menacingly and one said,

"It will go easier for you if you tell the truth Mr. Shipman. This is your last chance. Is your name Evan Shipman?"

"No, it's Urby Brown."

"Is that your final answer?" "Your final answer?" The guards echoed each other in chorus, glaring at me.

"Yes." They'd gone off and returned ten minutes later with my passport stamped for entry. They'd saluted me into Germany with iron smiles.

Remembering the border guards' attempts to scare me away from Germany back in 1934, I wondered if I could get into the country and make it back with some Jews now that Hitler was on the warpath.

"We've got time to go home before we get the nightclub ready. I want to show you the men I want to get out of Germany."

Back in our apartment, Hannah took my hand and led me to a montage of photographs of friends of hers which hung on the wall. I hardly noticed it most times, because I'd never met any of them. They were all people who'd either been members of the various classical groups that she'd played in or had been fellow music students or teachers. She pointed at the photos of two men.

"That's Jascha Cohen, my violin teacher at Juilliard and one of the greatest violinists alive. And that's Elam Rosenthal, a great young pianist, twenty-five years old." She paused, then said,

"I want to get them into France." She looked at me expectantly.

"You go set the night club up. I'll run by Stanley's again, see if we can find a way to get them here with Colonel Schulz-Horn's help," I said. Hannah threw her arms around me and kissed me. She was worried though.

"It's dangerous. What if your father finds out what we're up to?"

"Leave him to me," I said. "I'll get them into France, even if I have to kill him." Hannah's shocked expression made me regret my words.

"Don't say that," she said. "I know that you had no choice, but you've done too much killing already. During the Great War and then shooting Buster Thigpen to save Redtop."

"There's worse," I said. The time had come to confess to Hannah the killing I'd regretted the most in my life and that had changed me forever.

"When the Count learned that I'd killed Buster, he told me that Buster was my half brother. We had the same mother but he was her son by an earlier lover. Hannah, I killed my brother!" Hannah looked horrified, but kept holding my hand tightly. I went on,

"After he told me that, I threw the gun I'd used to kill Buster into the Seine. I vowed I'd never kill again. I've kept my word up to now. That's why it was so stupid of me to talk about killing the Count. I hate everything he stands for but I'll never break my vow, whatever happens. "

"That's what's kept you from going to Spain to fight the fascists?"

"Yes. No more killing. Ever."

Hannah let my confession pass without comment, saying,

"Imagine we get Cohen and Rosenthal to France. How soon can we get them to America?"

"Jean Fletcher knows Ambassador Bullitt; I think she can twist his arm to get emergency visas for them. I hope your friends still have their passports." I didn't say it to Hannah but I reckoned that their passports had been confiscated. "We can hide them in the empty maid's rooms upstairs," I continued.

"You sure you want to risk it? You told me you think the Count has your loony drummer spying on us."

"I'll have to make a deal with the Count to keep his spies off our backs until we get your friends out of France. Leave Lonny Johnson to me. I'll work out a plan with Stanley."

I knew what was running through Hannah's mind when she heard me talk about "making a deal" with the Count. It meant that he'd try even harder to get me to break up with her so that Pierre Lestage could "erase" her at his leisure.

⋏

I wasn't able to lay my head down on a pillow after the second set ended around midnight. Before leaving the nightclub, I phoned Stanley and told him I had something urgent to talk to him about that wouldn't take too long. After my rendez-vous with Stanley, I'd meet up with my journalist friend Jean Fletcher at one a.m. at La Coupole on Boulevard Montparnasse.

I walked to Stanley's place and took the elevator up to his living room. A beautiful redheaded English movie actress who'd caused a sensation at the nightclub a week ago was waiting to take the elevator down. I held the door open as she turned her aristocratic profile toward me to smile at Stanley.

"Later, baby," Stanley said to her. "You be back in fifteen minutes, hear?" She waved the sparkling diamonds on her bracelet at him, closed the elevator doors and went clunking down in it. It was 12:30 in the morning. Silver trays littered the table. It was weighted down with plates of thin sandwiches with cucumber slices in them, scones, the remaining pieces of three or four different kinds of cake, half-empty jars of jam and honey, silver tea and coffee pots and fancy cups and saucers.

Stanley's man Finn came in and cleared up. He looked like an Irish version of the giant Italian boxer, Primo Carnera, with his broken nose and cauliflower ears. He stood half a foot taller than my six feet. Finn had made a hasty exit from Ireland because he'd chosen the wrong faction of the I.R.A. Stanley had met him in a bar on the Champs-Elysées a few months ago and taken him in. Now they were inseparable.

"Sorry to barge in on you, Stanley. Wasn't that Sally...?" He waved me off and filled two glasses of water for us and lit a cigar. He laughed when he saw the look of disbelief on my face.

"You're drinking water now? I've never seen you drink water before."

"Mon petit, I need me a break. Sally real fancy and she got her a yen for some eats she call 'afternoon tea.' Lord have mercy, thank goodness you phone me. I need me some water real bad, which I ain't drank since I was a little sprout back in New Orleans. I don't feature makin' it with Sally with no taste of tea and cake still in my mouth," he said, frowning.

"What's happenin'?"

I gave Stanley a rundown of what Hannah and I had in mind. The more dangerous I made the business sound, the wider his smile grew. When I finished, he said,

"Don't you worry, Urby. I'm gone phone the Colonel and we work us out a plan. Now, if you excuse me, I gots to tend to my woman." Right on cue, she stepped out of the elevator, primping her flaming red hair. She held the elevator door open, sizing me up.

Since the announcement of the Munich Agreement yesterday early in the morning, the sense of panic and fear gripping the Parisians had been transformed into a carnival atmosphere. It was one a.m. on Saturday the first of October and Hitler wouldn't be sending his armies into Czechoslovakia after all. France wouldn't be at war again. The Parisians would party hard this weekend.

As I walked along Montparnasse Boulevard, black Renault, Citroën and Delage motor cars inched past, filled with shouting passengers waving wine and champagne bottles out of the windows. A traffic jam spread beyond La Coupole as far as the eye could see. Car horns were honking rhythmically, one-two, one-two-three, one-two, one-two-three.

I looked through the glass front of La Coupole, as the chill wind lashed my overcoat. My waiter friend Honoré spotted me and hustled over to hold the door open as waves of sound and heat and smells from sex-gorged bodies washed over me. He led me into the restaurant, past tables of people eating their way through huge seafood platters with waiters opening up so many bottles of champagne that it sounded like machine gun fire at the Battle of the Somme. The Argentine band was playing languid tangos as Honoré led me to my table.

In my private eye days, La Coupole had been my Left Bank headquarters for meeting up with customers, friends and informants when I was working the few cases that took me to the area.

What I liked most about La Coupole was drinking there with my journalist friend Jean Fletcher, who could tell me what was going on in Paris and in Europe. As a trade off, I filled her in on the happenings in Harlem-in-Montmartre and in other parts of the underbelly of Paris. Jean's knowledge and contacts had been as invaluable to me as Stanley's in bringing Daphne Robinson and myself back from Hitler's Germany alive.

Honoré escorted Jean to our table, her black leather coat draped over his arm. She was a no-nonsense brunette from Indiana, about my age and height. She always wore a red beret and usually a tweed jacket and corduroy pants. Most people would call Jean "imposing" or "formidable." She was all of that, if you overlooked the twinkle in her hazel-colored eyes and her gift for telling the outrageous stories and gossip recorded in her circus-stunt memory. I had met her at Chez Red Tops about a week before I took on the Daphne Robinson case and during the course of a boozy evening we'd become friends.

"Whew," Jean said, shaking my hand as she sat down, "People are going wild out there, Urby. Sorry I'm late, but the traffic was so blocked up that I walked here all the way from rue Jacob. People kept buying me drinks."

I let Jean in on what a "friend" had told me about Hitler's plan to attack Poland without letting her know that the Colonel was my source. Jean looked at me blankly for an instant. I knew that she was recording every word in her brain.

"No leaking of sources, right?" she asked. I nodded Yes, then said,

"The Nazis are planning to haul in the Jews and start killing them wholesale within weeks. Hannah and I need to get two of them out, by yesterday."

Jean went pale and said in her flat, rapid-fire voice,

"It won't be a picnic getting Hannah's friends out of Germany. But if the Colonel can pull it off and you and Hannah can hide them for a week, I'll work on Ambassador Bullitt to grant them an emergency visa to the States. He isn't as big an anti-Semite as most of our diplomats. I'll promise him to write a piece on his good works in France. Who knows? It might help his campaign for FDR to put him in the Secretary of State's chair and get rid of that horrible man Cordell Hull. If Lindbergh doesn't become President in 1940." Jean made a face and went on,

"Whatever you do, though, Urby, **you** must stay out of Germany. You'll be arrested as soon as you arrive. One of my newspaper pals told me that they've had you on a watch list since your escape with that lying blonde bitch Daphne Robinson. If they catch you, it could be the guillotine."

"The guillotine? Come on, Jean. I thought only the French still use it."

"I'm not kidding. Hitler's brought the Widow to Germany."

That really gave me something to think about. I'd stood in a crowd to see a man guillotined in the street outside of La Santé prison in the early 20s. The fellow's widow begged the executioner to give her his head. "Monsieur de Paris" as the French used to call the chief *coupe-tête*, just bagged it and started dismantling his guillotine with the help of his assistants. Knowing what I now knew about Hitler's plans for the Jews, I had to keep my head off the chopping block so that Hannah wouldn't end up like that woman. Jean was studying me and she said,

"Sorry about the gruesome stuff. But don't go to Germany. I bet Colonel Schulz-Horn would give you the same advice."

Thinking about the threat to Hannah if Hitler invaded France suddenly drained all the energy out of me. I felt dizzy, fearful for her safety and then exhausted, dead on my feet. I needed sleep fast. I asked Jean if I could walk her back to her hotel on the rue Jacob. Fortunately, she said,

"I appreciate your gallantry, but you look tired, mon ami. I'm going to stay here a while, soak up some atmosphere and a bunch of whiskey and then head home, ink up a safe version of the Colonel's story on Hitler's projects and cable my story to New York." Jean had guessed who my source was, as I reckoned she would.

We said our goodbyes. I gave up on finding a free taxi and the metro had stopped running hours ago. I trudged to the Seine through ear-splitting car horns until I spotted a taxi letting off passengers at Lapérouse restaurant on the Quai des Grands Augustins. I skirmished with a drunk man and woman to get into the cab. They were too ossified to put up much resistance and I muscled my way in.

In my reverie, the taxi's window became a movie screen showing me a guillotine and my severed head staring up at me from a basket held by a smiling Lonny Johnson. The Count's Oriflamme stormtroopers rained blows on Hannah with their rifle butts then my father's hit man, Pierre, slit her throat.

CHAPTER 6

Right after my quartet had finished its second set just past midnight, Stanley signalled for me to follow him into my office behind the stage. Hannah was standing at the bar watching me and I nodded for her to join us.

Inside the office, Stanley was sitting in Redtop's old leather armchair behind her desk. Hannah usually sat there, when she was running the business end of Urby's Masked Ball. Hannah and I sat down in armchairs facing Stanley, waiting to hear what he had to say about his and the Colonel's plans to get her friends out of Germany.

"A drink, Stanley?" Hannah asked, but he nodded No.

"Just a touch of water, I'm gettin' used to the stuff." Hannah looked at me, astonished, and I shrugged.

"Water?" she repeated, not believing her ears. She'd never seen him drink water before either.

"Bottle water, honey. You can't be sure about no French water come out of no faucet, I reckon."

"Seltzer water alright? It's the only bottled water we've got."

"Fine." Hannah went to the icebox, took a Seltzer water bottle out and spritzed some into a glass. She whispered to me,

"I wish you had your Leica camera here. To record this for posterity-Stanley meets H2O."

The silence continued as Stanley kept inhaling his cigar and stabbing at ever more elaborate smoke rings. He'd sip the water, brandish the glass at Hannah and chuckle at her astonishment as he smacked his lips in contentment.

"What time it be?" He finally asked. I looked at the clock and said,

"Fifteen minutes after midnight."

"Fine," Stanley said, "Just fine." He lapsed into silence again. The telephone rang and he grabbed it.

"Stanley talkin'!" he shouted, holding the receiver at arm's length. He smiled and said,

"Five minutes? Thank your folks for me. Tell 'em I won't forget, hear?" He hung up and placed the telephone back on the desk. He mashed his cigar out in Redtop's green jade ashtray. Stanley eased back in the chair, flexed his fingers, then said to Hannah,

"Honey, I'd love to have me a touch of yo' rye whiskey right about now. Why don't y'all join me?" Hannah opened the liquor cabinet, took out three whiskey glasses and a bottle of Hiram Walker. Relieved, she poured each of us a generous shot.

We tipped our glasses at each other. Stanley savored his rye contentedly, sighing "Ummph, ummph. Almost taste as good as seltzer water."

"Stanley..." Hannah wagged a finger at him then took a swig of rye.

There was a tentative rapping on the door. I stood up to open it, but Stanley gestured for me to sit down.

"Honey," he said to Hannah. "You best open it."

Hannah clapped and shouted with delight, hugging people I couldn't see. She led in two small, dark, dishevelled men, both wearing well-worn dark overcoats and crumpled up snap-brim hats. Hannah and the two men had tears running down their cheeks. One of them carried a battered violin case and the other a spit-shined leather briefcase. A third man, an American I reckoned, stood watching us. He slouched against the door-frame in a frayed black overcoat. He held a grey flatcap in his right hand.

There was something familiar about the fellow, but I couldn't put my finger on it. Stanley looked at him, clearly astonished for an instant before he zipped his poker face on. Stanley and I eyeballed each other, while I waited for the man to introduce himself. He held out his hand toward Hannah saying,

"Evan Shipman." While he shook our hands, my heart pounded so hard I thought it would jump out of my chest. Back in 1934, as I tried to enter Germany to hunt down Daphne Robinson, the SS border guards had mistaken me for this man. Hannah waited for him to go on.

"American Christian Rescue Society... ACRS," he said, tentatively. "Ever heard of it?"

"No," Hannah said. He smiled.

"We're a small group of concerned Christians, horrified by what Hitler's been doing to Jews and other minorities since he came to power in 1933. We try to get as many endangered people out of Germany as we can. It's never easy, but this time we got help from a gentleman who said he knew both of you." He bowed towards Stanley and me.

I knew that he meant Colonel Schulz-Horn but Evan Shipman was choosing his words carefully in the presence of Cohen and Rosenthal, not letting them know too many details about their escape.

"We've saved a number of people," he went on. "Unfortunately, the Nazis have cottoned on to us. When the Nuremberg Laws were passed in 1935, Jews lost their German nationality and their passports were confiscated unless they managed to hide them away in time. Some countries have been generous about issuing emergency passports or visas so we can sneak people out. I can't say that America has helped us a lot. Now it's become much too risky for us to keep operating in Germany and these gentlemen are likely to be our last evacuees."

"It must be tough on your wife, you being in such a dangerous place?" Hannah asked. Evan Shipman blushed and said,

"Never got married. Never had the time. During the Great War, they locked me up in a U.S. military training camp for a couple of years for being a non-religious conscientious objector, although I kept telling them I'm a Christian. A few years after it ended, I joined movements protesting against the injustice being done to Sacco and Vanzetti and against lynchings in the South. I got so sick of what was going on in America that I had to leave or end up turning to violence. I finally joined the ACRS and they sent me to Germany to help evacuate people targeted by Hitler after he came to power in 1933. I never had a chance to finish my work in the American South so I guess I'll be heading back there now."

Hannah was looking at him, full of admiration. I felt jealousy taking hold of me for the first time since we'd been together.

"How did you get our friends out of Germany so quickly?" Hannah finally asked. Shipman shrugged and answered,

"I'd better not get into that. Let's just say that they traveled mostly in the trunks of cars with just enough food and water to keep them going."

"How long has this ACRS been operating?" I asked. "I went into Germany four years ago and got stopped at the border by the SS because they thought I was you. They kept asking me if I was Evan Shipman, and I kept jabbing at the name Urby Brown printed on my passport. I thought that Evan Shipman was a name the SS dreamed up out of thin air to make me sweat."

Hannah looked us over and said,

"You're both the same height, six feet tall. And you're what, around 40, 45?" she asked. He said in his strong Yankee accent,

"Could you please call me Evan? You're right on both counts, Miss..."

"Just Hannah," she said.

"Hannah," he repeated, seeming to savor the sound her name made.

"One last question and I swear I'll shut up," Hannah said. "Has the ACRS got any operations in Spain? I mean getting Republican fighters out now that General Franco's got the upper hand?"

"We just don't have the resources, I'm sorry to say. Saving Jewish people from Hitler is our top priority now."

Hannah protested,

"I hate this French and English neutrality! They're letting Franco win by default. I hate just standing by and letting Spain fall to the fascists!" Hannah looked at me as if I should feel guilty about not going to Spain with her, as she'd asked me to. But she now knew why I'd vowed never to kill again and that I was war weary. I intended for the Great War to be my last. Evan Shipman and Hannah stared into each other's eyes, soul mates in fighting the good fight. I was growing more and more jealous of Shipman. Hannah suddenly said,

"Urby. Evan's got hazel eyes and yours are blue-grey. That's probably what got you past the SS border guards into Germany."

The two other men watched us, smiling nervously all the while we were talking to Evan Shipman. Hannah suddenly seemed to realize they were still in the room. She hooked her arms into theirs and introduced us:

"Stanley Bontemps, Urby Brown. I want you to meet Jascha Cohen, my violin 'maestro' at Juilliard," he bowed his head, "and Elam Rosenthal, one of the greatest pianists in the world." Rosenthal made a stiff bow, as if his joints ached. He was a very young man who, judging by his haggard face, had aged a lot in the past few days.

"Danke, Danke, tausend time to save uns," he said. Stanley patted him on the shoulder and Elam winced.

"Them Nazis beat on you, son?" Stanley asked. He rarely looked angry, but he was furious now. Elam nodded Yes.

"Don't you worry none, you safe now," Stanley said. He turned to Jascha Cohen. "Y'all need to get some good eats down you and some sleep. We gone talk when you rested."

"We sleep here?" Jascha asked, looking around him smiling, as if the tiny office was a luxury suite at the Ritz.

'No, "Hannah said. "We've got two empty maid's rooms at the top of the building. You can stay there until we can get you emergency visas to travel to America. Do you have your passports?" They searched in their clothes and then held them out to me. Although I couldn't understand German, their passports looked authentic.

"Are they real or fakes?" I asked. Cohen laughed for the first time.

"We gave the SS the fakes," he said. "Our friend Shmuel Blumberg made them. They're much better than these real ones."

"You'll fly to New York with entry visas to America within a week, if everything works out," Hannah said. "The maid's rooms aren't huge and you'll have to spend a lot of time in them until we can get you out. I hope you don't mind flying?"

"Mind?" Cohen said. "We swim to America if we have to."

Cohen and Rosenthal listened intently as Hannah explained the ground rules to them:

"Maximum caution. Please keep your curtains closed when you're in your rooms. There's a real danger that we're being watched here." The two men looked at her uncomprehendingly.

"Warum?" Elam asked. "Why?" Cohen translated.

"It's a long story," I said. "My father's a French Count, a fanatic who's the boss of the biggest fascist group in the country and friends with Hitler and Mussolini." They looked shocked.

"I'm sorry that you'll be here like prisoners but..." Jascha interrupted me, saying,

"One week, that is not long to wait. Still, I ask myself, how safe are you and Hannah, if your father is such a man as you describe? Should you not be leaving with us?"

"We'll be ready to leave when the time comes," I said. Evan Shipman had watched all of our exchanges in silence. He finally said he had an appointment with a friend from the American Embassy, after which he planned to take a train to Le Havre and then board a steamship for New York from there. He'd been away from America for five years, the last three on the run from Hitler's Black shirts. He said he planned to stop off to see his mother in New England and then head to the Deep South.

As Evan Shipman put his flatcap back on, ready to leave, Jascha Cohen and Elam Rosenthal tried to hug him. He shied away from them as if he wasn't crazy about being touched. He brushed off their thanks by saying,

"I did what any Christian would do when faced by evil." He nodded goodbye all around, then held out his hand to me and I shook it. He said,

"Mr. Brown, I'm sorry that the SS gave you such a hard time at the German border back in 1934, mistaking you for me. I was pretty active going in and out of Germany at the time."

"No apologies needed," I said. "And it's 'Urby.' You were working for much nobler causes than I was." He smiled quizzically at me, doffed his cap to Hannah and then left.

"The man's got guts," Hannah said. "You've got to hand it to him."

"He ain't the only one got guts. There be Urby too," Stanley said. I'd never seen him irritated by her before.

"Of course," Hannah said, suddenly on the defensive.

◢

The next morning, the police raided our apartment and dragged Jascha and Elam away. Before the police vans sped off, I caught sight of my father's chief stormtrooper Pierre Lestage getting into one of them. Hannah and I raged at the policemen, but it did no good. We phoned Stanley and he came rushing over. One of his contacts in the French government had told him the cops had received an anonymous tip that the men were holing up with us. Stanley's informant promised to give him more details within the hour.

I reckoned the Count was behind it all and guessed that he'd sent Pierre to my nightclub to supervise the capture of Cohen and Rosenthal. Hannah cried out,

"It's all **my** fault! I thought we'd get away with it because the police would never believe two classical musicians were hiding out in a jazz club in Pigalle."

"We done our best," Stanley said, comforting her. "Them Nazis was fixin' to make slaves out of 'em or kill 'em and we done our best to save 'em. But we ain't counted on no spy among us." The telephone rang and it was for Stanley again. He shook his head sadly and hung up the phone.

"It was Lonny, done rat them out to your daddy. Your old man done give them to the cops when they promise not to arrest you and Hannah."

"I'm going to bust Lonny's jaw, then kick his ass into the gutter!"

"You leave him to me," Stanley said. "Meanwhile, you best start lookin' for a new drummer, 'cause Lonny need more than a fist-beatin'. His drummin' wasn't no good no more nohow. Sound like two armadillos tap dancin' on a hot tin roof." When Stanley's voice turned to ice and his eyes froze over, death was lurking nearby. I reckoned that Lonny would probably soon be on the floor of the Seine, chained to a block of Corsican concrete.

Lonny Johnson wasn't at the nightclub that evening and we never saw him again. I found a Corsican drummer named Jacques Stefani to replace him. He couldn't keep time as well as Lonny, but he was the nephew of the head of the main Corsican criminal syndicate in Pigalle who'd been one of Stanley's best friends since the early thirties. Stanley had saved the life of the mobster's son by paying all expenses for an emergency flight to London and for an operation by the world's best heart surgeon, a friend of Stanley's.

Hiring Jacques Stefani would buy us extra protection from the growing number of fascist gangs marauding through Paris. They were stepping up their attacks on Jews and non-white people, waiting for Hitler to sweep into Paris and finish the job for them. Meanwhile, I reckoned we'd be safe around Montmartre, our mountain of martyrdom, because the fascist bully boys lacked the guts to go up against the Corsicans.

CHAPTER 7

I **stood before** my father's elegant beige stone *pierre de taille* building on the rue Boissy d'Anglas, a few blocks away from the American Embassy. Engraved on a gilded nameplate beside the door were the words "Le Comte Import-Export, Premier étage gauche." Extensive renovation work was being done on its nineteenth-century façade, which was covered by scaffolding. The Count's fascist-monarchist political movement was obviously coining more money from wealthy donors.

Articles in Le Populaire claimed that the "haute bourgeoisie" had started betting heavily on the Count again. Their wallets came out after Hitler and Mussolini flooded Spain's General Franco with weaponry and with planes flown by their pilots. Their aid had turned the tide of the Civil War in Franco's favor, despite the arms and matériel the Soviets gave to the Republicans. England and France sat on their hands, congratulating each other for having chosen the path of neutrality.

An armored security front door had been installed since my last visit. The bell-like contraption that I used to ring to enter had been replaced by an electric buzzer. I passed a bunch of other such new-fangled gadgets and doo-hickeys inside.

Because his movement was rich again, the Count hadn't tried to blackmail me lately for any of the one hundred grand in hush money that the Robinson family had paid me for shutting up about Daphne's escapades in Nazi Germany. Neither had there been any more demands that I cut him in on the inheritance left to me by Redtop.

What the Count thought he had to blackmail me with was a signed witness statement he'd tortured out of Redtop swearing that I'd shot and killed his former Oriflamme stormtrooper Bartholomew Lincoln "Buster" Thigpen, Jr. in cold blood in February 1934 in the Bois de Boulogne. According to the document, I'd then forced her to drive me to Argenteuil so that I could deep-six Buster's corpse in the Seine. The Count figured that he could use the statement to threaten me into doing his bidding if I didn't play ball.

He didn't know that the paper he'd forced Redtop to sign was worthless. She told me that she'd tricked him into letting her sign it with an "X," which you used to sign documents in France if you were illiterate. But she knew how to read and write. She even kept a diary, which she planned to use to write her memoirs. She said she'd told the story of why I killed Buster Thigpen, which was to save her life. Her diary also described how the Count tortured and bullied her into signing his statement by threatening to have the police deport her. Redtop planned to tell me where she kept her diary and her version of what went down, but she hadn't got around to it before her "suicide."

After the cops captured Cohen and Rosenthal, I realized that I needed to stop fooling around and lay my hands on Redtop's papers fast to deny the Count what he thought was his leverage on me. It was time to counterattack by proving he'd ordered Pierre to "erase" Redtop, because I was convinced that he'd told Pierre to kill her and make her death look like suicide.

Even if Redtop's papers helped me to build a solid case against the Count and Pierre, I grew surer by the day that the Count's backers in the Préfecture would never bring him to justice. But I could do some blackmailing of my own by threatening to leak the story to the left-wing press or to English or American newspapers. I doubted that even the Count's great benefactor, Marshal Pétain, would want to be linked to the man behind the murder of an American woman, especially Redtop who was a household name in America.

"Soyez le bienvenu, Monsieur le Comte," Pierre Lestage said.

"Welcome, Count," was the form of address that my father had ordered all of his men to use with me. In his mind, we had a signed and sealed deal that I'd agree to being recognized as his legitimate son some day soon and, in exchange, he'd leave Hannah, Stanley and the nightclub alone and keep renewing our papers. I'd agreed to that deal a year ago to buy time. But now that I knew the role he'd played in the capture of Cohen and Rosenthal in my club by giving them over to the cops after being tipped off by Lonny Johnson, the time had come to dot the i's and cross the t's again.

"So, you still restrain yourself from the violence, Monsieur?" Pierre asked. His eyes gleamed with malice as he led me up the stairs with his men trooping behind us.

"I saw you at my nightclub with the police yesterday morning when they arrested some friends of mine."

"Jews!" he spat out.

My rage took hold of me and I sucker punched him in the gut. He tumbled backwards into the arms of the three stormtroopers below him on the stairs. I climbed the steps two by two to the landing and walked to the Count's office door. The old wooden one had been replaced by an armored metal door with a buzzer beside it. Pierre used to knock on the old door three times, followed by another knock, which was the special signal to let the Count know that I was his visitor. I followed the same routine with the buzzer. The Count called out,

"Enter, my son." I heard his voice through a brand new loudspeaker hanging on the wall. Pierre's fellow stormtroopers were dragging him up to the landing. I heard the lock click open then entered the Count's office. He rose from his desk and held out his arms for the ritual four kisses on the cheeks, but I ignored him and sat. He stared at me with his left eye, the one without the gold-colored eyepatch.

"So, you're beefing up security," I said, looking around. "Metal doors, microphones, a button to unlock the door. Are you expecting an attack from the guards at the American Embassy down the street?" The Count laughed but stopped when he sensed my rage.

"No, I'm expecting to go **on** the attack, when our German friends march into Paris," he smirked. He pointed to the walls around him and said,

"This room is impregnable. It's also totally soundproof. I could shoot you with a cannon and no one outside would hear a sound."

"Maybe I'll bring a cannon with me next time I come," I said.

"I sense that you are somewhat angry, my son."

"Cops are arresting people **inside** my nightclub! Your spy, my drummer, is high-stepping in front of the pearly gates as we speak. If Pierre comes around again, he's a dead man. I'm not saying that I'll do the killing myself. I'm getting to be like you." The Count just laughed.

"It's only because of my...friendship with the Préfet that you and your... mistress are not sharing a jail cell with her friends." Then he looked pensive and said,

"Perhaps I should have turned a blind eye." He laughed at his awkward words, then said, "After all, it is, all of it, a joke of God."

"You're insane!" I raged. "We're not talking about jokes. We're talking about you sending two men back to Germany to be murdered."

The Count looked bored and pressed a button under his desktop. That meant I was dismissed. As I walked along the corridor with its newly repainted walls and new carpeting, I upped my estimates of how many more rich and powerful French people were pumping big money into the Oriflamme movement. I reckoned they were banking on a quick victory by Hitler's troops over their own armed forces.

⋏

Hannah and I began a frantic search for Redtop's diary. We spent the whole day, with Stanley helping us, turning the apartment inside out, searching for the writings that Redtop had hidden somewhere. I'd never seen a book in Redtop's apartment, so I knew that we'd struck gold when Stanley climbed up a ladder and yelled that he'd found one under piles of clothing on a high shelf in her walk-in closet. Hannah and I hadn't had time to search the huge apartment in the months that we'd lived there and re-opened Chez Red Tops as Urby's Masked Ball.

Stanley handed down a leather-bound edition of "Up from Slavery," by Booker T. Washington. I opened the book to find that it was hollowed-out and held a thin brown notebook with the words "Journal, January-March 1938" on its cover and a folded piece of paper inside it like a bookmark.

On the last day of her life, Redtop had written that the Count had prepared a new copy of the witness statement which he ordered her to put her full signature on or else "face a painful death." The Count's new statement was among her papers. In its legalese, he had her attest that she'd witnessed one Urby Brown, Private Investigator, shoot and kill in cold blood an unarmed musician named Bartholomew Lincoln "Buster" Thigpen Junior in the early morning hours of February 10, 1934. It further stated that I'd forced her to drive me, with the corpse in the trunk, to a place near a jetty at Argenteuil to dispose of the body by weighting it down with rocks and immersing said cadaver in the Seine.

Redtop had defiantly signed an "X" again on the Count's new statement. She'd written that the Count was sending Pierre Lestage to her apartment at two a.m. to fetch the new statement signed with her real John Hancock.

Near the end of her diary, Redtop wrote that she wasn't going to put her signature on any witness statement written out by the Count. I unfolded the paper that was inside the diary. It was her signed account of what really happened during the killing of Buster Thigpen. She wrote:

"Urby Brown wasn't no killer 'cause Buster Thigpen gone crazy and be armed with my shotgun he take off me, and he be squeezing the trigger to blow off my head when Urby Brown shoot him to save me my life. Urby Brown be a war hero and a fine, upstanding gent, innocent of all charges in the lying witness statement of the Count, which him and his gang try to force me to sign holding my head under water and holding they guns to my head." She'd signed her own statement and it had been witnessed by a retired Garde des Sceaux friend of hers and notarized at the U.S. consulate.

Redtop's last diary entries were that if Pierre Lestage tried any "monkey business" on her, she aimed to go down in a blaze of glory, *"putting my sawed-off shotgun onto Mr. Pierre Lestage."* She was sick of the Count's bullying and threats and she was *"ready to meet my Maker,"* rather than sign any more fake witness statements which would *"send Urby Brown to that thing the French cops uses to chop off your head like a chicken for the pot."*

Having found the diary and Redtop's notarized account of Buster Thigpen's death, witnessed by a retired Attorney-General of France no less, we all agreed that Stanley should keep the originals in his safe after I had a photostat copy made of all her writings. I planned to show them to Jean Fletcher as soon as possible. That way she'd know what had really gone down with Redtop if anything happened to Hannah and me. I'd hold onto an extra copy to show to the Count, if I needed to make him back off. Stanley had me write out instructions to his servant Finn that if anything happened to Hannah, myself or Stanley, the originals in Stanley's safe were to be handed over to Miss Jean Fletcher of the New York Knickerbocker magazine.

Fortunately, we were ready for our counterattack, because Hannah disappeared and things went crazy.

Chapter 8

A few days after we found Redtop's writings and made our arrangements for their safekeeping, I woke up to discover that Hannah wasn't in bed. I went into the kitchen and found a note from her that said, *"Gone to Spain. I'm sorry, but I didn't plan it. It's just that when Jascha and Elam were carted off by the police, I felt I had to do something to fight against fascism. If Franco and Hitler and Mussolini win in Spain, we're next on the list. Don't worry about me. I'm going with friends and I'll keep in touch with you somehow. I love you more than ever, but I have to do this. Forever yours, Hannah."*

I didn't believe it at first and I combed through all her old haunts in Paris looking for her. Her friends in the Latin Quarter knew a lot about her plans to go to Spain despite their attempts to convince her that Spain was a lost cause and that she was walking into certain capture and death. They said she kept talking about doing something to save the Republican forces from being slaughtered wholesale. I kicked myself for not taking her seriously when she started spending most of her free time meeting with like-minded friends in cafés on the Left Bank to scheme up ways to help the Republicans. Meanwhile, I was spending my free time cooling out from my growing fears for Hannah's safety by watching Pathé newsreels and movies at the Cinéma Max Linder and cutting up old touches with Stanley at his penthouse apartment.

Months passed as I divided my time between keeping the nightclub going, making frantic trips to the American and Spanish Embassies and the

French Foreign Affairs Ministry on the Quai d'Orsay. I read Le Populaire's accounts of the death throes of the Spanish Republic as its fighters were annihilated by Franco's men and the German and Italian air forces.

Early in February 1939, Stanley got word from Colonel Dieter Schulz-Horn that Hannah was being held prisoner in Cadaqués, a few miles from Portbou on Spain's border with France. Renegade troops from Franco's army were demanding five thousand dollars in cash for her release. If they didn't have the money within twenty-four hours, she'd be gang-raped by Spanish legionnaires and then garrotted. The Colonel gave me the name and telephone number of a Frenchman in Perpignan then he hung up. I phoned the man immediately and he knew all about the ransom demand. He said that, once we'd agreed to pay the ransom and picked him up in Perpignan, he'd telephone the Spaniards and she'd be delivered to the border checkpoint at Portbou two hours later. For one grand more, the Frenchman could get her back into France with no questions asked. I agreed at once and told Stanley, who said,

"Let's get goin'."

We jumped into his Rolls-Royce with Finn at the wheel. Stanley stashed his Colt M1911 in the glove compartment with extra clips of bullets and we burned rubber. The three of us took turns racing nonstop to Perpignan where we picked up the Frenchman, a retired gendarme. He knew the guards on both sides and we were waiting at the border an hour before the Spaniards arrived. Franco's officer crossed into France and took the cash, which was wrapped up in the front page of an old copy of Le Populaire. He opened it and thumbed his way through the ransom money, counting it. Our retired gendarme doled out bribes to the French border guards to look the other way and let Hannah through. The smoke from their cigarettes curled up into the bitterly cold air of the Pyrenees. They kicked a soccer ball around to keep warm while we concluded our business.

"Muy bien," the Spanish officer said, satisfied with his count. Then he strolled back into Spain, blew a whistle and three Spanish legionnaires dragged Hannah to a spot ten yards from the border and released her. She saw Stanley and me waving at her frantically and she stumbled toward us, finally collapsing into my arms a few yards inside France.

They'd kept me prisoner with her, because I feared that she'd never return alive. Hannah and I both trembled when I finally held her again and kissed her bruised face. I felt like racing back for Stanley's Colt and slaughtering the men who'd dumped her like a sack of potatoes, cowards ready to rape and kill her for five grand. Stanley and Finn looked like they felt the same as I did as we faced off with the Spanish officer and the legionnaires. They tightened their hands on their weapons.

"Take me home, please!" Hannah cried out. We all snapped out of it.

The Spanish officer and the legionnaires raced off in a camouflaged truck, while Stanley, Finn and I lifted Hannah onto the back seat of the Rolls-Royce and piled our overcoats on top of the thin grey blanket covering her. She fell asleep immediately. The French border guards continued with their banter and smoking and soccer playing as if we weren't there.

After we dropped off the retired gendarme, Finn floored the accelerator and we roared off to Paris. Hannah slept all the way back and she was still asleep when I carried her up the stairs to our apartment. I sat by her bedside until she woke up a day later. Her first panicked words were,

"Where are the others?" And then she seemed to remember and tears ran down her cheeks as I held her tight. She closed her eyes again and slept through another day and night.

⋏

I spent the next eight months helping Hannah to mend, but she healed herself mostly. She'd get up early and head to the Pigalle metro station to go to Place Saint Michel. She insisted on going alone. Hannah told me that she spent the morning hanging out with her fellow violinists and teachers in cafés near Place Saint Michel and the Schola Cantorum on rue Saint Jacques. Afterwards, she'd lunch with friends who'd fought in Spain or demonstrated for the Republican cause. They mourned the fall of the Republic when Franco announced the end of hostilities in April.

Hannah rarely talked to me about what had happened to her in Spain and I didn't want to make things worse by asking too many questions.

From what little she said, I learned that she'd been captured when she was fleeing across Catalonia with a band of Republican fighters trying to escape across the French border. They'd dug in to face the enemy at Cadaqués on the Mediterranean Coast, making them sitting ducks for the Messerschmitt fighters that swooped in from the sea to strafe and bomb them. After two days of resisting the attacks of waves of Spanish legionnaires, the handful of survivors had surrendered and then been garroted. They'd spared Hannah only because she wore a Red Cross armband and was an American. The officer in charge reckoned that they could arrange a ransom deal for her. The only good thing that Hannah had to say about Franco's men was that the officers knew enough about the ransom value of captured female Americans to restrain their men, and themselves, from raping then killing them.

The Count, who already hated her because she was Jewish, hated her even more now because she'd gone to war on the side of the Reds.

▲

On August 23, 1939, the "unthinkable" finally happened. As Colonel Schulz-Horn had warned me, the Foreign Ministers of Germany and the Soviet Union signed a non-aggression pact.

Fear descended on Paris again. With the Soviet Union now out of his way, Poland was next on Hitler's menu.

After Hitler's armies invaded Poland on September 2, 1939, France and England declared war on Germany within days. The world was at war again a few months past my forty-fourth birthday. It had been only twenty-five years from the start of one war to the start of the next. From what my French Foreign Legion buddies had told me about the development of the airplane and the tank over that time, we all feared that this new war might bring an end to the world.

On the day France declared war, Hannah and I sat among the silent patrons at the Café Paname, no longer wondering whether we should escape from France, but if we had enough time to get out if France caved in to an all-out assault from Germany. I was certain that America would declare war on Germany and Italy soon, which would make Hannah and me enemy aliens, subject to capture if the Germans marched into Paris. I was determined to get Hannah to safety even if it meant losing everything we had in France and returning to Jim Crow America. Getting her to safety also meant that we'd have to work out a plan with Stanley to keep my father from blocking our escape. To do that, we'd have to sneak past the plainclothes policemen and Oriflamme watching our nightclub.

Right away, Hannah and I started working out plans with Stanley for the two of us to get out of France, because Stanley himself refused to even think of leaving. But there were few signs of war, apart from the French and English army mobilizations that we read about in Le Populaire and saw in the Pathé newsreels. As time dragged on without major combat, Hannah and I started thinking of all the reasons that we didn't want to go back to America and Jim Crow. We lulled ourselves into believing that Hitler and Mussolini had come to their senses and would back down rather than take on the English, the French and, a short time later, the Americans. I grew all the more convinced that all sides would step back from the apocalypse because I remembered that in the Great War the first battles had begun days after the declarations of war at the end of July 1914. Five weeks later, the first Battle of the Marne had been fought in September, killing or wounding nearly a half million men on all sides.The German army had even reached the outer suburbs of Paris before being beaten back.

In May 1940, when the "Phony War," the "Drôle de Guerre" exploded into a real war, we were all taken by surprise.

Paris, June 11, 1940-Exodus

Paris started emptying as soon as word-of-mouth stories began to trickle into the city about big defeats suffered by the French, British and Belgian armies. Parisians turned a deaf ear to the French government's propaganda machine bragging about heroic French victories and massive German losses of men and matériel. Everything went downhill fast after the Nazis launched their lightning assault in the North in mid-May 1940 and swept through Belgium and the Netherlands supported by their Panzer tanks and Stuka dive bombers. They'd nearly trapped the Anglo-French armies at Dunkirk when an impromptu armada of British small boats had appeared out of nowhere to ferry hundreds of thousands of soldiers to England under heavy German air attacks. The Germans still captured over a hundred thousand soldiers, who were now prisoners of war.

By late May, nearly two million Parisians had fled the city, leaving it like one of those ghost towns you saw in American Western movies with tumbleweed blowing past deserted saloons. People commandeered buses and taxis and anything with wheels on it-from horse drawn carts to bicycles and baby carriages-to move their loved ones and their possessions out of the city. Hannah and I stayed on, trying to talk Stanley into leaving with us. He was in constant pain from arthritis now; he tried to ease it by chain-smoking reefers. He refused to budge.

From the foot of the Sacré Coeur basilica, Hannah and I could look out over Paris and see columns of smoke rising from the ministries clustered around the Eiffel Tower, the Quai d'Orsay and the Ecole Militaire.

"I read in Le Populaire that they're burning files and documents," Hannah said. "That means the government's going to get the hell out of here."

Still, Premier Paul Reynaud's new team of politicians kept up a drumbeat of propaganda about the gallant counterattacks of the French army and the heavy casualties that they were inflicting on the Reichswehr in the face of superior numbers with more modern weaponry.

We had a handful of customers each night until late May when the French started burning their fuel depots and the Luftwaffe attacked factories in the suburbs of Paris. The rank-smelling fumes from burning fuel and the gagging odor of paper smoke stank up the air and made it unbreatheable, even up in Montmartre. Three nights went by without a single customer.

"Let's shut down," I said to my two remaining musicians, one having vanished like a ghost. "I'll let you know when we reopen."

"You pay us two weeks mon ami," Jacques Stefani said, menacingly. Hannah handed over the money, because we knew we had to stay right with the Corsicans. Whatever happened and whoever ruled France, we reckoned they'd control the rackets around Montmartre forever.

Hannah and I left Paris on June 11, already late in the day, maybe too late. Stanley wasn't going anywhere, content to stay in his marijuana-fuelled paradise and "ride out the storm." Meanwhile, the French government had packed its bags and decamped to Tours the day before. Paris was declared an "Open City" and the American Ambassador, William C. Bullitt, was named Mayor of Paris by the departing government to negotiate with the Germans on its behalf.

The Le Bourget and Villeneuve-Orly airports had been knocked out by the Luftwaffe, which swelled the numbers of panicked Parisians and expatriates struggling to escape from the onrushing Germans by rail or road.

Hannah chose Bordeaux as our destination. Before Stanley started floating in his marijuana cloud he had friends of his arrange tickets for us on a boat leaving from there for Lisbon on June 13 at midday. He'd also booked passage for us on a ship leaving Lisbon for New York on June 15. It was a ten-day sea voyage instead of a two-day flight by seaplane, but Hannah had never flown and I couldn't talk her into taking to the air. I hesitated to fly too. I hadn't even gone near a plane since the end of the Great War. After crash landing in the Baie de Somme, I knew I'd never be able to pilot a plane again. But I was ready to fly in one to get Hannah to safety. Thanks to Jean Fletcher, we'd already obtained transit visas that would get us across Portugal to Lisbon, the last port left in Europe for escaping by sea to the Americas.

Closing up the nightclub took up the whole afternoon. By the time we finished hauling things down to the cellar and locking it up it was five p.m. There would be daylight until 8:30 or nine p.m. as we neared the longest days of the year. Hannah and I took the only two sets of keys with us, one of which we would leave with Stanley. I knew that Stanley and his Corsican friends would stand guard over our place.

Most of the colored residents of Harlem-in-Montmartre had already headed back to America. Colonel Schulz-Horn had told me to spread the word among them that, even if America wasn't at war with Germany, colored Americans could expect to be beaten up or even murdered by any Nazi soldiers they came across. Hitler had passed a second set of Nuremberg laws in 1935, two weeks after the ones aimed at Jews, which dealt with "Gypsies" and "Negroes." This second set confirmed our inferior status as sub-humans, like the Jews, and made it illegal for us to associate with Aryans.

My warnings, and the horror stories going around about how the Germans tended to execute, rather than capture, defeated soldiers from France's Black African colonies, had convinced most of my colored friends to leave. Heavy-hearted, they returned to Jim Crow America.

⅄

In the early morning hours, when we figured the "watchers" would be asleep, we'd started loading up the trunk of Redtop's Hispano-Suiza with gallon jugs of water, cans of meat and vegetables, baguettes, liter bottles of red wine and bottles of whiskey and calvados. We packed our suitcases with a few changes of clothing and other necessaries for a ship crossing from Lisbon to New York. At three a.m. on the day we planned to leave, we snuck our suitcases into the car and covered them with posters advertising the nightclub. We had two days to reach Bordeaux, to embark for Lisbon on June 13. Our strongbox fit into Redtop's custom-made giant glove compartments. It held twenty grand in US dollars, as well as gold ingots and most of Redtop's jewelry and precious stones.

We'd been stocking up on gasoline for a month on the sly and were able to cram enough ten liter jerricans of gasoline into the Hispano's trunk to get us to Bordeaux and further. The last things we packed were our musical instruments.

Without telling Hannah, I planned a detour towards Bagnoles-de-l'Orne in the Domfront region of Normandy, to see the ancestral castle of the d'Uribé-Lebrun family. My father wanted the "fruit of his loins," meaning me and any children from a marriage he arranged for me, to keep running things there for a thousand years, like Hitler's "Thousand Year Reich." When we finally hopped into the car to escape from Paris, we would have no luggage or picnic gear to pack. Any spies watching us would think we were just going out for a drive.

We had one more stop to make before we left Paris. Hannah and I went to say our goodbyes to Stanley and hand keys over. He was waiting for us with his man Finn who opened a bottle of champagne, filled our glasses and put them on the coffee table.

"Good luck and good travels," Finn croaked, a smile creasing his battered boxer's face. He left us alone with Stanley.

Stanley was high as a kite and he seemed to float over to his wall safe. It was hidden behind a painting of some kind of jungle. We heard the clicking of the combination lock, then Stanley came back with a blue velvet bag. He held it out to us and I grabbed it before his fingers seized up and pain brought tears to his eyes. I hefted it and recognized its weight.

"I got y'all a goin'- away present," he said with a sly grin.

I pulled out an M 1911 Colt with three clips of ammunition tied to it with a red satin ribbon. The gun was identical to the one I'd deep-sixed into the Seine four years ago, after I learned from a gloating Count that when I'd killed Buster Thigpen, I'd killed my half brother. Hannah looked at me, waiting for me to speak. Stanley broke the silence, saying,

"Take it, mon petit. You be needin' it to protect Hannah and yo' own self." When I hesitated, he went on: "I know why you gave up on shootin' irons after killin' that good for nothin' Buster to save Redtop. Then learnin' that he be your brother by Josephine Dubois when she rollin' with a different man and all. But these be different times. You gone be on the road and I hear tell that a lots of nasty things goin' down on them roads." Before I could refuse, Hannah took the gun and the clips of ammunition and stashed them in her handbag.

"Thanks," Hannah said and kissed Stanley's cheek. "Let's say this is your going-away present to me. I don't know how to use it, but I know we'll need it."

"I'll protect you," I said.

"I know, but I don't want you to die slugging it out with armed men and gangs of looters. I'll just keep pulling the trigger until they drop. At least, we'll take some of the bastards with us."

"Hand the stuff over Hannah, I know how to use it." Hannah handed me the hardware. Stanley watched us then lifted his glass.

"I'm beginnin' to believe y'all gone make it," he said.

I took out my Michelin map to show Stanley the route we planned to take to Bordeaux. From his jazz touring days, Stanley knew every nook and cranny of France. As I read out the names of the towns to him, he nodded his approval of the sinuous path we would follow to avoid main roads until we reached Laval in the Mayenne region. From there we would take major roads past Angers and Nantes until we hit Bordeaux. He questioned me about the hook west that I had made from Paris through Dreux and then a passage to Bagnoles-de-l'Orne in Normandy. Hannah overheard me when I whispered to him that the Count's castle stood there. She rolled her eyes and then exploded.

"Urby, this isn't a goddamned sightseeing tour! We've got to get to Bordeaux before the Nazis march down the Champs-Elysées."

I knew that Hannah was right, but I felt the pull of a place that, over the past six hundred years, had been home to the Count and his lineage, which included me, like it or not. I was drawn to it like cocaine in the old days. I knew going near it would hook me into heavier stuff, but I was fool enough to think it wouldn't.

We finished the champagne and Stanley said,

"Y'all best start drivin'. I reckon there be a long night ahead of you in heavy traffic. Don't fret about me or your business while you in America. I be waitin' for you in this here chair when you gets back."

I started to thank him for everything he had taught me about life and jazz but he stopped me cold.

"Y'all best go now," he said. "You got you maybe three hours of good light so git. And keep that Colt primed and ready."

As we approached the Porte d'Auteuil heading for the highway west, the traffic was inching ahead. We were surrounded by cars, trucks and buses, as well as horse-drawn carts and wagons-anything that could transport. They overflowed with people, mattresses, luggage, furniture, parasols, more mattresses and pets. By nightfall on June 11, after traveling for three hours, we'd reached the Carrefour Royal in the Forest of Marly-le-Roi, a distance of fifteen miles from Paris. The traffic had stalled as columns of infantrymen and military vehicles carrying exhausted and frightened French soldiers, limped past us in a deafening roar. They gave off the gagging stench of fear as they headed towards Paris to clash with the Germans racing to meet them.

Further westward, we crossed more columns of grimy, dog-tired looking French soldiers stumbling toward Paris like sleepwalkers with their rusty Great War weapons and vehicles. The soldiers were pushing the outgoing traffic into one lane and forcing larger vehicles off the road. In the columns of bumper to bumper traffic, any vehicle that lost its place had to wait a long time to get back onto the road, because the others refused to let them in. Some managed to force their way back when their passengers threw themselves in front of cars and trucks and dared the drivers to run them over. Fistfights were breaking out everywhere as the panicked French were blown asunder by the German whirlwind.

The noise was ear-splitting and the humid heat made you sweaty and thirsty. People ranted insults at each other in the night, as drivers jockeyed to get ahead of each other in fruitless attempts to go faster.

Rumors began to spread that the Germans had already entered the suburbs of Paris and that, at daybreak, they would send waves of Stuka dive bombers to attack the zombie-like French soldiers still shuffling their feet towards Paris to reinforce its defences. That meant that the civilians fleeing in the opposite direction would be massacred along with the soldiers, because there was no French air force to fight off the Stukas.

At about four o'clock in the morning of June 12, over eight hours since we'd left Paris, we reached Argentan in Normandy, a distance of some two-hundred kilometers, or 125 miles, from Paris.

Long unbroken columns of traffic stretched ahead of and behind us as the sun rose on June 12. We could sense fear gripping the long, winding lines of fleeing civilians. Daylight meant clear visibility for air attacks on the column from Stuka dive bombers, which had not, so far, put in an appearance.

CHAPTER 9

Horses now dotted the fields. We crossed through the spa town of Bagnoles-de-l'Orne and followed a sign that read, simply, "Le Château." To the southwest of Bagnoles, we saw an enormous white stone castle with a crenellated parapet. After waiting to see if there was movement inside, we drove up the long alleyway to the gates. If anyone was home, we'd tell them we were lost and ask for directions to Laval. We parked the car and walked toward the castle. We crossed the drawbridge which was lowered over an empty moat. I took the Colt out of my jacket and banged it on the heavy oak door until my arm ached. Finally, I said,

"Looks like nobody's home."

"This place is giving me the creeps," Hannah said. "Let's cut out."

"Let's take a quick look at the backyard first."

We walked around the castle and found, to our amazement, that the usual Le Nôtre style formal garden with ranks of trimmed hedges and an artificial pond with a fountain smack dab in the middle wasn't behind it. Instead, there was a large tarmacked airfield with an observation tower and windsocks hanging limply in the windless air. There were three hangars with airplane fuel pumps beside them. We walked up to one of them and spotted a small gold-painted single-engined plane with the Oriflamme insignia on it. The other two hangars were empty. I took the nozzle of the pump off its perch, squeezed the grip and airplane fuel splashed onto the tarmac.

"It's full of airplane fuel," I said. I tried the other pumps, which were also full.

"There can't be many private citizens in France with setups like this," Hannah said. "I wonder if your old man has his own air force to support his stormtroopers."

We drove back along the driveway and turned off it to hide the car in a copse where we had a clear view of the castle, but couldn't be seen from it or from the air if any planes flew overhead. For the first time in days, we were away from the panic of the exodus roads. A slight breeze was cooling us. We could see the white mass of the castle which dazzled through the swaying leaves of the giant copper beech trees scattered across its immense formal front gardens. Hugging each other as we gazed at its battlements, we stood on the bank of the Risle river stunned by the immensity of the d'Uribé-Lebrun castle. Then Hannah said,

"So that's what it all boils down to. Without you, your old man will be the last d'Uribé-Lebrun standing and all he'll have left is a giant six-hundred year-old heap of stones attached to a private airport."

There was a brook near us and we ran to it, jumped in and swam around naked, splashing each other. We dried ourselves off by rolling around in the grass and then brushing the motes of dirt off each other's bodies. When we put our clothes back on, Hannah opened the hamper and took out ham and butter sandwiches, which we ate beside the river, drinking its clear water.

"This is the blood of your ancestors we're drinking here," she said, pretending to have gone solemn.

"No it isn't," I said, "It's water."

Hannah laughed and shook her head,

"Unlike most great musicians, you lack poetry in your soul."

"You and your fiddle are all the poetry I need," I said.

"You dare to call **me**, the star pupil of Jascha Cohen, a fiddler?" Then her mood changed and she looked broken-hearted, remembering Cohen. I held her hand.

"I wonder if Jascha and Elam escaped," I said.

"Not a chance. I bet the French shipped them back to Germany a few weeks before Kristallnacht. With people like Evan Shipman gone, who would have helped them escape?" She looked into my eyes, hers softening.

"I love you," she said.

"I'll always love you," I said. "... As long as you promise not to run off to fight in a war again without me. Is that poetic enough?"

"Yes. Now, let's pack up and hit the road."

As we were climbing into the Hispano we heard the sound of two airplanes growing louder as they came in to land. We saw them streak over us and then heard their wheels braking on the tarmac. I drove the Hispano deeper into the copse so that its black form was completely hidden by the trees and high hedges lining the driveway. The planes' engines went silent. Hannah handed me a pair of binoculars from the glove compartment and I focused on the drawbridge in front of the castle.

A big blonde Oriflamme stormtrooper appeared from the left side, accompanied by two German soldiers with swastika armbands, their lugers holstered. Then the Count came into view, strolling between two heavyset German generals. They were all laughing and the Count was waving his arms around as if bragging to the generals about the extent of his grounds. Pierre Lestage was bringing up the rear peering around like a hunting hound sniffing the wind. He turned to stare in our direction, pulled a German soldier over to him and seemed to point directly at us. We both lowered our heads and hugged the ground. I was sure they hadn't seen us. After a few minutes, I looked up again and saw that the Count and the German generals had gone inside the castle.

I focused my binoculars on Pierre's beaming face as he exchanged Heil Hitler salutes with one of the German soldiers. The blonde Oriflamme stormtrooper and the two German soldiers shared Pierre's thermos bottle of coffee. Hannah and I were dying for a few cups of it to get us going but we had to settle for watching the men drink it all down.

I motioned for Hannah to take my place behind the steering wheel and I got out and strained and pushed at the Hispano to move it a few feet up a slope leading downwards away from the castle toward a dirt road. When we reached its crest, Hannah put on the hand brake and I took over at the wheel. The car coasted down the hill onto the road, far enough away for me to start up the engine without being heard at the castle. We bumped along in deep ruts until I saw a sign for Laval and we headed that way on an empty departmental road.

"That's one less thing to worry about," I said as we saw a few cars in the distance. " At least the Count isn't with the government members fleeing south. He'll be flying back to Paris to watch his Nazi pals goose-stepping down the Champs-Elysées."

"Better start worrying again, my love. Maybe he's made a deal with the Germans to become the new French leader himself. Have you thought of that?" I reckoned he was too faithful to Marshal Pétain to take the top spot, unless the Germans wanted a younger man in charge. I started worrying about what would happen to Hannah if my father took control of France.

⟡

Two hours later, at nine a.m. in the morning, just east of Niort, we turned onto the main road south. The traffic was building up again as what seemed like all of France fled toward Bordeaux.

We'd slowed to a crawl again. I asked some people pushing handcarts if there was any news. The latest rumors were that the government was planning to hightail it out of Tours and head to Bordeaux as well. Premier Paul Reynaud had cracked under the strain of the debacle of the French army. His young mistress, Countess Hélène de Portes, was running the government on his behalf. They were all due to arrive in Bordeaux by June 15 with the Premier's cabinet and the whole General Staff of the Army. Everyone I talked to felt that surrender was coming.

Bordeaux, a city of a quarter million inhabitants when Stanley and I held a jazz concert there four years ago, was expecting to grow threefold in population by the end of the day. The villagers on the roadside passed on the radio's news that every one of the nearly five hundred hotels in the city was already full and that we shouldn't expect to find a hotel room there. These announcements came with self-satisfied smirks from the villagers who offered to lodge the refugees in their cottages or barns for a king's ransom. The fleeing crowds ignored them and kept inching towards Bordeaux.

Hannah and I hadn't budged for an hour so we turned off the motor and picnicked inside the car on ham and cheese sandwiches. We uncorked one of Redtop's bottles of red wine. The hot and thirsty passersby glared at us enviously. We gave a sandwich to an old woman who was tapping feebly on our window, begging us for food. A young soldier in a tattered uniform, fleeing the Germans like us, snatched it out of her hands and tripped her. He stepped over her as she writhed in pain on the ground. He kept wolfing down the sandwich until another soldier on the run snatched it out of his hands and hot-footed it away, gobbling its remains. Having noticed that we'd handed out food, others rushed our car. When I signalled that we weren't dishing out any more food, they turned hostile and started kicking the side of the Hispano and spitting on our windshield.

I drew the Colt, rolled down the window and fired a round into the air. Everyone went silent when I shouted,

"La prochaine personne qui y touche, je la descends!" My warning that I'd shoot the next person who touched the car kept them at bay. Seeing the feral look in the faces turned towards us, I was glad we had a pistol and a lot of spare ammunition.

The first air attacks came as we were passing along the highway south of Saintes. I heard the roar of engines in the sky as we rolled slowly past stands of poplars lining the road. I squinted into the sun and saw the shark-like outline of planes and then heard a siren coming toward us from the sky as people scrambled off the road, leaping into ditches, clawing at the earth for cover. Wave after wave of Stukas screeched down, their sirens wailing as they spat bullets that kicked up the surface of the road. More people scattered for cover as the bullets pinged into metal and thudded into human and animal flesh, followed by screams of pain. Bombs launched by Stukas blew up houses and barns and set straight rows of poplars alight.

The Stuka dive bombers soared upward into the clear blue sky again then banked into a turn for another dive as people tried to pull their dead and dying off the highway. I yanked the steering wheel and headed toward the side of the road as the Stukas revved up their engines and dived. Their sirens screamed as they plunged toward us again. The wail of the sirens, the steady tap-tapping of the machine guns and the plinking of bullets against asphalt and metal rang in my ears like a jazz syncopation from hell.

Hannah tightened her grip on my arm as a column of machine gun bullet impacts skipped along the road heading straight at our car.

"It's over, Urby I love you!" she shouted and we held each other.

Then, as if the pilot had decided not to destroy Redtop's Hispano-Suiza but to keep it intact for later use by a German officer, he stopped firing for an instant and let loose again after he swooped over us.

Finally, the Stukas climbed, banked, made one final bullet free pass to inspect their handiwork then wiggled their wings and soared off as if flipping the bird at the survivors.

We started up the Hispano again and drove past the horrors slowly, both of us steeling ourselves to keep heading south to Bordeaux. That was the hardest part for me, because the screams of the wounded kept bringing back my nightmares of fighting in northern France during the Great War. I had a memory of rain, mud and the ever-present smell of rotting corpses in trenches dug into the earth like graves.

Today was beautiful and sunny, but death was raining on us, from planes swooping down from a cloudless blue sky. Suddenly, it was April 1917 again and I had the German Albatros fighter in my sights and my Vickers machine gun jammed and I rammed the Albatros and it lit up like a firework the night of Bastille Day. The human torch who'd been piloting it splashed into the Baie de Somme. I must have cried out because I felt like I was going to burn alive too as I saw the Bay rushing up to meet me. Hannah called out,

"Are you alright?"

"Yes. Let's keep moving," I answered, shutting out the horrors around us.

We followed our Michelin map of Bordeaux to the address of Stanley's friend Jacques Dieuzeide. It was in the old city, a few blocks away from the Groupe Mondial Travel Agency where we'd pick up our tickets for the boat leaving for Lisbon tomorrow at midday.

We pulled a bell at the gate of an old stone building and a grey-haired head popped out of the window two stories above.

"Qui va là?" the moustachioed man called down to us.

"Des amis de Stanley," I replied.

"Attendez que je descende," the man said and a minute later, the gate opened and he signalled for us to drive the Hispano into the courtyard. He was wearing an expensive-looking blue linen blazer with a monogram on it, an open-necked light blue shirt, spotless white pants, and white leather shoes. He looked like he'd just arrived from a party on a yacht. He gave us a gleaming smile and said, "Jacques Dieuzeide, à votre service." He brushed Hannah's knuckles with a rapid "baise-main" kiss that must have tickled his carefully trimmed moustache. He gave me a handshake that felt as if it had been weakened by shaking a lot of hands. I could see from the look on Hannah's face that she didn't like what she'd seen of him so far. I saw a pretty brunette peering down at us from the window frame where Dieuzeide had appeared a minute before.

"Suzanne, on arrive," he called up to her. Then, he said in British-sounding English,

"Suzanne de la Rochefoucauld is my assistant. You must be exhausted. She has refreshments awaiting you. Don't bother to unpack yet. Have a cocktail first. You must have come through hell."

"It wasn't a tea party," Hannah said, noncommittally.

I could sense desperation and smell fear in the man, behind his smooth manners and expensive cologne water. Dieuzeide owed Stanley his life, Stanley'd told me, because he'd paid his Corsican friends in Montmartre a bundle of money to persuade the *Unione Corse* mafia to back off killing Dieuzeide. All because Stanley had got friendly with him when he helped set up a jazz concert for Stanley in Bordeaux in the early thirties. At the time, Dieuzeide was a prosecuting attorney and had come close to dismantling a large network of the *Unione Corse* in Bastia. Now he was the leading magistrate in Bordeaux and had promised Stanley that he'd make sure that Hannah and I caught our boat to Lisbon tomorrow.

We followed Dieuzeide up the steps and entered his expensively furnished and decorated town house. I reckoned that if he made his living as a career lawyer and magistrate, there must be rich pickings in Bordeaux.

"I'm Suzanne," the brunette said, extending a manicured hand with dazzling dark red polish on her nails. She was casually dressed in a rich, elegant way, like her boss.

Dieuzeide was in his mid-forties like Hannah and me, but Suzanne was in her late twenties or early thirties at the oldest. It was obvious he was crazy about her but my gut told me that he was just a means to an end for her. Hannah's glances toward me were shouting that she wanted to get away from these people and take our chances on the streets of Bordeaux like the other refugees who'd swept into the city. We didn't need Jacques Dieuzeide or his assistant because we had plenty of food and booze to make it on our own until the boat left for Lisbon in less than twelve hours. I ignored her warnings and we stayed put because I was bone-weary.

"Martini Dry?" Suzanne asked. She made great dry martinis and light conversation and we passed the evening telling them about what had happened on our exodus from Paris.

"That must have been, comment dire, complexe," Suzanne cooed.

They were good listeners who made all the right sympathetic noises. Suzanne brought out cocktail canapés and kept the booze flowing. She had a new phonograph and kept a steady stream of records by Stanley, Louis Armstrong, Sidney Bechet and myself playing all evening.

Jacques gave us a rundown of where things stood with the German invasion.

"They're at the gates of Paris," he said. "The French government's falling apart. Paul Reynaud, the Président du Conseil, the Premier you would say, is determined to refuse an armistice with the Germans. But his Vice Président du Conseil, Le Maréchal Pétain, wants armistice. As for the ailing Reynaud, he's going up against his thirty-eight-year-old mistress, La Comtesse Hélène de Portes."

"Encore des drys?" Suzanne asked. She made us more martinis and canapés while Dieuzeide went on,

"Ah, cette Comtesse, quelle nature! She chairs cabinet meetings and bosses Generals and Ministers old enough to be her grandfathers around, while the poor Reynaud lies in bed in an adjacent room, listening to her screaming. Le pauvre." Dieuzeide said that his informants had told him that Maréchal Pétain and his allies were prevailing in their push for a rapid armistice with the Germans, despite opposition from people like the Junior Minister for Defense, Charles de Gaulle.

"I think France will fall within a few days and then the Germans will be doing their *pas d'oie* goose-steps on the Champs-Elysées. The armistice faction will force Reynaud to resign. Although la Comtesse wants the armistice, she will resist a takeover by Marshal Pétain. After all, he's an eighty-four-year old man, yesterday's man. The Pétainistes will stage a 'bloodless coup d'état,' against her lover, Reynaud." Suzanne had been listening, and changing the records as soon as each one ended.

"C'est très complexe," she said, repeating herself.

Jacques Dieuzeide knew all about Stanley's arrangements for Hannah and me to leave for Lisbon by boat at midday the next day and he told us he'd drop by the Groupe Mondial travel agency early in the morning to pick up our tickets.

"Mes amis," he said. "I'm afraid that if I do not go there bearing my authority as Magistrat, a corrupt agent will sell your tickets to the highest bidder. Thousands of people will pay any price for such tickets to escape from France, now that the Germans are days, maybe hours, away from capturing Paris. Once Paris falls, the rest of France collapses like a house of cards."

Dieuzeide kept saying in one way or another that tomorrow would probably be one of the last days left to escape from France. He finished off with a patriotic flourish, telling us that, as one of the top-ranking notables in Bordeaux, he felt duty bound to be the last man to leave the sinking ship of France, likening himself to the captain of a mighty ocean liner like the Titanic.

We handed over our passports and reservation vouchers to Dieuzeide. He told us not to bother fetching our suitcases from the car; he and Suzanne would bring them up. He led us to the master bedroom with its enormous double bed and ceiling fans stirring warm air through the room. He kissed each of us on our cheeks, embraced us with his blue linen covered, cologne scented arms and left us by ourselves. As soon as he closed the door, Hannah giggled and took a running header onto the bed like an Olympic high diver. She rolled around on the cotton sheets and threw a pillow at me.

"You got to give the guy credit. He's a gutless wonder, but he really knows how to live."

"Stanley's vouched for him, so there's got to be more stuffing in the turkey than we've seen so far."

Hannah pointed to what she called a Louis XV style cheval dressing table in the corner. Its top bulged with Coty, Guerlain and Caron perfume bottles, as well as silver-backed hairbrushes, hand mirrors and powder compacts with SdlR monogrammed on them. She asked, pretending to wonder at it all,

"Think these SdlR knicknacks belong to Jacques' humble assistant Suzanne de la Rochefoucauld?"

We lay in a clean, comfortable bed for the first time in days. The fans whirring in the ceiling overhead were hypnotizing us into sleep. Hannah told me in a drowsy voice that she was glad that Stanley had vouched so strongly for Dieuzeide because she didn't have a good feeling about him or Suzanne. I worried about her instincts as I drifted off to sleep. I woke up suddenly and tried to get out of bed but felt glued to the mattress. Hannah had already fallen asleep.

"Goddamn it, they've slipped us some kind of Mickey Finn" was the last thought that ran through my mind before I passed out.

When Hannah and I awoke the next day the clock read three p.m. We raced downstairs and found a note from Dieuzeide apologizing for "the course of action that I've been forced to take." He wished us good luck and reminded us that as citizens of a country that was not at war with Germany, we were in less imminent danger than they were. We could pick up our passports at the Groupe Mondial Travel Agency from a clerk named Henri Varnet. Dieuzeide had left us the keys to his townhouse and invited us to stay as long as we wished. He asked only that we lock up on leaving and drop off the keys with the concierge.

"I knew they were phonies and I let them screw us!" Hannah wailed as we dressed. I rummaged through the wardrobe and put on one of Dieuzeide's swanky blue linen blazers and slipped the Colt into its pocket, figuring that it might come in handy if I came across Dieuzeide and Suzanne. We rushed downstairs. The Hispano was still parked in the driveway. They'd taken one set of our strongbox keys off the bedside table when we were unconscious and had unlocked the glove compartment and helped themselves to half of the money, gold ingots and jewelry in our strongbox.

"The bastards!" Hannah shouted. "We paid a high price for yesterday evening's festivities. Over ten thousand dollars, plus gold and jewelry."

"At least they only took half," I said, trying to put a brave face on things and calm Hannah down. I checked the ignition, took the keys out and waved them triumphantly.

"Hey, Hannah. They were good people after all. They've left us our car keys." Hannah rolled her eyes and then said,

"Let's go after them. Maybe the ship's been held up and we can grab them and get our stuff back."

Hannah and I broke speed records driving to the Groupe Mondial Travel Agency. I fought my way through the crowded room to a receptionist by waving the Colt around and cursing loudly in English. People scattered in fear, probably thinking that we were Germans. The frightened receptionist confirmed that our tickets had been transferred to Monsieur le Magistrat Dieuzeide and his Assistant. It was authorized because he was bearing our passports and a note from me approving the transfer of our tickets to them. She showed me a note written in French but in my handwriting. Forgery was one of Dieuzeide's silky skills. We were told that the boat had left a half hour late but was now steaming toward Lisbon. All further bookings out of France were full. As Dieuzeide had promised, we were able to pick up our passports from Henri Varnet. He was a beady-eyed specimen who stared at my Colt nervously as he handed over our documents. I put the Colt away, thanked him and ran outside and jumped behind the wheel of the Hispano.

"I've got our passports!" I called out to Hannah as we roared off toward Dieuzeide's town house. We expected to be followed by a police car with its sirens wailing, but the police seemed to have vanished. They were trying to flee the country like everyone else.

Ⓐ

We spent the afternoon in the town house, listening to the news on the radio. The Germans were at the gates of Paris but the French army was making a heroic stand and had launched a counterattack. We laughed because the radio bulletin sounded like the propaganda we'd heard in the days before our escape from Paris. Then the radio went silent.

"The newscasters are probably rushing to the elevators to get the hell out of Paris," Hannah said. Then the likelihood that Paris was going to fall to the Germans suddenly dawned on us and we fell silent, holding hands as if we were at the funeral of a well-loved old friend. We mourned Paris by drinking our way through Dieuzeide's finest Saint-Emilion wines until we passed out.

We spent the next day, when we should have been embarking from Lisbon for America, desperately searching for a way out of France. Bordeaux was swelling with crowds of frantic people caterwauling in a babel of tongues in the blistering heat. The government started arriving from Tours in big black limousines accompanied by motorcycle police escorts. Boos filled the air of Old Bordeaux as the government passed. We both expected the crowd to start attacking the cars until we looked into the nervous faces of the gendarmes and soldiers escorting them. They held their rifles and machine guns at the ready and looked like they wouldn't hesitate to open fire. There seemed to be no way to escape from France. Too many people were ahead of us in the line.

My fears for Hannah's safety grew. I'd taken Jacques Dieuzeide at face value because he was a friend of Stanley's and I wanted to believe that he'd help me to protect Hannah. But the more I saw of his town house with its rich furnishings and tapestries and paintings, the more I cursed myself for believing that people like Dieuzeide and his mistress would put our safety above their own. Stanley had, unwittingly, set us up. We drank more wine to steady our nerves and then collapsed into bed not bothering to take off our sweaty clothes.

When Hannah and I woke up in the early evening and turned on the radio, the newscaster was describing, in a trembling voice, the German Army's victory parade down the Champs-Elysées the day before. The Germans had done their homework and their preparedness had shocked the Parisians. They were already putting up signs in German on all the major thoroughfares, signs that were Made in Germany. They possessed the blueprints and inventories of all the important ministries, companies and museums and of the homes and businesses of rich Jews, which they'd already begun to occupy and loot.

I knew Hannah had the blues as badly as I did, so I couldn't read the sudden mischievous smile on her face. She said,

"Let's get out of here and pretend we don't have a care in the world. I looked through Suzanne's appointment book. She's reserved a table for two at the Hôtel Splendid at 8:30 tonight. She's got some great outfits, genuine haute couture: Lanvin, Worth, Poiret, you name it. While you were sleeping, I tried on a few dresses and they fit me like a glove. Will you take me to dinner Count Urby? We'll put it on Dieuzeide's tab."

"I thought you only wear dresses you make yourself."

"I'll be a *bourgeoise* for one evening and wear haute couture and perfume... if you promise not to tell anybody," she said, smiling. "So, are we going to the ball, Count?"

"Of course," I said, bowing deeply, imitating Dieuzeide. I loved seeing Hannah smile again. If it took dressing to the nines and a fancy evening out to cheer her up I was fine with it. Remembering Dieuzeide's physique, I figured that I could fit into whatever swanky threads he'd left behind.

We rummaged through Dieuzeide's closets like swells looking for duds to wear to a "cocktail party avec jazz" at the Jockey Club de Paris. Hannah found a sparkly red evening gown by Lanvin, whoever that was, and I decked myself out in a beige linen suit and brown and white wing-tipped spectator shoes. An open-necked white cotton shirt and a beige paisley silk ascot completed my attire.

Hannah never wore perfume. She dabbed a *soupçon* of Coty's "Chypre" behind her ears and on the inside of her wrists, the way we'd seen actresses apply perfume in the movies. The cloying scent of mossy woods and citrus filled the air. She made a face and said,

"Coty was one of the Count's big bankrollers. I never should have put it on. It's going to bring us bad luck."

" Not tonight. You smell good," I lied, kissing her neck, hoping to see her smile again.

CHAPTER 10

We arrived at the restaurant a few minutes early and told the Maître d'Hôtel that Magistrat Dieuzeide had reserved a table for us under his name. Two waiters ushered us into the Hôtel Splendid's glittering dining room. Bordeaux had become the capital of France now that Paris had fallen. On the way to our table we passed diplomats and elegant women from every corner of the globe milling about in the hotel's salons, seeming to "talk in tongues" like people who'd already leapt over the edge of hysteria.

A waiter came to our candlelit table for two and offered us the hotel's publicity fans and, as friends of Monsieur le Magistrat, a complimentary apéritif of Mumm Cordon Bleu 1935 champagne. The constant murmur of voices went quiet suddenly when a ramrod straight white-haired old man of medium height, with a beautifully trimmed white moustache entered the room. He was surrounded by a phalanx of tough looking guards, some of them sporting badly concealed rods as they sweated in their summer suits. The old codger was wearing a tuxedo, but it was easy to recognize Marshal Pétain even in civilian clothes. Most of the people in the restaurant stood up to applaud the Hero of Verdun as he strode jauntily to his table, seemingly impervious to the heat. A few seconds later, Premier Reynaud entered, pastyfaced and clutching the arm of an elegant and fierce looking woman who looked like all the protection he needed.

"That must be his mistress, Countess Hélène de Portes," Hannah whispered. I heard polite, scattered applause as she and the Premier sat down at a table some twenty feet from the Marshal.

The diners grew quiet, fanning themselves and scrutinizing the members of the government as they filed into the restaurant. I reckoned the diners were trying to read the tea leaves and figure out who was in and who was on their way out. I kept count; there were a lot more people coming up to Marshal Pétain's table than to Reynaud's. Countess Hélène had gone red in the face as she eyed the number of men lining up at Pétain's table to bow and scrape before him. Hannah nudged me and said,

"Reynaud's woman's going to strangle the old-timer."

Suddenly, a giant of a man with dark hair and a pencil-thin moustache marched in lighting a new cigarette from his last one. He handed the still lit butt to a beetle-browed man behind him, who, in turn, passed it on to a subordinate for disposal. The giant was Charles de Gaulle. I recognized him from the Pathé newsreels I'd seen at the Cinéma Max Linder. He dwarfed his bodyguards, who walked a respectful distance behind him. I said to myself that they wouldn't do him much good if an assassin took a potshot at him.

De Gaulle and his men were escorted to a table right next to Marshal Pétain's. The old man rose to his feet and waved his arms around when he spotted de Gaulle. The "Temporary Brigadier General and Junior Minister for Defense" looked annoyed and then strolled over to Pétain. He stood towering over him as if posing for another newsreel moment for the cameramen and photographers who'd suddenly broken through into the dining room. The two men shook hands without speaking and de Gaulle returned to his table as the waiters frog-marched the reporters out of the room. De Gaulle's guards sat at his table with their sweaty hands hovering near the guns holstered inside their jackets. They scanned the guests in the dining room and the people milling around by its doors as if they were expecting to make a quick draw any minute. One of de Gaulle's flunkies would light a new cigarette for him each time he finished one.

Meanwhile, Hannah was watching Countess Hélène de Portes like a hawk. Clearly outraged by the attention that Marshal Pétain was getting, Reynaud's mistress stood up and started working the tables as if rallying the troops to support her lover, Premier Reynaud. After a few minutes of glad-handing, she turned and headed toward the WC at the end of the long dining room. Hannah leapt to her feet, saying,

"I'm going to see if she's our ticket out of Bordeaux." I saw heads turn as Hannah ran after her and the babble of conversation ceased until they disappeared through the door of the WC.

Ten minutes later, the two women walked back arm-in-arm, smiling like they'd known each other all their lives. The Countess took Hannah over to de Gaulle's table and whispered in his ear. He stood up and planted an awkward "baise-main" inches above Hannah's hand and then motioned to his men to get lost while they talked. The old Marshal was leaning toward them but he'd have needed his ear trumpet to pick up their words.

They talked for a few minutes and, for the first time since he'd arrived, de Gaulle cracked a smile. When Hannah stood up, de Gaulle cranked himself up to his lofty height and fumbled a card out of his jacket pocket. He palmed it and wrote something on it. Then he bent like a crane on a building site to give Hannah another airborne baise-main. Hannah gave a thumbs up sign to Hélène de Portes and received one back from her as she returned to our table. I watched these goings-on in wonderment. Hannah sat down with a self-satisfied smile and then said,

"We're leaving for England with de Gaulle at dawn tomorrow. The Countess wants him out of the way, because he's still refusing an armistice with the Germans. He wants to fight on from France's colonies in Africa."

"He's going to Africa from England?" I asked, amazed.

"Not right away. First, he's going to see Churchill and get his backing for his plans...Hélène's words. He's stiffened Premier Reynaud's spine so much that she's furious."

"He's got to fight back. That's the only way to put a bully down," I said. I remembered how I'd turned the tables on Buster Thigpen at the Saint Vincent Colored Waifs' Home what seemed a lifetime ago.

"Hélène's arranged for a plane to take de Gaulle to England and she's plotting to keep him from returning to France. The problem is she can't lay her hands on enough airplane fuel to get him to England without arousing Pétain's suspicions that she and Reynaud are sneaking off to rally to Churchill.

There's only enough fuel to get him as far as Normandy." I suddenly realized the deal Hannah had struck.

"So you told her that you know a place in Normandy where there's loads of airplane fuel?" Hannah nodded Yes.

"What if the Count's still at the castle? Or is having his airport guarded by his stormtroopers?"

"No problem," Hannah said. " Hélène said that he was in Paris when the Germans marched in, just like you guessed. She's's going to phone him tonight and instruct him to make sure that he and every one of his men, *sans exception*, is at the Ministry of Defense in Paris first thing in the morning waiting for a phone call from Premier Reynaud."

"There's a problem with the plan you and the Countess have cooked up. Reynaud's government might not last until tomorrow morning. Then Pétain will be the boss, if Dieuzeide's right. I think we should get out of France now-we're a short hop from the Spanish border and we can pay smugglers to get us to Portugal. We've got transit visas through it, so we can make it to Lisbon and..." Tears started rolling down Hannah's cheeks. She held my hand and said,

"You're right but I can't face Spain again right now. Besides, I don't trust Franco. Hitler helped him to win **his** war so he'll probably help Hitler. Franco will probably start rounding up Jews-anyway, that's been a Spanish specialty since the Inquisition. We're better off hitching a ride to England in de Gaulle's plane."

"I thought you never wanted to set foot in an airplane."

'I said I didn't want to spend **two days** flying from Lisbon to America in a **seaplane**. A flight to England will only take a few hours."

"Alright," I agreed. I didn't want to press her further about Spain and re-open old wounds. "I saw de Gaulle give you a card he scribbled on. What was that about?"

"He just wrote the number of the hangar at Mérignac airport where we're meeting him at eight a.m. Then a short flight to your castle for refuelling and we're off to Heston Airport London. Voilà!"

"Amazing," I said admiringly, not reacting to her calling the Count's château "my castle." "Countess Hélène must really want to get de Gaulle out of the way. What if she double-crosses us and sends French fighter planes to shoot us down on the way to Normandy? Or between Normandy and England? " Hannah said,

"The French pilots are too scared of the Luftwaffe to take to the sky. Besides, she's hedging her bets. If de Gaulle makes it to London and wins in the end, she and Reynaud will be national heroes for 'saving de Gaulle.' She'll let Pétain do the dirty work of denouncing him as a traitor."

I turned the plan over in my mind and didn't see anything wrong with it. I expected we'd be under heavy German attack in England, but I reckoned that the English would fight the Germans to the bitter end, the way they had in the Great War. Hannah was right: between trusting our lives in a throw of the dice to the Spanish, the French or the English, England won hands down.

"Let's go to England with de Gaulle," I said, finally. "How did you work things out with the Countess so fast? You two were only gone for ten minutes."

"Easy," Hannah said. "I told her that, when we cut out, I'd leave the keys to Dieuzeide's town house under the doormat. I also mentioned that his mistress had left behind some great clothes and cosmetics and jewelry when she fled to South America. I explained the children's rhyme 'Finders, keepers; Losers, weepers' to her and she said she was happy to finally find one custom to like in the 'Anglo-Saxon' world." From Hannah's expression, I knew there was more to come.

"The clincher was that we turn Redtop's Hispano over to her for safe-keeping." I laughed and said,

"Good move. If everything works out, we won't need it."

♈

Hélène de Portes came by early the next evening to commandeer Redtop's Hispano and we invited her up for a drink. She made an inspection of the premises, going through Dieuzeide's clothes closets and taking a few of Suzanne's outfits down from hangers and folding them over her arms. She swiped a few of Suzanne's perfumes, put them in her handbag, then sat down in the living room with us.

"What will you do when the government falls?" Hannah asked as we sipped Lillet apéritifs. Hélène suddenly looked older than her thirty-eight years.

"Paul and I plan to drive to his country house in Grès in the Hérault and then escape to North Africa," she said. "We want to retire from politics while Pétain, Weygand, Laval and the others make their little arrangements with the Boches. Paul Reynaud and I could have found a more honorable solution for France than the one the senile old goat Pétain is planning." She shrugged her shoulders and went on,

"But how can one expect a fossil who can hardly make pee-pee by himself to be able to deal with a savage like Hitler?" She finished her drink and stood up.

"Thank you for lending us your beautiful car," she said. "Paul Reynaud and I appreciate it. If you would help me put these clothes in it, I would be obliged. I saw some nice coats that I may come back for later, after you've left, if you don't mind."

"Not at all," I said. "Why don't you hang onto the key? I'm sure that Magistrate Dieuzeide and his assistant Miss Suzanne de la Rochefoucauld won't be needing the place for a while."

"Merci, et bon voyage," she said.

We helped the Countess take more of Suzanne's clothes and a few rare bottles of Bordeaux wine that took her fancy and then waved goodbye to her as she roared off in Redtop's Hispano-Suiza.

"That's one tough frail," I said. "France will be losing one of her best people when Reynaud goes. And I don't mean Reynaud."

We called for a car to come at seven a.m. in the morning to take us to Mérignac airport for our rendez-vous with General de Gaulle. Sometime tomorrow we would be in England, safe from my father when Pétain came to power.

The next morning, we waited for de Gaulle in a hangar beside a ten-seater passenger plane with no markings on it. We'd put our luggage and our instruments next to the aircraft steps leading up into the plane. It was parked just outside the hangar, with its engines revving up. The motors sounded strong and steady. The pilot, in a French Air Army jumpsuit, came down the steps to shake hands.

"We leave fast," he said, "As soon as mon géneral arrive."

We saw a black hearse race across the tarmac and drive into the hangar to stop a few feet from us. General de Gaulle stepped out of it, dressed in full military uniform. The pilot ran over to him and saluted. The General took off his képi, shook my hand and gave Hannah his unusual baise-main. Then he said,

"Bonjour. Ou devrais-je dire, Good Morning?" His heavy French accent made it hard to understand him but he was already practicing his English and he refused to converse with us in French. "Thank you for what you do for France! You were legionnaire in Great War?" he asked me. "You fight much battle for France and she award you the Croix de Guerre with Palme, non?" De Gaulle had done his homework. I snapped to attention and saluted him.

"Oui, mon général," I barked. He returned my salute and patted me on the shoulder. He looked at Hannah and said,

"You are very brave, vous deux. Many would not help de Gaulle. But to help him is to help France, for I am the France who fights. Bravo! You go now, yes?" he asked. An aide stepped out of the hearse and passed him a pair of binoculars. He stuck his head around the hangar's door as if checking whether he'd been followed. His back to us, he didn't see the astonishment on our faces.

"Aren't you coming with us, sir?" Hannah asked.

"No, that is trap of Countess de Portes. She expect me to go now, but I stay in hiding here one more day, to try to save France from shameful armistice with Germany. You go now. My pilot, he fuel plane at aerodrome of Count d'Uribé-Lebrun and fly it back here and hide it. If I do not stop armistice, I fly to England."

Hannah and I looked at each other, realizing that the General was pulling an elaborate double-cross on Countess de Portes and on us.

"Where can we go, sir?" Hannah asked.

"You return Paris, my friends. I arrange government car to take you there. It awaits you at noon at Hôtel des Bains in Bagnoles-de-l'Orne. I pay your lunch." He started reaching into his pocket for some dough and I stopped him.

"Vive la France," I said. He kissed us on both cheeks and then looked into our eyes, his expression suddenly solemn.

"De Gaulle and France will not forget you," he said. "If I fail to stop Pétain and Laval from armistice, get news to me in London any way you can."

He lit a cigarette from the one he was smoking, saluted and then clambered back into the hearse, which roared off across the tarmac.

"We go now," the pilot said.

The moment we were seated, the motors revved up to screaming pitch and the plane shot down the runway and took off for the Count's castle. We saw the hearse far below us, racing back toward Bordeaux. "The double-crossing bastard!" Hannah shouted over the engine noise. "What if the Countess has the last laugh and shoots **us** down?"

"She won't do that. She wants de Gaulle out of her hair so that she can play her double game of pretending to stiffen Premier Reynaud's spine against the armistice, while working with Pétain and Laval to make it happen. Pétain takes over and she heads off with Reynaud in Redtop's Hispano to his country house and then on to North Africa where they wait for Pétain and his bunch to stumble. Everyone will blame France's defeat on 'deserters' like de Gaulle who've joined up with Churchill, Public Enemy Number One. No, Hannah, the Countess wants this plane to make it to England today with us and de Gaulle on board. De Gaulle's pulled a double-cross on us, but he's really pulled a fast one on the Countess if he manages to block Pétain's armistice."

I was right about Countess Hélène. There was no ambush. We landed at the Count's château and it was deserted. The pilot holstered his sidearm and smiled from ear to ear as he refuelled General de Gaulle's plane.

"On aura presque assez de carburant pour aller de Bordeaux jusqu'à Manhattan." He was saying that he would have almost enough fuel to go back to Bordeaux and then fly General de Gaulle to Manhattan. Heading to America would land them in the middle of the Atlantic, I reckoned, but it would be easy for de Gaulle to escape by plane to England tomorrow, June 17, if he failed to block the armistice and Pétain took charge of what was left of the French government.

As Hannah and I were making our way along the road dragging our strongbox, instruments and suitcases to the Hôtel des Bains in Bagnoles-de-l'Orne, we saw General de Gaulle's plane fly over us on its way back to Bordeaux. We waved at it and the pilot dipped its wings in a salute and then soared up into the cloudless sky.

The car and the military escort General de Gaulle had promised us were waiting at the Hôtel des Bains. Gendarmes stowed our things in its trunk and then the Renault shot off toward Paris, the escorts' sirens wailing, sweeping everything off the roads in front of us.

On our arrival back in Paris, we'd gone by the nightclub and found nothing missing. I walked to Stanley's to let him know we'd returned. Stanley had come down from his marijuana cloud and was his old self again. The pain from his arthritis seemed to have died down, he said. When I told him about Jacques Dieuzeide and Suzanne's betrayal, he wanted revenge. He said they wouldn't last long. He had friends in Brazil who'd deal with them.

CHAPTER 11

Bastille Day in Paris, July 14, 1940

Ten days after my forty-fifth birthday, Bastille Day 1940 was more like a day of mourning France's defeat than one of celebrations and fireworks. Marshal Pétain had been anointed as the supreme leader and savior of France. Germany's favorite, Pierre Laval, had been appointed Vice President of the Council of Ministers of something called simply "L'Etat Français" or "The French State." Pétain was the President of the Council, but Laval was its real chief and, effectively, the Premier of France. The Third French Republic had been dissolved, having survived for nearly seventy years since its founding after France's last great defeat by the Germans during the Franco-Prussian War.

Under the terms of the armistice, the German occupiers had allowed the new government to set up shop in a spa town called Vichy in Central France at a safe remove from the politically fickle Parisians. Then the Germans had drawn up a "Demarcation Line," reserving the strategic parts of France, including Paris, Northern France and the Atlantic Coast for direct German rule and leaving most of the rest as a "Free Zone" under the control of the French State hunkering down in Vichy.

General de Gaulle had escaped from France on June 17 and made an appeal to the French from London on June 18 over BBC radio. He called on all Frenchmen to reject the armistice and keep fighting Germany and Italy. The Vichy government had stripped him of his rank and declared him a traitor.

Premier Reynaud and Countess Hélène de Portes had been in a car accident as they tried to escape from Bordeaux to his country house on June 28 before making their way to North Africa. The car had run into a plane tree which had become Hélène's personal guillotine, nearly decapitating her. Reynaud had survived the accident with minor injuries and then been arrested as he left the hospital.

Just before Bastille Day, radio announcements started calling on the multitudes who'd fled Paris to return so that France's economy and way of life could return to "full dynamism."

The announcers said that, until further notice, Jews and other non-Aryans wouldn't be permitted to cross the Demarcation Line. They made vague statements that exceptions would be made on a case-by-case basis. Hannah and I had returned to Paris before the Line was set up, but we wondered how long it would be before the French police came knocking at our door now that they were under my father's authority.

⚓

Hannah and I settled back into life in Pigalle. After lunch on Bastille Day, Hannah sat at the piano, called me over to give her a kiss and then said that she felt like playing Erik Satie's "Gymnopédies" for a while. I liked what I heard and applauded at the end. She sat down beside me on the couch.

We held hands, finally at peace. We tried not to think of the new horrors that faced us with the Germans occupying Paris and my father now Minister for National Security in Marshal Pétain's government. The telephone rang.

"Five dollars says it's Stanley," Hannah said.

"My money's on the Count." I got up to answer it. I'd won. The brief conversation over, I hung up and said,

"He wants to meet me in his office. At 2:30."

"Goddamn him!" Hannah said. "He really wants to rub your nose in it. He's never telephoned here before but now he summons you to turn up in an hour. He wants to announce that he's closing our nightclub and forbidding you to have anything to do with me! I'll probably be doing jail time by this evening!"

Hannah flung her empty wine glass against the wall and was going for the crystal vase on top of the liquor cabinet. I stopped her, held her and kissed her hard and then she started kissing me back. She looked up at me and I said,

"Remember. We stick together, whatever happens."

"Go get him," she said.

⅄

As I climbed the steps to the entrance of the Count's now fully renovated building with its new armored door, I saw Pierre staring at me from a window on the second floor. His expression was filled with a hatred that he dared not show in my father's presence. He pointed his Beretta at me, then holstered his firearm.

I leaned on the buzzer until Pierre opened the door. He was wearing a black stormtrooper uniform with the lightning bolt badge of the Oriflamme du Roi over his heart and the fleur de lys insignia of his rank as lead stormtrooper pinned to his collars. His black leather belt and jackboots were polished to a high sheen. He'd dyed his hair and moustache black and now looked like Charlie Chaplin's Hitler in the film "The Great Dictator." Before I could burst out laughing, he straight-armed a Hitler salute at me and said in a voice dripping with sarcasm,

"Soyez le bienvenu, Monsieur le Comte." He ushered me to the Count's office, his face betraying none of the hatred that he'd shown me from his window only seconds before. He rang the buzzer using the special signal and my father's voice instructed him over the loudspeaker to leave the two of us alone. I heard a buzzer unlocking the door to the office and I went inside.

The Count remained seated, trying to impress me with his power.

"It's been a long time since I last saw you," he said, in a husky voice, barely looking up from the pile of papers on his desk. "Much has happened."

"That's an understatement," I said. "I guess you must be happy that your Nazi friends have occupied the country you and I fought so hard to defend during the Great War." He smiled, saying,

"France was a different country and Germany was our enemy then, not our best friend."

"You call a country that's killed, wounded or imprisoned a million Frenchmen in the last few months France's best friend? You've got a funny notion of friendship and patriotism."

"Yes. It's all a joke of God, like the two of us." Hearing those words again enraged me. I was about to stomp out on him when he said,

"I call it a joke of God because you and I are doubles of each other, two halves of a whole. Through a series of God's jokes on humankind, you were raised in New Orleans, not Paris. If I'd had enough sense to listen to Father Gohegan's pleas, I should have fetched you from New Orleans when you were a baby and raised you here."

Before I could speak, he turned around in his chair and lifted a gold-colored box file beside him onto his desk. The file had the d'Uribé-Lebrun crest stamped on it, along with the name "Le Comte Charles-Emmanuel d'Uribé-Lebrun," which was the moniker that the Count planned for me once I was legitimized by Marshal Pétain. He scrabbled around inside the file and handed me a letter, yellowed with age, dated July 17, 1895. I recognized Father Gohegan's handwriting which I'd copied when he taught me how to write.

"Read it," he ordered, easing back in his chair to watch me.

In the letter, Father Gohegan referred to correspondence he'd sent the Count a week earlier in which he described finding a newborn baby in a Moses basket on the front steps of Saint Vincent's Colored Waifs' Home for Boys on July 4, 1895. He'd written that a quadroon prostitute named Josephine Dubois had told him in the sanctity of the confessional that the baby was hers and that a white Frenchman, the Count, had fathered her son. That made the boy an octoroon, of one-eighth African blood and thus a Negro, by the racial codes prevailing in Louisiana. She'd begged Father Gohegan to write the Count imploring him to come and take their son to France to save him from Jim Crow. Father Gohegan stated that, normally, his conscience would forbid him from bowing to such a request but that the wretched creature had committed the unpardonable act of suicide in the meantime.

I just stared at the Count when I finished reading the letter.

"Where's his July 10 letter?" I asked.

"Consigned to the flames of woe, no doubt," he said, grinning. He went back to searching in the box file then asked, feigning indifference,

"Are you ready for another one?" Sensing that I was closing in on the answer to the question of who I was and where I came from, I said,

"Just keep them coming."

"Are you sure?" he said. I nodded yes. The Count frowned, then handed me another letter. It was dated September 15, 1895.

In that letter, Father Gohegan described how he felt personal guilt over my mother's death. He couldn't understand why the Count had not seen fit to reply to his earlier letters. In light of the woman's tragic suicide, Father Gohegan expressed the hope that the Count would now heed the teachings of Mother Church and show Christian charity by accepting responsibility for the son that he'd fathered. To my astonishment, Father Gohegan had described me as a "white" baby in appearance and assured the Count that no one need ever know that I had a "modicum of black blood" flowing in my veins. He swore on the Virgin Mother that he, Father Gohegan, would never divulge this. He told the Count that, after praying long and hard, he was now more convinced than ever that the best path was for the Count to come take me and raise me in France. Otherwise, he had no alternative but to install me until my eighteenth birthday in Saint Vincent's Colored Waifs' Home which he headed. There, I'd be brought up as a colored man, "...sharing, as you are aware, the fate of that benighted race in America."

"Let me see the next one," I said. The Count retrieved the letters and slipped them back into the box file and put it next to his chair out of sight.

"Bah! The file is filled with letters like those. I ignored them at first and then I decided to act because I could never trust a priest so ready to deluge me with letters about a being of African descent, albeit one with my blood coursing through its veins."

"Then why didn't you just leave me alone?"

"I was interested in how you would develop, the kind of man that you might grow up to be. At the time, I was fascinated to see how a *métisse* with my blood in its veins would fare. On the eve of the Great War, I felt it was time to arrange for you to come to France. I was right to do so. As I've told you, my war wounds have made you the sole blood heir to the d'Uribé-Lebrun lineage."

The Count studied me and then said,

"You may find it ironic, given your short but lucrative career as a private investigator, that I hired one to look into every aspect of the events surrounding your mother's suicide."

"Why? Father Gohegan explained everything in those letters I just read." The Count shrugged and then said,

"I never believe anything I read. Not even what I write myself."

I suddenly remembered something Stanley had said a long time ago, when I met him for the first time in Madame Lala's Mahogany House in New Orleans. Stanley had made me doubt, for an instant, the truth of the story Father Gohegan had told me about my history. I couldn't remember what Stanley had said. Something about a woman named Claudette who I resembled.

"Only I, and now you, know about my hiring a private investigator. Not even Pierre is privy to our secret, because it's a matter between you and me alone." The Count took his gold-plated Berthier pistol out of his desk and placed it on the table. He'd bragged to me once that the rifle maker Berthier had only ever made two pistols, both gold-plated, one for him and one for Marshal Pétain.

"There's no need to flash your fancy shooting iron around. I'm unarmed." He ignored what I said and continued,

"The private investigator's final report, which I received only very recently, confirmed many of my suspicions about your birth." The Count's mood had turned somber now. I waited for him to go on, because I felt that I was drawing closer to finding out more about my mother, Josephine Dubois.

"All I'll say for now is that I should have sent a positive reply to Father Gohegan's letters and brought you to France immediately. Lives would have been spared."

"You couldn't have stopped me from asking questions about where I came from." The Count waved my words away with his cigarette holder, saying,

"I commissioned the investigator to look into the circumstances surrounding the death of one Josephine Dubois in 1895. I always appreciated her at the Mahogany House bordello. She was...special." He gazed off into space as if suddenly seeing her face before him. Then he went on,

"The investigator worked in my employ on and off for over twenty years after the Great War ended. I gave him no deadlines for arriving at the truth, because I didn't want him to give me the answers that he thought that I wanted to hear...I know how such people operate and so do you." He lit another cigarette, then asked,

"Do you feel like tasting your favorite Domfront calvados?" I nodded Yes and he went over to his sideboard, busied himself pouring out the calvados and brought back two large snifters of it, placing one on the desk before me.

"Tchin Tchin," he said, touching my glass with his and sipping the calvados with appreciation, before going on,

"The only conditions I placed on the investigator were to be thorough, to tell no living soul about any facet of the investigation and to deliver the definitive truth to me in his final report. I let him know in no uncertain terms that violating any of my conditions would bring about his immediate demise. In return, I paid him a generous monthly fee, so that he would give my affair priority over everything else."

The Count laughed suddenly and then said,

"The man learned enough about me to take my warnings seriously...that is, no doubt, why it took him twenty years to deliver his final conclusions. Also, I provided him with a steady income for all that time. Perhaps he hoped that I would die at the hands of Jews or Red terrorists before he had to submit the report. No such luck for him, I'm afraid. I don't plan to die anytime soon."

"Sounds like he was gypping you," I said. "The man strung you out and pocketed your dough for twenty years. Pretty clever shamus, if you ask me."

"No doubt," the Count smiled at my words. "Finally, I grew tired of his cat-and-mouse game and I had to...summon the investigator to deliver the report to me personally in Paris, two weeks ago," he chuckled as he remembered the scene.

"He was shaking with fear when he handed the document over to me. I installed him in the Hôtel de Crillon right down the road, while I perused his report then considered its implications. The villain ran up large expenses on food and whiskey, like a condemned man on an American Death Row allowed to order any meal he desires before his execution."

The Count set down his snifter of Domfront calvados. It was the one we drank when we met in his office and the best I'd ever tasted. It was distilled, he'd bragged to me many times, from apples and pears picked by "nubile country maidens" at a farm attached to his Château in Bagnoles-de-l'Orne. He didn't know that I'd been to the castle twice since Hannah and I left Paris in the exodus just over a month ago, fleeing the onrushing German troops.

He picked up his pistol and went to a portrait of a d'Uribé-Lebrun ancestor with a powdered wig and a harelip which hung on the wall near the door. He laid his gun on the floor and removed the portrait from the wall. A safe was hidden behind it.

He'd never shown me the safe in all my visits to his office. It was almost as if he were now letting me know where the family jewels were hidden. He clicked out the combination as I watched him and my ears tuned in the sounds the lock was making. There were four turns to the combination: three clockwise, four the other way, then three more clockwise and four counterclockwise. I stored the sequence in my memory, 3, 4, 3, 4 by remembering that the Count had opened it using a waltz tempo.

I didn't know his starting number, but it would be pretty easy to crack the safe beginning with any number and then using the sequence I'd just heard. I knew that I'd be doing that soon to find out what was inside. First, I'd have to find a way to break into the office, with its new armor-plated security door. With special picklocks, I was sure that I could crack it. Stanley's Corsican buddies would find the necessary hardware for me. As if reading my mind, the Count reached into the safe, pulled out a folder, opened it and waved a sheaf of papers at me.

"This is the report," he said. "As you can see, it isn't very voluminous."

"That doesn't look like twenty years' worth of work. What did the gum-shoe find out?" The Count laughed at my slang word, and waved a No at me with his finger. He returned the report to the safe, spinning the lock, putting the ancestor's portrait over it again and picking up his pistol.

"You were a 'gumshoe' once so you know the rules: the report is confi-dential and it's my sole property. Only I know the truth that the safe holds."

I looked at the tight ranks of paintings of famous d'Uribé-Lebrun Constables, Lord Chancellors and Admirals and Marshalls of France which hung from head height to the ceiling on every wall. The wall behind the Count must have had over fifty paintings on it. I scanned them, remember-ing the exact portrait which concealed the safe. The Count had his good left eye fixed on me, as if reading my thoughts, perhaps already anticipating the break-in that I was planning. Was he manipulating me? I wondered. Then he said,

"I prefer the expression 'private eye' to 'gumshoe.' I paid for an eye to search out the truth for me, for over twenty years, because this eye here..." he pointed to his good left eye "...could not be in New Orleans and Paris at the same time. It's sad to think that my 'private eye' met with a tragic death by fire in New Orleans soon after he transmitted his findings to me a few weeks ago and returned to America. A fine servant of the truth, he was." The Count wasn't making any pretense of sympathy for the dead shamus. I said,

"It's strange how many of the people you come across end up dying by fire or water." He laughed and said,

"Don't speak to me of death by water after your friend Redtop's confes-sion that you murdered my colleague Bartholomew Lincoln Thigpen, Junior in cold blood and sank his body in the Seine at Argenteuil. An interesting choice for a watery grave. Did you know that the town was a favorite haunt of those decadent Impressionists?" I didn't know what he was talking about but protested,

"I didn't murder Buster Thigpen in cold blood and you know it! And Redtop didn't make any 'confession' that I did. You tortured a fake one out of her!" I pretended to be angry, knowing that if the whole affair came to light in American and British newspapers, I was holding the upper hand. He seemed untroubled by my outburst. I continued,

"You said that Pierre wasn't wise to you hiring a private eye?"

"No. And Pierre was here with me when the 'eye' met his fiery demise. I understand that the man was a heavy smoker. No doubt he fell asleep smoking in his bed and set it on fire. The conclusion of the investigation of the New Orleans Police Department, 'Death by misadventure,' points in that direction."

I was sure the Count had sent Pierre to kill the shamus. I was amazed that his reach still extended to the police in New Orleans, a city which he told me he'd left for good in 1895.

"I don't believe you," I said. "Torching places and people is your man Pierre's specialty." He shrugged indifferently, then asked,

"Did Father Gohegan make you religious?"

"No," I answered.

"Good! I'm not religious in the way of your Father Gohegan. But I believe that men of destiny arise from time to time to steer mankind in the direction we are meant to go. If we're taking the wrong route, such men right the direction of the Ark we all voyage in to cross the ocean of life."

"Very poetic," I said. "And you're one of these men of destiny, of course?" He nodded yes and sipped his calvados.

"Bien sûr," he answered. "So are you. Potentially."

"So what do these Destiny Men do?"

"Our role is not to dispense love or charity to mankind but to be... 'erasers,' I think you say. We exist to erase the mistakes of the past, to wipe them away so that the proper destiny opens up before mankind."

The man's lunacy was overwhelming me. Ever since I'd seen Pierre aiming his gun at me as I approached the Count's headquarters, I'd felt my urge to violence returning to the same level it had reached six years ago when I flung my Colt into the Seine after finding out that Buster Thigpen was my half brother by a man my mother had been with before the Count. His words were turning my rage up another notch.

"And I suppose that the men in those autographed photos on your desk-Hitler, Marshal Pétain, Mussolini and General Franco-are Destiny Men too?"

"Bien sûr," he repeated, smiling. "I knew you would understand. And there you have the answer to any questions you might have about what my 'cher Adolphe' is doing in Germany and in the rest of Europe. He's **erasing** the greatest mistake in history: our Aryan forefathers allowing the arrival of the 'chosen people' from the Middle East into Europe."

He was exalted now, once again the madman I'd seen ranting into a lollypop microphone in the newsreel at the Max Linder movie house. I was anxious to leave him before my rage went white hot and I strangled the man in his soundproof office.

"Be patient, my son," the Count said. "We will soon laugh at God's joke together and shed tears as well."

"You'd better keep your boy Pierre away from my nightclub. If he turns up again ..."

"Do you think I care about your threats?" he thundered, interrupting me. "There are many Pierres. They will disappear for good when you give me your final word that you will remove the Jewess from your life and accept my legitimizing you as my son and heir. My patience is exhausted. You must marry a suitable bride I will propose to you." To buy time, I said,

"It's a deal, except for giving up Hannah right away and taking over your band of Nazi stormtroopers. That isn't on the cards."

He peered into my face then laughed. His "Joke of God" seemed to be tickling him again.

"I'll find other successors to lead my Oriflamme movement," he said. "But I would have preferred to keep its leadership 'in the family.'"

The Count held out his hand and we shook on it. He embraced me and I let him kiss me on the cheeks four times, sealing the deal. He grew emotional.

"Your nightclub can count on my protection now. No one bearing malice toward you will come near it. If any one of my men becomes overzealous, you have only to report to me and I will punish the offender. Severely!" He smiled at me and then went on,

"You're a middle-aged man now. It's high time to give up this child-ish nonsense of being a jazz musician running a decadent nightclub," he scolded me. "It's time for you to put your hands on the plow. Giving up your mistress is a small price to pay for the wealth and power that can be yours."

"No chance," I said. "Hannah and I have more wealth and power than we need." He laughed dismissively, saying with a sneer,

"That's the kind of communist claptrap she spouts? Your jazz and that woman are obstacles to your founding a family and becoming a grown-up 'à part entière.' I can accept your situation for a little while longer...say, a week? Then she must go."

"Then our deal's off." I stood up to leave.

"Touché," he said, laughing. "You called my bluff. You and your Jewess can carry on as before until I decide when and where Marshal Pétain will le-gitimize you. As for your mistress, all I can offer is that she won't be expelled from France, for now. After all, America is still our ally. Yet, time presses on for us, my son. You're forty-five years old, if I'm not mistaken. I'm sixty-eight. I want to see grandchildren before I die."

"You'll leave us alone? I'll agree to having Pétain wave his magic wand over me as long as you keep your hands off Hannah and Stanley Bontemps and my nightclub. If your man Pierre or any of your thugs set foot inside it, the deal's off. Hannah and I will contact the American authorities in Vichy to let them know we're heading home." Now that I'd made the threat, I knew he'd have his Oriflamme, the police and the Gestapo watching the airports and the train stations, ready to stop us if we tried to leave France. I went on,

"I get to choose my own musicians. That's the deal. Take it or leave it."

"Granted. Of course, were you to employ musicians who were not ac-ceptable, they will be proscribed."

"One last thing. Stanley Bontemps gets to play at my club any time he's healthy enough. He's got arthritis but he's still the best musician in town." The Count hesitated before saying,

"He's a bad influence on you, but he's non-political and has a certain folkloric amusement value for the Germans as an American Negro stereotype. He's free to play in your club and stay in the area, as long as he stops associating with undesirables...like his Corsican criminal friends."

"It's a deal then," I said, with seeming finality. I reckoned that I'd bought Hannah, Stanley and me time to figure out a new route to safety, because we thought that America would be at war with Germany within weeks. We'd then be enemy aliens, subject to imprisonment, or worse, by the German occupiers.

"So our pact is sealed this time?" He asked. "No going back on our commitments?" He held out his hand again and I shook it.

"It's a pact with the devil, but I'll shake on it." He laughed.

"If **I'm** the devil, who are **you**?" He came around the desk and stood in front of me, his arms wide open for another embrace.

"Please," he said. I folded my arms around him and we exchanged cheek kisses. It all made my blood boil. I'd have killed him with my bare hands then and there, except his death would've made Pierre Lestage the Oriflamme leader and he'd have tortured then murdered Hannah, Stanley and me to avenge his master's death. Not being able to read my mind, the Count said,

"Welcome home, my son Charles-Emmanuel." I recoiled from him and he chuckled.

"You'll get used to your real name. As, in time, you'll get used to taking control of our family affairs. I'll need to lean on you more, now that I'm so busy helping the Marshal deal with the monster Laval the Germans have forced on him." The Count raised his hands in protest before I spoke.

"I know that you'll have nothing to do with my Oriflamme movement, but I ask one favor from you..."

"No!" I said, interrupting him.

"Wait. You'll be pleased to know that the favor concerns my second in command, Pierre Lestage. I need you to keep an eye on him." He smiled seeing the shock on my face.

"I thought he was your top attack dog," I said.

"My sources have recently confirmed that Laval is trying to enlist him in a plot to undermine my position with Marshal Pétain and to take control of my Oriflamme movement away from me. I want you to report to me on everything Pierre does. You'll be my 'private eye', my 'gumshoe' as you say. I have to deal with Pierre very soon. He knows too much about our history to stay alive."

"I want a two hundred dollar retainer and fifty dollars a day, one week up front, plus expenses, say one hundred dollars a week. In cash. Now."

"Surely you jest?" he asked.

"If you're hiring me as a private eye, that's what you pay."

"But you're my son," he complained.

"It's a question of principle, if you know what 'principle' means." He laughed and reached into his pocket.

"Will you take French currency?"

"No, just dollars. In case you break our deal and we need them when we get to New York." He wasn't happy about it, but he shelled out my fees, taking the dough from a folder in one of his desk drawers.

Chapter 12

I gave Hannah and Stanley a rundown of my interview with the Count. They both cracked up when I told them I'd turned the screws on him to fork out over six hundred bucks up front to be his shamus and keep an eye on Pierre Lestage. I turned my fees over to Hannah who fanned herself with the brand new bills.

"They're probably counterfeit," she said. Stanley took the bills from her, closed his eyes and riffled them next to his ear. Then he said,

"They ain't fake, Hannah. They be righteous money." He handed the dough back to Hannah, who smiled at Stanley and stashed it in her handbag.

Stanley was happy that I'd managed to buy time for Hannah and me to try to get out of France again. He thanked me for getting him elbow room to go on living his life and playing his soprano saxophone in Urby's Masked Ball whenever he wasn't in pain.

Stanley said he wasn't bothered that his best cars had been taken by the Germans, because he planned to stay put inside his apartment when he wasn't at the Café Paname or the nightclub. He said he was sick of seeing German soldiers everywhere in their field grey uniforms. They crowded the cafés on the Place Pigalle, reminding him of white American tourists in Pigalle cafés in the nineteen twenties who spewed out their bigoted insults at the colored Americans seated near them. They made threats and stomped off if a colored man was sitting alone with a white woman. Most of the French patrons would

ignore them or mock them, but some café and restaurant owners tried on seg-
regation to attract the Americans, until the French government cracked down
on them hard. Stanley said he "felt the same draft" from the German occupiers
that he felt from most white folks back in America. The Germans would stare
at him like they wanted to beat the "Neger" to death right on the sidewalks of
Pigalle. Others recognized him because he was still famous in Germany from
his gigs in Berlin before Hitler came to power; they'd ask him on the sly where
he was playing. He'd flash his toothiest smile at them and make funny faces to
get them laughing, all the while pretending not to understand their English.
Stanley didn't want any Germans turning up at Urby's Masked Ball.

We agreed it was high time to tell my journalist friend Jean Fletcher about
Redtop's written account of Buster Thigpen's death, which would clear me of
the murder "in cold blood" charge that the Count was dangling over me. There
was also her diary which would implicate Pierre and the Count in her murder.
I had no illusions that the French police or the Germans would bring them to
justice now, but Jean Fletcher could get the story out to the American and British
press if anything happened to us. That would put an end to my father's influence
with Marshal Pétain and the Germans because they feared that anything that
upset the Americans would convince them to enter the war on England's side.

Now that the Count saw Pierre Lestage as a danger and was even paying me to find a pretext for eliminating him before he sold the Count out to
Laval, I reckoned that, if I got to Pierre first, I could make him sign a confes-
sion that he'd killed Redtop on the Count's orders. It might take torture to
drag it out of him, but I was ready to do anything to stop them destroying
Hannah.

I told her and Stanley about the twenty-year-long investigation of the
suspicious circumstances surrounding my mother's suicide which had been
carried out by a private eye hired by the Count. Hannah asked,

"Why is her suicide suspicious after all these years? The Count seems to
specialize in suspicious suicides-look at what happened to Redtop."

"I don't know. That's why I've got to see the private eye's report. It's in a
safe in his office. He waved it in front of me."

I could see a flicker of worry cross Stanley's face.

"What's the matter Stanley?" I asked.

"I think they be things in the past that ain't worth diggin' up. Ain't we got enough to worry about with these Nazis struttin' 'round in Paris? And figurin' out how to get revenge for Redtop?"

"I've got to know my past, Stanley. Who I am. The Count called me some kind of 'Joke of God.' I've got to know what he means. I've got to get into his safe and get my hands on the report." Stanley sighed and then said,

"Well, if you got to, you got to. No safe alive can't be cracked."

"Sure. But it's getting into the Count's office that's the problem. He's put up so many metal security doors and locks that breaking into his building is harder than getting into Fort Knox. If I can get past that stuff, I reckon I can crack open his safe and get at the report. I know exactly where he's hidden it."

"Then we got to trick the Count into leavin' his doors unlocked."

"How?"

"We get my Corsicans in on it. I reckon they pretend they be attackin' the US Embassy a few blocks down from the Count's politics headquarters. They can say they doin' it cause America ain't backin' the Germans to take over England and end the war. That get them a pat on the back from the Boches." I liked Stanley's plan. The Embassy staff had been relocated to Vichy, but an anti-American demonstration at the Embassy building was a powerful symbol that would draw the Oriflamme stormtroopers to it like bears to honey.

"I don't even have to steal the report. It looked real short. It won't take me long to read through it and learn what the Count's shamus found out. Then I can put it back in the safe and cut out. The Count won't know I've been and gone."

"When's your old man going to get Marshal Pétain to turn **you** into a Count?" Hannah said, mockingly.

"He didn't say, but I figure it'll be very soon. That's why I want to read that report and see what cards he's holding. How soon do you think you can get the Corsicans to fake an attack on the American Embassy?" I asked Stanley. He thought it over, taking a long drag on his cigar.

"Let's do it tomorrow night," he said. "Tonight we reopens Urby's 'cause it be Bastille night. We gone have us some customers to bring back, so let's do it tomorrow. My fingers ain't been givin' me no trouble for a few days, so I can take the first set, while you slips off to the Count's office. The Corsicans can start whoopin' and hollerin' at the Embassy around eight p.m. and that's gone smoke out your daddy's Nazis. Shoot, they so dumb, they gone want to join the Corsicans picketin' the Embassy and such and you know the Germans gone let them have a free hand for a while to shame America. The Count's man Pierre be the danger 'cause he gone stay inside. So I reckon we gets our Corsicans to make such a ruckus at the Embassy, throwin' smoke bombs and firecrackers and whatnot, that old Pierre gone come out to have himself a look-see. Then you picks the lock at the entrance and the Count's office. You cracks that safe easy as pie and reads them papers. Then you gets yourself back here in time to kick off the second set."

Wrapping up the mystery of the gumshoe's report was something that I had to do before the Count railroaded me into a ceremony with Marshal Pétain to make me "legitimate." I figured that, if I was ever going to find out why I was a "Joke of God," it had to be now.

I was excited that I was moving towards answers to my questions about who I was. What was my mother Josephine Dubois like and had my father, the Count, ever had any feelings for her? I'd have answers within twenty-four hours if Stanley's plan worked.

I spent the rest of the day rounding up the rest of my quartet, all three of them white Frenchmen, including my Corsican drummer Jacques Stefani. His clan had bribed their way back to Paris across the Demarcation Line.

There were no good colored American sidemen left in Montmartre. They'd returned to America tired of being attacked by the fascist French thugs now beating up Jews and non-Aryans in broad daylight, while the police stood idly by, probably obeying my father's orders.

Our reopening was a flop, despite news of it having spread throughout a dead quiet Paris by the "*téléphone arabe,*" meaning by word of mouth. By the time the second set began, we were only a quarter full. Our usual colored customers were either on their way to America, staying out of sight or hadn't been able to return to Paris across the Demarcation Line.

The few white patrons were wondering if it was safe to be seen in a jazz club during the Nazi occupation, especially one with two colored American musicians and an American Jewish woman running the show.

⋏

At 7:30 p.m. on July 15, I was sitting at the bar with Stanley Bontemps and my ragtag quartet, filling them in on how the evening would play out. I told them that Stanley would lead them during the first set while I was away taking care of some urgent business. I'd return for the second set at 10:30 p.m. and we'd play as a quintet with Stanley.

We'd gone through the rehearsals early in the afternoon. During our re-opening the night before, I had the feeling that the musicians were changed men. Stefani and my two white pickup musicians had already become skittish from the drumbeat of Nazi and French fascist propaganda attacking jazz and other forms of "degenerate art." They were looking over their shoulders, fearing attacks by fascist vigilantes because they were playing in a jazz night-club. Even though I assured them we had solid protection, I didn't know how long I could keep them from bolting. Hannah and I had heaped money on them, but I felt that they could disappear at any time and I'd have big trouble finding replacements.

⋏

A half hour later, I exited the metro, on the Place de la Concorde. Red and black swastika flags flew from all of the flagstaffs where the French tricolor had flown a month before. Direction signs in German had been placed everywhere and groups of German soldiers strolled around like tourists, brandishing their Leica and Rolleiflex cameras. They wanted to photograph the Place's great fountain before they ran out of daylight.

The Stars and Stripes hung from the American Embassy's flagstaff like a tri-colored bedsheet in the still, hot air. Noisy demonstrations were going on in front of the Embassy and on the rue Boissy d'Anglas beside it. These were Stanley's friends with their wide-brimmed hats pulled down to avoid having their mugs on photographs taken by Gestapo posing as tourists. The German soldiers who'd been standing at attention in front of the Crillon Hotel and the French Ministry of the Navy, which had been taken over by the German Kriegsmarine, had approached to check out the demonstrators. They made no move to disperse them when they found out that they were having a pro-German demonstration.

More "demonstrators" were pouring out of the metro on their way to the Embassy and I started sprinting up the rue Boissy d'Anglas and crossed the rue du Faubourg Saint Honoré heading toward the Count's headquarters. I ducked behind a car and watched dozens of Oriflamme stormtroopers running toward the Embassy, echoing the shouts of "A bas, l'Amérique" "Down with America" roaring from megaphones. I used parked cars as cover to make my way to the Count's headquarters as the last of the Oriflamme stormtroopers left it chanting "A bas, l'Amérique." Pierre Lestage stood hesitating on the sidewalk. The door to the building was wide open and he looked at it and then toward the Place de la Concorde. Finally, he sprinted after the others. When he'd moved fifty yards down the street, I darted into the building and paused, waiting to hear if he'd left a guard inside.

I called out, "Y-a-t'il quelqu'un?" There was no answer. The building was empty.

I ran up the steps to the Count's office. To my surprise, the door was wide open and I shut it as I stepped inside. When I found the d'Uribé-Lebrun ancestor I was looking for, I took his portrait down to get at the safe. I knew the sequence of the code on its combination lock, but not the starting point. Four, was the date in July I was born, so I started with four and followed the sequence I'd memorized. My tug on the handle opened the safe's door. I peered inside, saw a bound sheaf of papers with the name "Le Comte Charles-Emmanuel d'Uribé-Lebrun" printed on the cover and opened it. A handwritten report was inside, its lettering like old-fashioned penmanship done with a ruler, a pencil and an eraser. The title page read:

INVESTIGATION INTO THE CURIOUS
CIRCUMSTANCES OF THE DEATH OF
JOSEPHINE DUBOIS (INCLUDING IMPORTANT DETAILS
CONCERNING MARY GOODYEAR , ALIAS "CLAUDETTE,")
FORMER EMPLOYEES OF THE BROTHEL NAMED "MADAME
LALA's MAHOGANY HOUSE" IN NEW ORLEANS, LOUISIANA,
PREPARED BY DEWEY LAFONTAINE, DIRECTOR OF THE
LAFONTAINE PRIVATE INVESTIGATION AGENCY, AND
SUBMITTED TO GENERAL COUNT RENE D'URIBE-LEBRUN,
ON THIS DAY OF
JULY 1, 1940

The name "Claudette" jumped out at me, reminding me of the name Stanley had uttered the first time I met him at Madame Lala's on Mardi Gras day in 1911. I was surprised to see her name in the title of a report that I was expecting to be all about my mother, Josephine Dubois. I skimmed through the thin document, my amazement growing as I hurtled toward its conclusion.

When I finished reading the last of its annexes, my whole body was shaking. What I'd read would change my life completely if it was true and not another of the Count's tricks. I decided right away to keep the report and make a copy of it. I rolled it up, closed the safe and placed the portrait back over it. I stole out of the office and the Count's headquarters, walking on the sidewalk on rubber legs. The noise from the demonstration was dying down. I glanced toward the Embassy as I crossed the street and hid behind a car when I saw Pierre loping back to the Count's headquarters, laughing at some joke a big blonde Oriflamme was telling him. I turned left onto the rue du Faubourg Saint Honoré and disappeared around the corner without being spotted. When I stopped at a café two blocks away on the rue Richepance, I put the report on the chair next to me and ordered a glass of red wine. My hands were shaking as I stared at the report's cover. I spilled more wine than I drank and apologized to the waiter when I ordered another glass.

He frowned at me with contempt as he wiped up the mess that I'd made. I started laughing so hard that I couldn't stop. The waiter stared back at me angrily, which made me laugh even harder. I'd never laughed like that in my life, a laugh that came all the way from my belly, a laugh that tasted like bile in my mouth. The other customers in the bar looked at me indifferently, all lost in their own thoughts. The Parisians had seen so much madness in the past six months that a new lunatic among them made no impression. I was laughing because I now realized that the Count had been right. I'd been a joke of God from the moment I first drew breath. I remembered that I needed to return to my nightclub in time for the second set. I wondered if Stanley had been able to get through the set without arthritis turning his fingers into claws. I left the waiter such a huge tip that he looked at it astonished then threw me a salute as if he thought I was a Gestapo undercover agent.

I walked all the way home clutching the report because I didn't trust myself to take the metro or a taxi. I feared that someone might steal the report or I might rip it to shreds in a sudden onset of madness. If that happened, I was afraid that the real story of my life would vanish forever, leaving only a memory shared by the Count and me. Dewey Lafontaine, the shamus who tracked down the truth like a bloodhound for twenty years, had been rewarded for his work by a fiery demise, if the Count wasn't lying about his death.

I arrived at the nightclub at 9:45 in the evening. Hannah was standing in front of the door, looking around anxiously. When she spotted me, she ran to me and held me tightly in her arms.

"I thought something bad had happened to you. That the Count was holding you prisoner." Her words almost started me up laughing again because Hannah was right-the Count **was** holding me prisoner. I handed the report to Hannah and said,

"Could you hide this in the cellar? Don't try to read it, I'll explain later. Hide it well, Hannah, the Count's men might be coming here to get it back." Hannah took it and ran past me into our nightclub. I waited for a few minutes and followed her in. I noticed that there were even fewer customers tonight for the second set than the night before.

Jean Fletcher, who I wasn't expecting to be there, came up to me, pecked me on the cheek, and said,

"I came running because Stanley phoned to tell me that Redtop's suicide was a murder and you've got proof that you want me to hold onto for safekeeping."

She looked at me expectantly but I answered,

"Sorry that you came all that way for nothing. I'll have to give it to you later."

"No problem," she said. "But I've got to run. Can we meet at La Coupole around ten tomorrow morning?"

"Sure. A demain," I answered. Jean's driver escorted her to the black Citroën Traction Avant that her magazine had laid on for her when the Germans marched into Paris.

Stanley was hanging out at the bar with the members of my quartet, who were scanning the few faces in the audience, trying to spot undercover Gestapo agents or cops. Stanley looked at me, trying to read my mood. He raised a questioning eyebrow and I nodded a Yes. He smiled and lifted his glass of rye to congratulate me.

"How did the set go, Stanley?" I asked, pouring out a glass of calvados from behind the bar, which was unattended while Hannah was off hiding the report. He held his right hand up waving it in a "comme ci, comme ça" gesture that meant that it had gone alright but not great.

Stanley leaned over to whisper,

"Your boys playin' like they scared to death. They wonderin' if they be Gestapos or police in here and it's got them spooked. I don't know how long it be before they gone."

Stanley was right. Even the Corsican drummer, Jacques Stefani, with his crime syndicate connections, looked fearful. He was sweating like he'd just finished running a marathon in the stifling heat outside. It was cool in the club because of its thick old walls and the overhead fans, but Jacques kept mopping his face with a big white handkerchief. I was looking forward to playing again but wondering if what I'd learned from the report would make a difference to my music.

I went over to Stefani and the pickup musicians, Quentin and Louis.

"How did it go?" I asked them. They wouldn't look me in the eye. From my experience, whenever a French jazz musician wouldn't look you in the eye or drink your booze, there were only two possible explanations: that they felt you weren't paying them enough dough or that they were worried about cops.

"Alright," Jacques said. "But I not come again. My family go back to Corsica, too much Germans in Paris now. The others too will not come again." I'd have to start looking for new musicians in the morning.

"Sorry to hear that you're going. I'll pay you before you leave. Let's make the last set our best."

We'd just started on Cole Porter's "Night and Day," when I looked up and saw Pierre Lestage come into the nightclub accompanied by a big blonde man I'd first seen through binoculars, hobnobbing with Pierre and German soldiers when Hannah and I stopped off at the Count's castle during our exodus to Bordeaux.

The two men were dressed in identical white linen suits and wearing black-banded Panama hats, making even their casual summer clothes look like some kind of Oriflamme uniform. They sat down at a table in the corner and watched us while we blew our way through some Cole Porter standards. Stanley was conjuring up a masterpiece of sound, arthritis and all, but Jacques Stefani was even more off tempo with his drums than usual and Quentin and Louis sounded like condemned men playing while their executioners looked on. After one drink, Pierre and his blonde Oriflamme buddy left. I reckoned that the Count was testing whether I'd report ro him that Pierre had turned up at the nightclub.

I didn't think that their presence meant any more than that because I guessed that the Count wouldn't discover that the report was missing for a while and I'd figure out some convenient lie to tell him when the time came. Pierre didn't know that I was working as the Count's shamus, checking on him on the Count's dime while he was hassling me.

I could feel the music flowing in me like lava. I was relieved to find that nothing of what I'd learned about myself in the report had changed my music. The music was part of me, whoever I was. I kept pushing myself and Stanley and suddenly the three French musicians started to play jazz. It was the best swinging our group had ever done. Jacques Stefani had found his groove at last and was rapping out the best drum lines I'd ever heard him play. Quentin and Louis were wailing their hearts out. Tonight was the end of the line for us, but we were going out in style. Stanley was watching me over his saxophone, then he winked at me and we started blowing incredible harmonies together with riffs and runs that we hadn't played since the days when we were fronting Johnny Sutton's band at the Blue Heaven Club in Harlem back in 1914. At the end of the set, the sparse audience gave us a standing ovation as if they'd witnessed a miracle, which they had.

We walked into my office and I gave the three French musicians some extra dough as a going-away present. They still wouldn't look me in the eye when we shook hands as they filed past me leaving the nightclub.

I closed the door and took a pint bottle of rye out of my desk. I poured a big helping for Stanley and he sat back contentedly, smiling at me wearily.

"Those boys only ever played one good set, their last. You got some cats lined up for tomorrow?" Stanley asked.

"No. You got anybody in mind?"

"Yeah, I'll phone them to get their butts here after lunch tomorrow. They the best left in Paris."

"Your Corsican friends sure did a fine job at the Embassy," I told him. "They raised a ruckus that cleared out the Count's headquarters. I cracked the safe and stole the private eye's report. Hannah's gone to hide it in the cellar." Stanley said nothing; he just kept blowing smoke rings into the air and stabbing at them. After a while, he asked,

"You read it?"

"Not every word, but enough to find out what happened." He looked away from me and took some more puffs on his cigar, waiting.

"You let the name 'Claudette' slip at Madame Lala's Mahogany House the first time we met, the first time we ever played music together. Way back in 1911. You remember?" Stanley nodded Yes. I went on,

"Josephine Dubois told Father Gohegan that she was my mother and he believed her. The Father told me what he believed was true. But you knew there was more to the story all along, didn't you?"

"I was hopin' your memory ain't be as good as mine. You tell me you fetched the name 'Claudette' out your head, from hearin' me say her name when you was 15 or 16 years old? Ga..od...damn!" he said, admiringly.

"Yes. Claudette's real name was Mary Goodyear." Stanley took off his Italian straw hat and stubbed out his cigar.

"You angry at me somehow?"

"No. You had your reasons for not telling me and I wouldn't be the musician I am today if it hadn't been for what Father Gohegan and you taught me. I'm glad that I could learn the truth when I was ready for it. It's never changed anything for you, has it?"

"No. You the son I wished I had. But I never had the time for all that family business, because I gots to music. When our music's in you, it take you over body and soul. I known you got the music in you first time I hear you blow. I known you was Claudette's boy, what Josephine Dubois stole away from her. Josephine done come to me with you early in the morning a little time after you was born and told me she swapped her baby for you 'cause she didn't want her own baby raised in no Jim Crow cathouse. Josephine was actin' crazy. She was swingin' you around in a basket like she gone throw the whole shebang into the Mississippi. So I done told her about St. Vincent Colored Waifs' Home and to go by there and just leave you on the steps. I known that the Father gone take you in and do right by you like he done by me. Tell you the truth, I didn't want Josephine to have no trouble for stealin' a white baby and anyways I reckons one cracker less in Louisiana be a good thing. Josephine done what I told her and I swore myself to keep an eye on you all my life." I rubbed his arm and he looked at me as if begging for forgiveness.

"You kept an eye on me good, Stanley." He frowned and then continued,

"Josephine upped and left town. Trombone friend of mine told me he done seen her in Natchez, Mississippi a few years later. Me, I never hear from her again. "

"Father Gohegan told me she committed suicide."

"Naw. She were scared and sorry for what she done, but suicide her own self? Catholics s'posed not to do that and she were one solid catholic."

"What about Claudette? The shamus said Madame Lala kicked her out of the Mahogany House. You know where she went?" Stanley shook his head No. His slight hesitation made me suspect that he knew more than he was letting on. Stanley kept trying to justify why he did what he did. He said,

"Urby, I known that Father Gohegan was teachin' you music like he done with me before. He told me how good you was, even before I hear you stretch out on the clarinet at the Mahogany House that first time. I just had to make sure that music in you come out right, I just had to. I reckoned that if your dues to play righteous music be livin' as a colored man when you really is a white man, you gots to pay them dues. 'Cause you got a gift in you sent from up yonder." I put my hand on Stanley's shoulder; I'd never seen him so upset. He went on,

"You gots to pay them dues and you shapes yo' sufferin' into music. You done pay your dues just like me and Louis Armstrong and Sidney Bechet and all them's been gifted by God."

"I'm fine with what you did Stanley. Music made me human again after the war."

"So what you goin' to do now, Urby? You come full circle. Your gift all cut and polished like a diamond." He held up his hands. His fingers were trembling, trying to tighten up into claws. He looked at them and then wiped tears away with the back of his hand and said,

"I ain't nothin' but a sick old man who ain't goin' to play no more. No part of my body ever pain me before, but these here hands be hurtin' most times now and I be missin' notes. I be one dead musicianer, mon petit, but you done got a lot of life left in you."

"You sounded fine tonight," I said, fearing that Stanley had given up. I'd never have believed that anybody or anything could stop him.

"Fine ain't good enough. You gots to carry on with what I learned you, you hear? If I was you, I'd point my size tens towards America and take Hannah to safety. Start all over again as a white man who be colored inside." He went on,

"You a man be colored in his music, heart, blood and bones. Only white thing 'bout you be your skin."

"It's going to get a lot worse for Americans here when Uncle Sam turns up." Stanley made a cricket laugh in his throat and wagged a finger at me.

"No way I'm leavin', mon petit. I ain't goin' nowhere else but Pigalle."

"Let's talk things over in the next few days, Stanley. Just you and me and Hannah. "

She came back into the nightclub then and signalled to me that she'd hidden the report. She started bagging up the takings. As Stanley turned to leave, she hugged him and he said, his voice raw with emotion,

"You take good care of your man, Hannah, he be special." She looked surprised at his words and the sound of his voice. She said,

"I will Stanley, but I'll need your help."

"Don't say that honey, you doin' fine. You and Urby got a long road from Paris ahead." Stanley went out of the door and we stood at the curb as his chauffeur/bodyguard Finn opened the door of the banged up Panhard coupé that could just about make it to Stanley's apartment around the block.

"Let's go upstairs," I said, when they'd gone. "We've got a lot to talk about...tomorrow morning."

"No, now," Hannah said, and I started telling her the whole story as we walked into our apartment. Hannah didn't say a word.

"Wait here," she said and disappeared down the steps, heading toward the cellar. She returned a few minutes later with the report in her hand.

We sat down in our armchairs and she handed me the folder. I asked Hannah if she wanted a drink and she said no, she wanted to be cold sober to hear what was in the report.

"I'll skip the whys and wherefores," I said. "He just kowtows to the Count and begs his forgiveness for taking so long to finish the job."

"Read it out loud," she said. "Read what I need to know."

PART II

PART II

Chapter 13

So I read out loud:

"*Therefore, to verify what are the known facts of the circumstances surrounding the presumed death of Josephine Dubois I had to investigate the even more mysterious events attending to the birth of the person your Excellency refers to as Charles-Emmanuel d'Uribé-Lebrun. In the interests of simplification, I shall refer to him in the present report using his alias "Urby Brown." When you assigned the present investigation to me some twenty years ago, you had assumed that your natural son, Urby Brown, was born out of wedlock to the woman you presumed to be his mother, namely the quadroon, Josephine Dubois. I can now affirm that the facts to the contrary revealed in the present report are true beyond a shadow of a doubt. I regret, sir, that a number of the Witness Statements annexed to the present report, which I copied verbatim from my notes of interviews with the subjects concerned, refer to yourself in what may be deemed an unflattering light. Please understand that these are the words of the witnesses themselves and I have appended them only to ensure the completeness of the present report. I have checked and cross-checked the statements contained herein over the past twenty years.*

Your Excellency may wish to note that, when you confided the task of investigating this delicate case to me on June 5, 1920, a number of the protagonists were recalling from memory events that had transpired in most cases more than a quarter of a century before. Given their line of work and the lives most of them had lived since their "retirement," most of the witnesses were in very bad physical and mental condition by the time I concluded the interviewing process. Several of them were clearly in the terminal stages of venereal diseases such as syphilis which are a frequent consequence of prostituting themselves. Personally, I deem their maladies just retribution for violating God's laws and the teachings of our Lord and Redeemer, Jesus Christ. However, in furtherance of His own teachings, I feel it incumbent on myself to repeat our Savior's injunction (John 8:7) "He that is without sin among you, let him first cast a stone at her."

Moreover, a number of the witnesses have either dispersed from New Orleans or passed on to the Hereafter since I began my task. Following your instructions, sir, I tracked down a number of key witnesses all over the United States of America and, in one instance, in Mexico in order to lay their earlier testimony before them and to offer them the chance to forswear or gainsay any of it. I can say with some pride that, out of the four direct witnesses concerned from the ill-famed "Madame Lala's Mahogany House," situated in a veritable spider's web of vice and iniquity which garnered a sinister renown under the name of "Storyville", not one of them wished to change any part of their previous testimony. You may wish to note that I have had them affix their signatures or their mark on the relevant pages in the Witness Statements annexed to the present report.

The task of collecting evidence from the negroes connected to the sad case of Miss Mary Goodyear was even more complex, as your honor may have ascertained in any dealings you may have had with members of that race. In many cases, the witnesses changed their testimony or were too afraid to give it, fearing that I, a white man, would pass said testimony on to the local authorities. The negroes rightly feared that the police would exact reprisals on their brethren. I pray your Excellency to forgive my digressions, but I only wished to underline how difficult and time-consuming it was to collect evidence, particularly from the negroes caught up in this most delicate of cases. So I will now return to my summary of the known facts:

I had repeated conversations with the proprietor of the establishment in question ("Madame Lala's Mahogany House"), Madame Laurence de Lavallade, née Thigpen (referred to in the present report by her alias of "Madame Lala"), a quadroon spinster, born in 1868 in Baton Rouge, Louisiana. She was the fruit of an act of foul miscegenation between her mulatto freed slave mother and her mother's former white master. Madame Lala affirmed when I interviewed her in 1922 that your Excellency was a regular patron of her establishment from approximately early 1894 to early 1895. During that time, your choice had fallen upon two of the "finest girls"(her own words, sir) in her establishment, one being a near-white quadroon named Josephine Dubois, born in 1875 in New Orleans and the other a pure Caucasian female of old English stock, Miss Mary Goodyear, known in Madame Lala's establishment as "Claudette." A French-sounding name was given to Miss Goodyear to whet the lusts of her clientele but she was in fact a Yankee girl born in 1876 in Wellfleet, in the Commonwealth of Massachusetts. It would appear that she came from a strict Episcopalian family of some means. However, the wayward Miss Goodyear decided to strike out on her own, being an adventuress by nature. Unbeknownst to your Excellency, before you became attached to this beautiful but miserable creature, she had become addicted to opium as had many of Madame Lala's girls. This was a deliberate policy of Madame Lala who sold the foul Chinese drug to her charges for the purpose of keeping them in thrall to the demonic poppy. They paid for it at exorbitant prices out of their wages of sin. The prostitutes ensnared in Madame Lala's web of vice spent most of their wages to feed their addiction, paying them directly to Madame Lala. This wretch kept raising the prices of the opium, thus, in effect, enslaving her charges. In fine, under the "Madame Lala system," Lala became wealthy by forcing her girls to engage in increasing numbers of acts of sexual intercourse and degradation to pay for their opium and other less harmful and (then) legal drugs such as cocaine and hemp. They also were forced to perform increasingly bestial sexual acts because these were remunerated at a higher rate than the more natural forms of sexual congress. I regret to say that this system, sustained by her beautiful stable of drug addicted pure white and exotic mixed-breed fillies, brought increasing renown to her establishment for the wantonness of its desperate inmates. In its heyday, it attracted many honorable gentlemen, including, it is rumored, the Mayor of New Orleans, the Chief of Police, a congeries of Justices of the Louisiana Supreme Court, the Governor of Louisiana at the time and even several Senators and Representatives from the United States Congress visiting our fair city of New Orleans. At the risk of sounding obsequious, I dare to contend, your Excellency, that you must number among the most well bred of the influential gentlemen who frequented Madame Lala's Mahogany House. It is my dependence on your sense of honor that has finally convinced me after much soul-searching and meditation to submit this report to you, because general knowledge of the names included in the testimony set forth in the attached Witness Statements would doubtless bring shame upon many prominent families in the State of Louisiana and in many other places, despite the distance of such events from this time in late June 1940, forty-five years after the events which are covered in the present report. Thus, were this report to fall into the wrong hands, it could be used to blackmail a

plethora of prominent families, desirous of protecting their repu-
tations and those of their members, even though many of the
persons mentioned herein have long been deceased. I have full
confidence that you will not disclose the information contained
in this report to anyone and that you will keep its contents safe
from prying eyes.

To continue with my report, your Excellency, the "Madame
Lala system" of using drugs to create a form of sexual slavery in
her establishment, depended on her having access to a plenti-
ful supply of drugs, the main one being opium. This drug was
procured for her by her quadroon brother, Bartholomew Lincoln
Thigpen, who also served as a pimp and recruiter of girls for
his sister. He used his swarthy Latin looks to lure women of
the mixed breed persuasion into a life of dissolution and sex
slavery at Lala's bordello. He had, for example, recruited the
quadroon Josephine Dubois into his sister's bordello late in 1892
and she promptly fell pregnant by him and was delivered of a
son, who was "christened," so to speak, Bartholomew Lincoln
Thigpen Junior and given over by Madame Lala to be raised by
their mother in a squalid area referred to by the negroes as "The
Battlefield" of which more later.

Unfortunately for Miss Goodyear, she fell into the clutches
of the said Bartholomew Lincoln Thigpen (hereinafter referred
to as Thigpen the Elder) who, breaking God's laws and those of
the State of Louisiana, personally recruited her, a white woman,
for his sister's establishment. The Yankee, Miss Goodyear, igno-
rant of our superior Southern ways as regards the preservation
of the purity of the White Race by severely punishing the crime
of miscegenation, engaged in sinful fornication with Thigpen
the Elder. Madame Lala managed to keep this miscegenation se-
cret from the white and mixed-breed prostitutes who, schooled
in our Southern way of life and racial codes, would no doubt
have reported such a transgression to the proper authorities

and received due pecuniary reward. However, the quadroon Josephine Dubois learned of it from the lips of Thigpen the Elder who had fathered her first child, Bartholomew Junior, later to become a drummer of some renown under the alias "Buster Thigpen." Fearing retribution if this criminal act became known to the authorities, Madame Lala persuaded the above-mentioned quadroon Josephine Dubois, to swear that she would not divulge the unholy sexual relations between her brother, Thigpen the Elder, and the misguided Mary Goodyear. The latter quickly learned the error of her ways under the severe tutorship of Madame Lala. In exchange for Josephine's silence, she heaped on her privileges which far surpassed any accorded to her other charges, even those most in demand by the clientele. For example, Josephine was provided with opium at cut-rate prices. As you may imagine, her privileged treatment went to Josephine Dubois's head. She began to give herself airs and to think of herself as superior to the other girls, even the pure Caucasian ones. Josephine's delusions were further strengthened by the fact that she had been "broken in" by Thigpen the Elder years earlier than Mary Goodyear had and she had already given birth to his quadroon son, Bartholomew Lincoln "Buster" Thigpen.

When your Excellency appeared on the scene at Madame Lala's in 1894, the above testimony by her girls Isabelle, Blanche, Marie and Fantine, which is reproduced in the annex, reveals that you "showered your favors," beginning later in that year, on Mary Goodyear and that you even paid Madame Lala a substantial bonus to ensure that her services were reserved for yourself on an exclusive basis for a period of roughly three consecutive months. After that time, you dispensed with her services, reportedly (by Madame Lala) because Mary Goodyear, alias "Claudette," began to demand that your Excellency should, in Mary's reported words, "make an honest woman out of her." Unbeknownst to you, sir, Mary Goodyear had become pregnant during your *period of exclusive usage of her services. As her pregnancy became more noticeable, Madame Lala sequestered her in quarters that she used in her establishment for such exigencies and plied her with opium to maintain her in a state of passivity. She explained to all clients who requested Mary's services that she had returned home to Massachusetts to visit her ailing father, a consideration which the clients found laudable. The testimony also reveals, sir, that you also had recourse to Josephine Dubois from time to time during your period of exclusive usage of the services of Mary Goodyear and Josephine Dubois also fell pregnant. Madame Lala sequestered her in a similar manner to Mary in the suites reserved for this purpose. Both of them being pregnant and sequestered in proximity to each other, they quickly learned that they were both pregnant by your Excellency. This awakened a great enmity between Josephine and Mary because they were both deeply enamored of you, according to the testimony of the above-mentioned girls. Josephine Dubois, being already used to favorable treatment by Madame Lala as described above, now completely lost her head and began to harbor dreams and ambitions far above her station. She became deranged by the notion that you would also "make an honest woman out of her" and take her to France and raise your octoroon child by her as a white person.*

At the appointed time, there intervened the birth of Mary's child, a blonde, blue-eyed pure Caucasian baby, a birth which all of those interviewed, including Madame Lala, confirmed. The explanations provided by the above-cited witnesses have convinced me that the Caucasian prostitute, Mary Goodyear, was delivered of your son in the early morning hours of July 4, 1895 by Madame Lala herself.

Approximately an hour later, Josephine gave birth to your octoroon bastard, a blonde, blue-eyed baby also delivered by Madame Lala.

According to the Witness Statements annexed hereto, some three hours later there was screaming in the house when Mary woke up to find that her baby had disappeared. After a thorough search of the house, no trace of the baby was found. Given the circumstances of the birth and in order to avoid causing problems for her business, Madame Lala chose not to inform the police to initiate a search, despite the fact that a white baby was missing.

Madame Lala and her charges had quickly determined that Josephine Dubois was also missing. She returned later that morning, as testified by one Blanche Theroux in the annex, "with the smile of the cat that ate the canary." Josephine explained her absence by boldly stating that she had cast her newborn baby into the Mississippi River because your Excellency had broken a vow you made to her, to whit, that you would take her to Paris. You would marry her there and make her a Countess and raise your child by her as a white man and a Count. When you didn't live up to your promises, Josephine claimed that she had wreaked her revenge by drowning your bastard son.

In the meantime a baby presumed to be Mary Goodyear's, had been found in a linen closet in a seldom visited room and this calmed the battle that was beginning to rage between the white pensioners of her establishment and the negro-descended ones. All of them were united in horror of Josephine's wanton act of barbarity toward what she avowed to be her own baby (to throw them off the scent). Josephine nevertheless continued to defend her unspeakable act. She had the temerity to advance as fact that her rival had gone to a conjure woman whom she paid to cast a hoodoo spell on you which lured you into impregnating Mary Goodyear. She also claimed that Mary had not protected herself from pregnancy in the usual manner employed by women who ply her trade but had tricked you into inseminating her in case the hoodoo spell proved faulty.

Josephine's barbarous act, as well as her wild claims and haughty and unrepentant demeanor (including her insistence that all address her as Countess Josephine) provoked hostility from all of the prostitutes be they whites or mixed-breeds. Madame Lala herself became so furious at Josephine that she stripped her of her privileges and her drugs. Afraid of the damage to her business that the continued presence of Josephine might cause, she ejected Josephine from her house and cast her onto the streets along with her baggages and meager possessions. Madame Lala told her never to appear in her establishment again and to clear out of New Orleans altogether, or else she would set her brother Thigpen the Elder onto Josephine and he would "carve up her pretty face." All this notwithstanding the fact that Madame Lala was the aunt of the child, "Buster" Thigpen, whom Josephine had given birth to by Madame Lala's own brother.

Madame Lala learned from her client, the Chief of the New Orleans Police Department, that Josephine had shortly thereafter disappeared from the city. Nevertheless, the badly burned body of a mixed breed woman covered with fragments of clothing with a fabric identical to that in a dress owned by Josephine Dubois was found hanging from a tree in the early morning hours of July 11, 1895 in the French Quarter. The corpse was so badly disfigured that a totally positive identification was rendered impossible. But, after a thorough investigation, the New Orleans Police Department concluded that the corpse was that of Josephine Dubois and that she had most likely committed suicide. Some vandals bearing ill will and grudges toward the negro race had most likely discovered her body hanging from the tree and then set it alight with

some flammable substance as an expression of their exaspera-
tion at the continued presence of such a numerous population of negroes and mixed-breeds in New Orleans in July
1895, more than thirty years after the abolition of slavery. The
Police Department treated her death as a suicide followed by
an incident of vandalism on her corpse. The story of the supposed suicide of Josephine Dubois, who was a very renowned
woman of easy virtue, spread through the city's circles of vo-
luptuaries very rapidly.

However, further investigation by your humble servant
has revealed that Josephine was still alive as of August 1931,
eleven years after you assigned me the task of investigating
the circumstances described in the present report. Her last
known address was in Natchez, Mississippi. I tried to locate
her there, but to no avail. If still alive, she is doubtless living
under an assumed name, somewhere in America or in Mexico
or even Canada, where her light complexion would facilitate
her "passing" as a white woman from America.

As for Mary Goodyear, the whole sorry incident of
Josephine murdering her own baby, though fictitious as
you shall read in my conclusions below, seemed to awaken
some slumbering moral fibers in her. Madame Lala agreed
with her that it was best for her too to leave the establishment and indeed to leave Louisiana in order to draw a
line under events. If known, such goings on would bring
Madame Lala's enterprise tumbling into ruin and even
lead to her incarceration and that of her brother, Thigpen
the Elder, if indeed they were not lynched for defiling
white womanhood. Mary Goodyear duly left with what she
thought was her own newborn baby and returned to her
native New England.

FINAL CONCLUSIONS OF THE PRESENT REPORT

1. *A high ranking acquaintance of mine on the New Orleans Police force revealed to me the following when I related the above story to him: one of his patrolmen who kept an eye on the Saint Vincent's Colored Waifs' Home in the Gentilly parish saw a woman, bearing a strong resemblance to the subject Josephine Dubois, leaving the area in the morning of July 4, 1895 empty-handed, whereas he had seen her enter it with a Moses basket some ten minutes before. When I later asked the patrolman in question, at that time long retired, whether the basket could have contained a baby, he said that he thought it could have. Conversations with other persons on this matter make me duty bound to relay to you my ninety-five percent certainty that Josephine Dubois was carrying Mary Goodyear's white baby in that Moses basket. I learned that Father Gohegan, the head of the Colored Waifs' Home, bestowed the name Urby Brown on the white infant, by which name he is still known. He is, as you know, a longtime resident of Paris. Having been raised in a negro environment, he is unaware that he is of pure white descent. Like your Excellency, he too thought that he was your natural son by the quadroon prostitute Josephine Dubois, until I brought the true story to your attention by submitting the present report to you after a painstaking and thorough investigation. The five percent of uncertainty on my part is only due to the fact that I was unable to question personally Father Gohegan, the priest having burned to death on July 5, 1913, when the Colored Waifs' Home was destroyed by fire.*

2. *Therefore, your Excellency, my final conclusion is that the said Urby Brown is of pure white racial origin and is your son by the aforesaid Caucasian female Mary Goodyear.*

3. *The foregoing leads me to my inescapable second conclusion that the baby whom Mary Goodyear took north with her was indeed the child of your loins, but with Josephine Dubois and not Mary Goodyear. That child is an octoroon negro in accordance with the system of racial classification prevailing in the State of Louisiana.*

AFTERWORD

Your Excellency might wish to know that I have not made any attempt to make contact with Mary Goodyear to alert her to the fact that the octoroon negro baby whom she has raised is not in fact her own child, but Josephine's. I felt that it would be untoward of me to do so since I deemed that any further action in this respect falls outside the scope of my mandate. I will only voice the hope that she has sought redemption for the evil acts which she committed as a young woman and that she has offered up her soul to our Lord and Savior, Jesus Christ, and begged for His forgiveness for her past sins. Our Lord has given her a heavy cross to bear, being punished by unknowingly bringing up as her own the child of a devious negress, whilst the pure Caucasian child of her womb was raised as a negro in a Home for Colored Waifs.

So, as far as I am concerned, with this report and the detailed Witness Statements annexed hereto, as well as the above conclusions, you can rest assured that, as so commissioned by you, I have turned over every stone in search of the truth of the circumstances surrounding the birth of "Urby Brown" and the purported "suicide" of Josephine Dubois.

I doubt that, without my intensive investigations, you would have learned about Mary Goodyear or perhaps even known of her other than as "Claudette." The present report will have served its purpose if it brings to light the fact that your natural son, known as "Urby Brown," long a resident of Paris, is indeed of pure Caucasian descent and not an octoroon as claimed, you informed me, by the late head of the Saint Vincent Colored Waifs' Home, Father Aloysius Gohegan. I hope that you will be satisfied with my arduous investigative work and that its conclusions, though long in coming, will bring balm and solace to your soul as they have to mine.

With my very best and sincerely respectful good wishes, I remain, your Excellency, your obedient servant, Dewey Lafontaine, Director of the Lafontaine Private Investigation Agency and formerly Detective in the New Orleans Police Department.

⚓

I finished reading the report and looked up to see the shock on Hannah's face. Like me, she couldn't believe what I'd just read. Then she said,

"So, what I get from Dewey's report is that the woman who you thought was your mother, Josephine Dubois, must have taken Mary Goodyear's white baby by the Count, namely you, to the Saint Vincent Colored Waifs' Home and left you there. She passed by a few days later and falsely confessed to Father Gohegan that you were her child by the Count. She pretended to beg him to ask the Count to send for you, but she reckoned that Father Gohegan, a white Southern man, wouldn't agree because of the 'one drop' rule.' You'd become just another colored waif, like her quadroon son, Buster Thigpen." It suddenly dawned on me that Josephine had even fooled Stanley. He thought that he'd been the one to convince her to leave me on the steps of the Home instead of throwing me into the Mississippi. But leaving me there had been her plan all along. She knew all about the Waifs' Home, because her son, Buster Thigpen was already there. I stopped Hannah to ask a question but I'd already guessed the answer,

"Why would she do it?" She thought for a while and then said,

"I suspect she had two motives, revenge and hatred. Josephine's love for the Count turned to hatred and a thirst for revenge, because he'd promised to take her and their baby to France, but left her instead with a near-white baby who'd grow up as colored in the same Jim Crow world she'd known. She hated Mary Goodyear because Josephine reckoned her rival had left herself unprotected on purpose, and then had the Count's white baby out of spite towards her. To make matters worse for Josephine, she and Mary had given birth to baby boys at nearly the same hour on the same day, as if they were twins born of the same father but with two rival mothers. Josephine must have really hated Mary and her white baby. She knew that baby, you, would have a better life than her own baby. She could never have imagined that you'd end up in France with the Count doing everything in his power to make you his heir."

"What about Josephine's suicide?" I asked. "Father Gohegan always said that he felt responsible for Josephine's suicide because he hadn't written in time for the Count to send for me."

"Josephine got someone to help her fake her suicide on July 11, 1895, probably Thigpen the Elder, Buster's father. That way, she figured she'd get off scot free and she did. Her octoroon son by the Count must have lived his life as a white man. He's probably still in touch with your mother, Mary Goodyear, if she's still alive. Josephine may not have been Einstein, but she had a genius for avenging herself on a system and people she felt had wronged her." Hannah paused then asked me,

"Do you feel any different, because you're white? I'd probably feel different if I found out that my Jewish parents had kidnapped me from a Presbyterian couple at birth and brought me up as a Jew. I don't know if not really being Jewish would tear me apart or make me happy that I was an 'Aryan' and didn't have to run from Nazis anymore."

"I was shocked at first, but I don't know what I feel now," I answered. "There's nothing I can do about it. What gets me is that Stanley knew about it all along, but never came out with it. Except for one slip he made the first time I met him."

"What slip?"

"We'll talk to him about it and he'll tell you."

"Do you hate him? He's known all along what the Count only learned from the report what, two weeks ago?"

"How could I hate Stanley? I'll always be in his debt for helping me to find my music. Maybe he helped me to find you too." Hannah looked doubtful, then said,

"It's going to take me a while to get used to you. Before I knew that, for us to stay together, we had to fight to make the world a better place. Now that you're white, I don't know if you'll just blend into the white world and stop fighting for the things I believe in. Will you turn into one more bigoted... French aristocrat?"

"Look, Hannah. I'm a colored musician from New Orleans who became a white man at forty-five. I feel like someone's slapped a new coat of paint on me, that's all. It won't last as long as the old coat."

"I don't want you to change."

"I understand now why the Count's been putting so much pressure on me to set a date for our meeting with Pétain. He wants to make me his legal heir before Premier Laval gets Pierre or some other Oriflamme to betray him to the Marshal who'll take all his power and wealth away. He figures that once I'm legitimized I'll have to work to keep him in power or go down with him. He would've had his man Pierre rub you out the moment he got the report, except he doesn't trust him anymore. He hasn't even told Pierre about it."

"Why doesn't he just tell Pierre that he's got proof that you're white and be done with it?"

"He doesn't operate that way. Now that the Count doubts his loyalty, Pierre's a dead man. He's just giving him enough rope to hang himself so he can watch the traitor as he swings from the noose. That's why he's hired me as a private eye to spy on him. Pierre's gambling all his chips on Premier Laval. The biggest one would be telling Laval that I'm the Count's octoroon bastard son by a Storyville whore. That won't go down well with Marshal Pétain and his 'crusade to return France to virtue and racial purity.' Laval could use that stuff to bring the Count down."

"Laval's got spies everywhere. He must know that you're the Count's bastard son. And you've never tried to pass for white."

"If Marshal Pétain doesn't have proof in hand that I'm the non-Aryan son of a murderer and raving lunatic, he'll stay loyal to the Count. After all, the Count made him the 'Victor of Verdun,' which is why he's now France's leader. Pierre could have given Laval enough ammunition to destroy the Count's standing with Pétain, **if** I was colored. Unfortunately for Pierre, it looks like I'm not."

"Let's go to Stanley's," Hannah said. "I won't be able to sleep until I have some answers from him." I phoned Stanley and he told me to come over and bring Hannah. He sounded as if he was expecting my phone call.

⚓

After a long silence, Stanley asked,

"Hannah, you done read it?"

"Urby read it out to me," Hannah said. "I want to hear it from you. Is it true that Urby's mother was Mary Goodyear and not Josephine Dubois?"

"Yes. I done told Urby that already. Now, I'm tellin' you. Urby's mama be Mary Goodyear, who was white. Urby be white. White."

"Alright," Hannah said. "I believe it now."

"You angry at me?"

"Never happen," she said. "You love Urby as much as I do."

"I love you too, child," Stanley said.

CHAPTER 14

La Coupole was full of German officers drinking café au lait and eating butter croissants when I met Jean Fletcher there the next morning at ten a.m. Signs had been pasted all over the façade warning Jews and other non-Aryans that they weren't allowed inside.

Jean was sitting at our favorite table. Our usual waiter, Honoré, was talking to her and gesticulating with the free hand that wasn't holding his tray. As I approached the table, I could hear him telling Jean how good it was to have customers again and she was asking him whether he was sad that so many of his customers were German officers. Honoré was treading carefully, aware that many of the Germans sitting nearby could understand French.

"A customer is a customer," Honoré shrugged. "I'm only a waiter. Maybe something good will come of it in the end."

"Hope you're right Honoré," Jean said, pouring water into her glass of Pernod and watching the liquor go cloudy. She lifted the glass in a toast to Honoré, saying in an exaggeratedly American accent, "Vive La France!" The German officers turned around warily to size Jean up. They relaxed, seeming to have decided she was an American floozy who'd started on an early drunk. Some of the Germans smiled at Jean, derisively lifting their cups of coffee to her, answering her toast. A few of them called out "Vive l'Amérique" or "Vive la France nazie!" Honoré took my order and rushed off to get my Pernod although I was a non-Aryan, as far as he knew. Jean gave me a peck on each cheek and said, waving her glass to encompass everyone in La Coupole,

"It's scary how quickly the French have taken to being occupied by the..." she cupped her hands and whispered into my ear "...Boches."

"Yes," I said. "I can't believe France and her allies whipped their tails during four years of mutual slaughter just twenty years ago and now Pétain's waved the white flag after just six weeks. Except for de Gaulle's bunch who are waging war with radio waves beamed from London." Jean lifted her glass as Honoré put my Pernod on the table. I clinked glasses with her as she whispered,

"To Temporary Brigadier General de Gaulle." Then she went on in her normal voice,

"I wish I could write that story about how you and Hannah helped him escape. Did you know that Churchill made him fly in the last RAF plane to leave France for England? Reynaud and Countess Hélène de Portes could have escaped by flying to England in de Gaulle's plane which was gassed up and ready to go thanks to the Count's fuel supplies. She'd still be alive and Reynaud wouldn't be in prison. Alright if I write the whole story after we win the war?" I nodded Yes and looked around: the Germans were pretending to ignore us, but they were listening intently.

"A penny for your thoughts," she said.

"It's going to cost you a whole lot more this time, Jean. What I'm going to tell you isn't for publication, deal?"

"Deal." She crossed her heart, but I reckoned that, if she said she would keep a secret, nothing, not even torture, would get it out of her.

"Jean, I'm white. The Count hired a private eye from New Orleans to make an investigation of everything about my birth and..." She gulped down her Pernod and signalled to Honoré to bring her another one, while she stared at me without saying a word. Only after a swig of Pernod did she say, mockingly,

"Pity, Urby, I was just beginning to like you. Still, it sounds like a great story. Give."

I told Jean about Dewey Lafontaine's report and how I got my hands on it. I asked her if she thought the Count had been manipulating me to steal it because he'd shown me exactly where he kept it and left his headquarters wide open during the fake protest that the Corsicans staged at the American Embassy.

"Possible," Jean said, downing her Pernod. I went on,

"It was too easy for me to crack his safe. He chose a combination that a child could've worked out. After I stole the report, two of his top storm-troopers showed up at my nightclub, despite the Count's promise they'd stay away if I went along with his plans for me. Maybe he was sending me a message that he knew I had it."

"The Count's really going to rush to get you legit with Pétain now that you're in the 'pure Aryan' club. Which means that Hannah's in more danger than ever because she isn't a club member." She paused and added, "I'm going to have to start calling you Count Charles-Emmanuel d'Uribé-Lebrun, son of one of the top five contenders for the title of 'deadliest lunatic in France.' Change that to one of the top **three** contenders."

"Call me Urby Brown. That's who I am."

"I hope so." Despite the way Jean was staying calm, I could see that my revelations had stunned her. She said,

"If I've got your story straight, it means that Buster Thigpen, who you killed to keep him from blowing Redtop's brains out, wasn't related to you. He was the son of a quadroon pimp who Detective Lafontaine called 'Thigpen the Elder' and a Mahogany House quadroon prostitute named Josephine Dubois who it turns out wasn't your mother." I hadn't thought out all the angles of Dewey Lafontaine's revelations. I was still horrified that I'd killed Buster, but relieved that he wasn't my half brother after all.

Jean went on,

"Think about it Urby. Somewhere out there you've got a real half brother, Josephine Dubois's son by the Count. He's an octoroon brought up as a white man by a mother who doesn't have a clue he's not her son. You've lived the life he would have lived if Josephine hadn't switched her baby for Mary's and he'd been handed over to Father Gohegan instead of you. I wonder what kind of man he's turned out to be. You'll have to track your mother and him down and find out. You're like me. You won't let it rest until you find out. You'd make a good reporter if you didn't already have a day job."

"More like a night job," I said.

"Seriously, I think you'll make a beeline for New Orleans as soon as you get back to America. You'll check out everything in Dewey Lafontaine's report because, deep down, you think the whole thing is another one of the Count's tricks to get you 'legitimized' by Marshal Pétain so that you become his recognized son and heir." I remembered that I wanted to see Jean to show her my photostat copy of Redtop's diary and her witness statement, so I handed them over. She read through the papers and whistled.

"This is explosive stuff, Urby. If it get's out that the Count ordered Redtop's killing, the Americans will make a protest, even if she's colored, because she's so famous. Hitler's still cozying up to America and Premier Laval's trying to shaft the Count anyway. The State Department will put so much pressure on Pétain that he'll drop the Count like a hot potato."

"That's the way I figure it too," I said. "If you hear that Hannah and I are dead or in prison or in America, could you get the story out?"

"It's a swell story... I'll get it out if it's the last thing I do. Meanwhile, you and Hannah should get the hell out of France. Pronto."

"We're trying to get Stanley to leave with us, but he's not budging."

"I'll keep an eye on him when you're gone. You'll have to plan your getaway very carefully. Your old man won't let his Aryan son waltz out of here with Hannah. You're the future of the d'Uribé-Lebrun line, Count."

Just then, I heard the sound of new patrons and turned to see Pierre walk into our area with the big blonde Oriflamme. They flicked a look over at our table and, with their backs turned toward us, sat down opposite two German officers who'd reserved places for them. I nudged Jean and said,

"See those two fellows over there? The ones in the white linen suits and Panama hats? The one who looks like a cheap stand-in for Adolf Hitler is the Count's hitman Pierre Lestage who Redtop wrote about in her diary. The blonde fellow seems to be a big buddy of his." Jean looked at them over my shoulder.

"They look out of place in here with all the Nazis lounging around sweating in their grey uniforms," she said. "Are they the men who came into your nightclub last night after you stole the report?"

"Yeah. Maybe they followed me here."

"Urby," Jean said, looking over my shoulder. "Pierre and his buddy are leaving without ordering anything." I turned around and saw Pierre and his blonde friend and the German officers staring at me. The big blonde said something in German to the Nazis and they fell about laughing. Then Pierre doffed his hat towards us in a sweeping gesture. He and his friend turned on their heels and strolled past us whistling Lili Marleen.

"What's that all about, Urby? Pierre was looking at you like you were dog turd. I don't speak German, but I'd bet his buddy wasn't exactly singing your praises."

The German officers opposite us were obviously talking about me as they whispered to each other and laughed among themselves. They were mugging gestures as if they were musicians, one of them holding his hands over the stops of an invisible trumpet and the other doing a bug-eyed imitation of a colored jazzman playing a clarinet, rolling his eyes and stretching his thin lips as far as they would go. I reckoned he was supposed to be me. If they smeared black greasepaint over their faces, they'd be putting on a minstrel show.

"The Count hasn't told Pierre about the report," I whispered to Jean. "He still thinks I'm colored. That's what his buddy must have been telling those Nazi clowns." What they were doing was catching on, because all of the German officers around us were calling out "Lawdy, lawdy" and trying to outdo each other with King Kong imitations.

"That's disgusting!" Jean shouted at them. "You call yourselves German officers?" They ignored her and kept up their shenanigans making shoe shining gestures and scratching at their scalps. I had to keep Jean from attacking them.

The German officer who'd been talking to Pierre's blonde friend came over to our table. His pale grey eyes bored into mine and he looked me up and down with disgust as if I were something nasty he'd brought into the Coupole on the soles of his shiny black leather jackboots.

"Papieren!" He barked out. I kept holding Jean back as she spluttered and fizzed at them like the fireworks kids throw at you on Bastille Day. I took my residence permit and passport out and he looked them over, disdainfully.

"Amerikaner?" he sneered. "Du bist kein Amerikaner, Du bist ein Neger." The German officers around us stood up and came over to our table, staring at me like a pack of wolves, all their fake hilarity gone now. They started shouting "Raus!" and shoving me toward the exit. Honoré and the other waiters looked embarrassed for me or shook their heads in sympathy as the cries of "Raus!" rose higher from all the German officers in La Coupole.

"They won't get away with it Urby, I'll phone Ambassador Bullitt's stand-in, Bob Murphy," Jean shouted. At the door, the Germans grabbed me by the arms and legs, counted "eins, zwei, drei" and heaved me out of La Coupole. I did a belly flop and the sidewalk felt like a kick to the stomach. Pedestrians stepped over me and kept on moving like robots with their eyes staring ahead, unseeing. I shook the cobwebs out of my head and got to my feet slowly. No bones felt broken. The German heave-ho party stood at the door, making a big show of wiping their hands to rub the filth, me, off them. One of them pointed at the signs on the façade that told would-be patrons that no Jews or other non-Aryans were allowed inside. The civilians, who'd watched in silence, resumed their conversations.

A terrible thought came to me all of a sudden. I'd left Hannah alone at home when I went to meet up with Jean at La Coupole. Once they'd left La Coupole, Pierre and his friend might have gone to our apartment to harass Hannah. I grabbed a passing taxi and headed to Pigalle.

⋏

One of Hannah's handkerchiefs was lying on the landing. I picked it up and ran up the stairs to our apartment. She was gone and the intruders wanted me to know that they'd taken her by force. Our sheet music and scores had been ripped up and flung around the living room. The big wooden radio had been knocked off its stand and kicked across the rug, leaving a trail of broken glass tubes. Most of our record collection had been smashed and scattered over the floor. I raced downstairs and made a quick search of the nightclub and then went down into the cellar. I was hoping that Hannah was hiding there, but she was gone.

I ran around Place Pigalle in the sweltering mid-July heat, passing sidewalk café terraces teeming with German officers and soldiers basking in the sun. Some of them stood up to take photographs of me as I passed. People who recognized me from nightclub posters called out my name and waved their Suze liqueur publicity fans at me.

I finally gave up my fruitless search of the cafés on Place Pigalle and returned to our building to see if Hannah had come back. I started by looking in the office of the nightclub. Light streamed through the window. I remembered that the desk lamp was off when I left to look for Hannah but it was on now. Its light shone onto a sheet of paper that was plunked down in the middle of the desk. I read the words on the paper:

"I want to see you at two p.m. today, July 16 in my office. Don't be late. Your Father." I had a half hour to get to his headquarters, so I had to move fast.

I started to take the Colt M1911 Stanley had given us for my exodus from Paris with Hannah then thought better of it. If the German soldiers or the French police caught me with it, I figured they'd march me off to La Santé prison or stand me up against a wall and gun me down. There was no way that I was going to leave Hannah on her own, so I left the gun behind when I went to see the Count.

At the Count's headquarters, Pierre and his blonde friend bowed and scraped before me, as if they hadn't abducted Hannah or got me thrown out of La Coupole four hours ago. They were gloating because they reckoned they were doing the Count's bidding. I was looking forward to seeing the Count's reaction when I told him what had happened at La Coupole. I was also wondering if the Count knew that Dewey Lafontaine's report was missing from his safe. I walked up to Pierre, thought of punching him in the belly and then asked him, nodding toward his blonde buddy,

"Does he have a name?" Pierre nodded and said,

"Monsieur le Comte, let me introduce my friend, Jean-Pierre." The big blonde clicked his heels and bowed rapidly from the waist like Erich von Stroheim's Prussian officer in Jean Renoir's film, "La Grande Illusion."

"I prefer Hans-Peter," he said. "I was born German in Alsace, when it rightfully belonged to the Reich. Now it's been returned, thanks to the Führer." Pierre winced. I could see that even he didn't like what his buddy was saying.

As we walked along the corridor to the Count's office, Pierre bragged to Jean-Pierre/Hans-Peter that the reinforced concrete walls of the Count's headquarters would withstand the explosive force of the bomb that the Oriflamme were planning to detonate at the nearby American Embassy if America dared to declare war on Germany some day.

The Count was sitting at his desk polishing his Berthier pistol when Pierre and Jean-Pierre ushered me into his office. I slammed the door shut on the two men and the Oriflamme stormtroopers milling around them.

"Where's Hannah?" I shouted and he gripped his pistol and waved it at me, motioning me to sit. He laid the Berthier down within easy reach of him and checked his watch.

"It's two p.m.," he said. "She should be arriving at the Gestapo's 'experimental women's and infants' transportation center' in Pithiviers as we speak."

"You sent her there?" I lunged for the pistol and he whipped it away and slammed it down on my right hand. In pain, I sat down hard in a chair and flexed my fingers to feel if any of them were broken. When I looked up, his icy blue left eye was fixed on me and he was aiming his gun straight at my heart.

"Shut up and listen to me! I had nothing to do with it. The Gestapo and my intelligence services had a café near the Sorbonne under observation. She got caught with some of her Red friends when we raided the café. The same kind of friends who talked her into going to Spain to enlist in a lost cause. We know what happened to her there. It's her fault for consorting with dangerous Reds and anarchists. And yours for not keeping her in line after I warned you that I could only protect you from our German friends if you were discreet." Ignoring his lies, I asked

"Where's Pithiviers?"

"On the way to Orléans. Nothing to admire around there except wheat fields, if you like that sort of thing."

"You get on the phone and tell them to bring her back! She's an American, goddamn it!" He smiled and said,

"Are you sure? She seems to have mislaid her passport. She may be a Stateless Jew for all we know." I balled my hand into a fist, ready to attack him when I had an opening.

"Your people must have stolen it. She has a residence permit too."

"Are you referring to this?" He slid Hannah's *carte de séjour* across the desk to me. "ANNULEE" was stamped on it.

"You ordered your cops at the Préfecture to cancel it, didn't you? She doesn't have any papers on her?" He shrugged.

"It's the prerogative of France to determine who should reside here."

"Tell that to the Boches." He recoiled as if I'd uttered a blasphemy.

"I advise you not to say 'Boches' again. Our Teutonic friends urged us to deal harshly with utterers of such blasphemy and we've passed a new law."

"You'd do anything to claw your way to the top, wouldn't you?" I asked. "Betray France, kill anyone who stands in your way? I'll say it once and you'd better listen. If you touch Hannah or Stanley, I'll destroy you. I've got solid evidence that your thug Pierre killed Redtop. On your orders." He looked worried for an instant, then decided I was bluffing, which I was. He wagged his pistol, mocking me.

"No such proof exists. Anyway, who would believe you? Even if it were true, who cares about some lesbian American negress who ran a nightclub for European, Jewish and Negro degenerates? Bravo and good riddance, I say."

"Redtop is a household name in America. Marshal Pétain won't touch you with a ten-foot pole after the story hits the newsstands in America with headlines calling you a killer, on a par with the worst Nazi thugs. I'd get rid of you, if I was Pétain." I'd finally got his attention.

"Tell me about your so-called evidence."

"I've found a written statement from Redtop that I didn't murder your friend Buster Thigpen in cold blood, but to stop him from blowing her head off. I've also got stuff pointing the finger at your man Pierre Lestage for killing her and staging it as a suicide. The newspapers' stories will link him to you."

For the first time, I sensed fear in him. Then his bluster returned.

"Your Miss Korngold is an illegal alien in France, now that her *carte de séjour* has been cancelled. She has no passport. Ergo, she has no valid legal identity here. Such illegal non-persons worry the French authorities and, of course, our German friends. And she is a Jew. All of these factors complicate her situation." He leaned back and lit a cigarette. His hand holding the pistol was rock steady.

"Why did they take her to Pithiviers?" I asked.

"Ah, the Germans are transforming its train station into a center for the... uh ...processing of foreign Jews for...internment and transport. Your friend is part of a test of possible new procedures by our German colleagues and my police..."

"Stop lying!" I shouted at him. "What are you doing to her?"

"Sorry, but it is out of my hands now." At my roar, he tightened his finger on the trigger.

"I won't kill you, because that would not be in my best interests." He aimed the gun at my right hand.

"However, a well-placed bullet into your right hand would put an end to your so-called musical career. And you will still be able to produce heirs to our lineage. I'm tempted to shoot. Before I do, tell me what you thought of the report that you stole from my safe last night." He laughed out loud when he saw the look of surprise on my face.

"You made it easy to steal, leaving your office door unlocked," I said.

"I did so, because I **wanted** you to read the report. You wouldn't have believed what it reveals if the news came from me. Well?"

"It makes no difference to me," I lied. "I've got one question though. Did you ever feel anything for Mary Goodyear?" He was pensive for a while, then said,

"It was a long time ago. I remember that she played the piano beautifully. You take after her in your...musical talent. Otherwise, as prostitutes go, she was unremarkable. Now, as for Josephine Dubois!" His smile transformed him into a young man for an instant. "She was special, ma Joséphine. She knew exactly how to give me pleasure. That's why I believed she was your mother as Father Gohegan said in his letters. Of course her racial and social origins made it quite unthinkable for me to bring her to France. But I was intrigued, so I sent Pierre to New Orleans several times over the years to see how you evolved. When he told me that you continued to look white and resembled me more and more as you grew older, I was determined to bring you here. As things have turned out, I was right to do so."

"You also have another son, an octoroon, by Josephine Dubois. He must have been raised as a white man by Mary Goodyear. Are you going to track them down? You might need him as a spare, if anything happens to me." He looked thoughtful for a moment and then said,

"To hell with them. It turns out that **you're** white, not him. That makes things easier for me than if it was the other way around. The woman was just a frigid whore. She believes her son's white. She's probably a proud grandmother of his children by now. Why should I care? Besides, nothing's going to happen to you."

"How did you know that I'd read your private eye's report?"

"I enjoyed tricking you into stealing it. Immensely," he said. He chuckled, remembering. "When Pierre told me about the demonstration at the American Embassy, I ordered him to deploy our forces there. I stayed behind, waiting for you to appear. I watched you from an adjoining office as you prowled along the corridor. The look of surprise on your face when you saw that my office door was open was priceless!" He laughed out loud, clearly enjoying his memories. Then he said, "For your future guidance, I check my safe every morning. You wouldn't know that, because you haven't been involved in our family's affairs up to now. That must change."

"You want the report back, I guess?"

"Of course not," he said. "Your real name's on the cover of the file. It's yours to have and to hold, 'til death us do part.' Besides, you've probably made copies of it. That's what I'd do in your...desperate situation as you try to save your Jewess from deportation. Or death. Give up, her days are numbered."

The Count had wound an ever-tightening web around Hannah. Now that I'd read the report and we both knew I was white and "Aryan," he intended to get rid of her fast. I had to find a way to get her to safety, while he was looking the other way.

"Let's stop playing games," I asked. "What do I have to do to get Hannah back from Pithiviers?"

He picked up his pistol again and pointed it straight at my heart. I looked into the eye of a madman. I feared that if he killed me, Hannah would disappear and be erased forever, one anonymous Jew without papers among the hundreds of thousands of Jews that the Nazis had already rounded up in Europe. I decided to play my trump card.

"When are you planning to tell Pierre and his blonde pal about Dewey Lafontaine's report and how things have changed? They got your German friends to throw me out of La Coupole this morning." That rocked him. He lowered his pistol.

"What? That's preposterous!" he shouted, his face scarlet with fury.

The time had come for me to turn up the heat on Pierre. I lied that Pierre had stirred up the Germans and that his blonde friend had tried to calm them down. The Count listened, looking like his head was fixing to explode. Something seemed to resolve itself in his mind and he stood up and paced up and down before me. He slapped his pistol against his thigh like a swagger stick, gazed at the portraits of d'Uribé-Lebrun ancestors crowding the walls, then turned to me.

"Pierre's insult is too great to bear. You are an Aryan and a Count descended from one of the oldest lineages in Europe!" His words told me that he already looked on me as legitimate and no longer as his bastard octoroon son.

He was nearly whispering, but he could have screamed if his office was as soundproof as it was cracked up to be.

"My informants have told me that this morning Premier Laval made a promise to Pierre that he can take over my political movement and confiscate our d'Uribé-Lebrun assets in return for information that will discredit me with Marshal Pétain. Laval will then intern you and me and liquidate both of us in due time. Pierre will be taking a train to Vichy to see Laval this evening." The Count paused and then asked,

"What was Jean-Pierre's role in the events at La Coupole?"

"The big blonde Alsatian with the duelling scar on his cheek?" He nodded Yes. "That's one *type* who really wants to be a German," I said.

"Pierre must have divulged something to him about us. He too must die."

I knew that he'd kill Pierre and Jean-Pierre rather than risk the loss of his power and the destruction of the d'Uribé-Lebrun lineage. Pierre had rampaged and burned his way through my life doing the Count's bidding. He'd lit the fire that destroyed Father Gohegan and the Saint Vincent Colored Waifs' Home in New Orleans and set me on the long road that led me to Paris in July 1914 on the eve of the Great War. He'd killed Redtop. Now his hatred was directed at Hannah as much as at me. I reckoned that the Count needed a number two man to run his day-to-day operations. My gut told me that if Jean-Pierre was that man, he'd pose less of a threat to Hannah than Pierre so I hammered more nails into Pierre's coffin.

"Pierre was egging on the Germans to insult me and throw me out of La Coupole. I can't speak German, but I think Jean-Pierre was trying to get the Boches to cool down." I tried to look on the verge of tears. I'd have tried to cry real ones if I hadn't run out of tears.

"What he did was the worst humiliation of my life," I said theatrically, pretending to rub tears away from my eyes. "I thought you and I had a deal and that you'd told Pierre to leave me be."

Flecks of spittle had formed on his lips, as if he'd been so deeply humiliated personally that he'd gone completely nuts.

"I have to be sure of the loyalty of Jean-Pierre if I spare him."

"My bet is that you can trust him." He nodded, then pressed a button under the desktop and kept on doing it as if making a call for help. I heard the sound of Pierre's voice coming through the loudspeaker.

"Monsieur le Comte, je suis là." The Count switched off his rage like an actor and unlocked the door by pressing another button. When it opened, he pointed his pistol at me, saying, with a warm smile on his face,

"Entrez. Only Pierre is to come in." Pierre, back in his stormtrooper uniform and jackboots strode into the room with his hand poised above his Beretta, ready to gun me down. Grinning Oriflamme stormtroopers, with Jean-Pierre standing at the front, watched us from the corridor, expecting to see my swift and bloody execution. Pierre was glowing with happiness like a gold panner who'd found the mother lode after a lifelong search.

"Close the door, Pierre, approchez-le." Pierre obeyed and he stared me down with his hate-filled eyes. I couldn't hear a sound from the stormtroopers crowding the corridor. The Count's voice was steady as he pointed the gun straight at my heart. Pierre smiled wolfishly and said,

"Ah, Monsieur le Comte, I see your patience is gone and the time has come for the bastard to die. I've waited too long for this moment."

"I've finally had enough," the Count said. Pierre was splitting his sides with his sinister high-pitched laugh as he drew his Beretta. It was probably the last sound that Redtop ever heard, I thought to myself. It was time to avenge her. He asked, wheezing with laughter and with tears rolling down his cheeks,

"May I...have the honor, your Excellency?" The Count waved him away with a smile and a pat on his heaving shoulders.

"That will not be necessary, my dear Pierre, I have him under control. We must ready him for torture before execution. Do you have your handcuffs?" Pierre was still wiping the last tears of laughter from his eyes as he dangled them in front of me.

"Do the necessary," the Count said. I held my wrists up in surrender. Pierre's smile widened as he prepared to click a cuff over my right wrist.

"Negro!" He spat into my face. The Count had tiptoed around his desk to aim his gun at the back of Pierre's head.

He shouted,

"He's not a Negro and you're a traitor!" Then his Berthier boomed like an exploding hand grenade.

I threw myself to the floor as I saw the Count squeeze the trigger. Pierre's smile lingered as the bullet drilled through his brain. His last sight was of falling handcuffs.

The Count stood over Pierre's corpse, unpinning from his collar buttons the fleur de lys insignia of his rank as leader of the Oriflamme stormtroopers.

During the Great War, I'd killed men in the mud of No Man's Land and in the sky to stay alive. I'd shot Buster to save Redtop. But the cold-bloodedness of the Count's execution of his longtime right-hand man jolted me. Pierre's life had been swatted away as if he was nothing more than a pesky fly. The Count hid his pistol behind his back and pushed a button on the loudspeaker on his desk.

"Entrez Jean-Pierre. And close the door behind you." As soon as Jean-Pierre spotted Pierre's lifeless cadaver spilling its blood out on the rug, his body started jerking all over as if he'd suddenly become a child with Saint Vitus's dance. When the Count trained his pistol on him, Jean-Pierre must've been thinking that he'd be bleeding out beside his buddy within seconds. The Count's eye drilled into Jean-Pierre's eyes as he rubbed the Berthier across the big man's temple. Jean-Pierre clenched his jaws, waiting for the bullet.

"Why did you and Pierre insult my son at La Coupole this morning? Tell me exactly what part you played in getting our German friends to expel a Count of the d'Uribé-Lebrun lineage from that establishment? I understand that you spoke to them in German." Jean-Pierre was sweating now, his eyes riveted on his dead comrade. I ratcheted up my best French and hypocrisy and said,

"Father, Pierre was the instigator."

As I thought he would, the Count smiled with pleasure when I called him "father." I went on, "Jean-Pierre was doing his best to stop the German officers from humiliating me. I'm sure that's why he was speaking to them in German." The Count and Jean-Pierre bent their heads toward me, listening.

"Besides, neither Pierre nor Jean-Pierre knew that your services are about to provide you with a certificate of my ancient Aryan racial origins before Marshal Pétain confirms me as your legitimate son and heir in a public ceremony in Vichy next week." The Count's smile widened the more I kept riffing on about how soon I would be "legitimized" and how there would be a public ceremony. I could see that Jean-Pierre knew that I'd thrown him a lifeline. He could dodge a bullet if he said the right thing now or just kept his trap shut and let me keep laying it on thick. The Count interrupted me to ask him point blank,

"Jean-Pierre, did the dead traitor Pierre insinuate to you at any time that my son was not a pure Aryan?" Instead of just saying No, which I expected, the cleverness of Jean-Pierre's next move made me wonder if I should've let Pierre take the fall alone.

"Yes, Monsieur le Comte," he said. "I never believed him, of course, but in the last few days, he kept on insinuating that your son had some African descent. When he told me he was going to repeat that lie to Premier Laval in Vichy tonight I was planning to tell you so that we could stop him." Except for the puckered duelling scar on his right cheek, Jean-Pierre looked like an altar boy. He had the guileless blue eyes of the angels Hannah had shown me in religious paintings in the Louvre. I knew he was neither one nor the other.

"It pleases me that you weren't enticed by his lies because my son is as pure an Aryan as you or I. Still, I'm somewhat disappointed that your German words didn't convince our friends to stop my son's public humiliation."

"I'm sure he'll do a better job next time, Father," I cooed. Jean-Pierre hastily said,

"I swear to do everything in my power to ensure that such an outrage never occurs again, your Excellencies." The Count took the barrel of the gun off Jean-Pierre's temple and said, "Garde à vous!" The man snapped to attention as ordered, clicking his heels and throwing us a Nazi salute. He smiled at me gratefully and I winked at him. I could see he was confused by that, but I wanted to keep him off balance.

"Bien," the Count said. "Jean-Pierre, never forget that my son saved your life."

The Count aimed his gun at the door and pressed the loudspeaker button again. He said "Entrez tous" and unlocked the door.

A platoon of Oriflamme filed into the office tentatively, their bodies in various postures of frightened obedience. They all looked horrified as they eyed Pierre's gory remains. They looked from the Count to me and I held my thumb in the up position, like the Roman emperor Nero in the silent film "Quo Vadis" that I'd seen at the Cinéma Max Linder in the 20s. The Count kept his pistol trained on his men as he pointed toward Pierre and said,

"There lies a traitor to our Oriflamme cause. He'd been plotting to assassinate me and my son, Count Charles-Emmanuel, to take control of our movement for base financial gain. His is the fate reserved for all traitors to France, to Marshal Pétain and to myself. Those who contemplate treason or cover up the treason that other comrades are even thinking of committing should know what awaits them. Who among you knows of a comrade who has contemplated treason against me or my son? This is your last chance to be pardoned." The men looked at my raised thumb. They'd probably seen "Quo Vadis" too and knew that a thumbs-down meant death by hungry lions. All pointed their index fingers at Pierre.

"Bien!" the Count said, satisfied. "Remove the cadaver and dispose of it in the usual manner. If even one of you leaks a word of what has transpired here, all of you will meet the fate reserved for traitors. I promise you, your new chief will carry out my death sentences without mercy. Exécution! -Step to it!" he shouted by way of concluding his pep talk.

The Oriflamme stormtroopers, relieved to be alive, aligned themselves in formation, clicked their heels and gave their Heil Hitler salute to the Count.

When the office was spotless and Pierre's corpse had been removed, they stood at attention before us, awaiting orders. They stared at my hand as if expecting me to do the Roman Emperor thing with my thumb again.

"Rompez! Dismissed!" the Count ordered. "Burn the trash," the Count said to them. "Not a trace is to be left of Pierre's treachery." The "erasers" and the rest of the Oriflamme marched out of the office, saluting smartly and saying in unison,

"A vos ordres, Monsieur le Ministre."

"Wait," the Count called out and they stopped on a dime and wheeled around in formation to face him.

The Count held up Jean-Pierre's hand as if he was the winner of a prize-fight. He barked out,

"Jean-Pierre, you stay with us." The Alsatian saluted with his free hand. It was rock steady now. Although he'd felt the Count's pistol brushing his temple, he now knew that the Count would let him live. I'd vouched for him.

"Ecoutez-tous," the Count announced. "I'm promoting Jean-Pierre, or Hans-Peter Kaltenborn to use his birth name, to replace the traitor, Pierre Lestage, as your chief." He pinned the insignia of leadership that he'd removed from Pierre's collar buttons into Jean-Pierre's. The big blonde glowed like a high voltage light bulb suddenly switched on. He seemed transformed by the knowledge that he was now number two in the Oriflamme du Roi movement. The Count kissed him on both cheeks and Jean-Pierre knelt in front of him and kissed the d'Uribé-Lebrun crest on his gold signet ring.

"Dismissed!" the Count barked out and the men filed out of the office behind their new leader, Jean-Pierre/Hans-Peter.

When he'd shut the door, the Count sat down and stowed his Berthier. "You were right, my son. Jean-Pierre knows nothing of our past." I wasn't as sure as the Count. I planned to keep a close eye on the Alsatian. He went on,

"Despite Pierre's recent treachery, which I blame on Premier Laval, he served me faithfully in the past and with discretion. His behavior at La Coupole was an aberration. Laval's enticements must have gone to his head. Tant pis, c'est fini pour lui." He blew on his fingertips, sending Pierre's soul into the afterlife like a speck of fluff on his lapels. He continued,

"Jean-Pierre isn't as bright as Pierre, but he's less ambitious. He'll serve us well. With Pierre dead, a large part of your history is erased like a misspelled word in a school dictation. There will be other erasures, I assure you." He paced around in front of his desk and said,

"There **is** a very slight possibility that we may be able to convince the Germans to put Miss Korngold in my custody. Would you like me to try? As a sign of my good faith and my desire to heal any breach between us?" The Count's words gave me hope that Hannah could still be saved.

"I'd really appreciate it," I said, sincere for the first time.

"We must leave for Pithiviers immediately." He made a telephone call and asked, "Quand?" He looked at his watch. Then he signalled for me to follow him and he marched out of his office like a conquering hero.

We took the trembling straight-armed salutes of the Oriflamme lining the corridor as we hurried past them towards the stairs. They stared ahead like robots but I looked back once and saw a few of them turning hard, angry

glances toward us. I'd seen that look before during the Great War, from legionnaires who hated their officers and assassinated them under cover of
battle. The Count seemed unaware that by killing Pierre he'd turned his men
against him. The two of us might end up being slaughtered by them.

We walked to the Count's official black Mercedes convertible limousine.
Its top was down. It had flags flying on the fenders on either side with what
the Count said was a preview of what would be Marshal Pétain's personal
flag, the French tricolor with a two-headed "Francisque" axe in the middle.
Jean-Pierre opened the doors for us and I looked into his choirboy eyes.
There was more going on in them now than blind obedience and gratitude.

We climbed into the back seat and Jean-Pierre closed our doors and
snarled at the chauffeur,

"Drive well or I'll have your head." The man cringed and a machine gun-
toting guard sat down next to him in the passenger seat.

CHAPTER 15

We drove past the American Embassy and the obelisk and turned right on the Cours la Reine and followed the Seine westward with the Palais de Chaillot on our right and the Seine and the Eiffel tower on our left. The air whistled past us as the chauffeur turned on the siren and accelerated, which blew some cool air over us as I wilted in the mid-afternoon heat. The Count looked cool and crisp, beaming from ear to ear, looking around as if he had all of Paris at his feet.

"I'll phone le Maréchal tonight and arrange the public ceremony you've suggested. It will serve as useful propaganda for the new regime. You do realize that you'll have to renounce your American nationality to become French? I suggest that you profit from the occasion to denounce America publicly for giving support to English imperialists instead of to the forces of progress embodied by mon cher Adolphe Hitler."

His words stunned me. Twenty years ago, I'd have given anything to be French and I'd wanted nothing to do with America. But now, renouncing America to become French meant I'd be knuckling under to a German occupier I hated. I might even be called upon to fight against Americans when the country declared war on Germany. Above all, once America joined the fight against Germany, I wouldn't be an enemy alien, but Hannah would. We'd no longer be on the same side. There was no way I could tolerate that. But I had to keep the Count believing I'd given him an ironclad guarantee.

"Wait to phone Marshal Pétain until Hannah's set free."

He sat back satisfied like a man holding a Royal Flush in a game of high stakes poker. The Count tapped the chauffeur's shoulder and said,

"Step on it, Marius. I want to reach Pithiviers before four p.m." As we raced along the road bordering the quai, the nervous guard in the passenger seat scanned the gawkers, machine gun at the ready.

Forty minutes after leaving Paris, it was hard to believe that a modern world capital was so near the rural countryside we passed through. It seemed frozen in eighteenth century pre-Revolution France. The roads showed few traces of the chaos and death of the exodus of a month before. We passed peasants wearing rags and wooden sabots who doffed their cloth caps or bonnets respectfully as we sped past, a blur amidst the parched wheat fields.

We passed identity control points manned by French gendarmes and a handful of German overseers as we approached Pithiviers.

At the first check point, I had started reaching for my papers, but the Count stopped me.

"That won't be required, my son," he said. "The border guards have been observing this car with their binoculars from the moment we came in sight of them. They have recognized that this is a car which must not be stopped or delayed." He pointed to the small flags on either side of the car with the "Francisque" axes on them.

When we were within fifty yards of the checkpoint, the gendarmes snapped to attention and saluted as we roared past, showering them in dust. The Count leaned forward displaying his well-known profile to the saluting gendarmes. I was sitting on his right, staring at the gold-colored eyepatch covering his right eye when the thought occured to me that I would make a perfect decoy for him because I resembled the Count so much. At forty-five, my hair was streaked with grey which made me look even more like him. All I needed to **be** him was an eyepatch. If I were crazy enough to wear one, our resemblance would make me a sitting duck for an assassin's bullet on the day America entered the war and the French rose up against the Pétainistes and their German masters. The limousine streaked past more saluting guards and peasants watching us warily. I could sense the anger behind their smiles and dutiful shouts of "Vive l'Etat Français! Vive le Maréchal Pétain!"

A church spire separated itself from the dusty wheat fields and the Count shouted over the noise of the motor and the wind whistling past us,

"That's Pithiviers, where you see that vulgar spire." He checked his watch. "We may be too late. The Germans tend to keep to their schedules."

We careered past the main square until we reached the train station. The Germans had installed what looked like ticket booths outside the station's entrance. The Count had said that they were carrying out a train transportation experiment at Pithiviers. I saw long lines of women and children waiting in front of the booths, shading themselves from the sun which was still scorching at four p.m. After the driver parked, the Count and I got out and walked past lines of silent women calming their moaning children. The women were handed blank pieces of paper but no money was exchanged. Once the women received their paper, they joined waiting lines inside the station. French policemen shoved women and children into train wagons like cattle. German soldiers stood by, their rifles at the ready.

There must have been a thousand people sweltering on the station platforms. I heard the sound of a train whistle and saw an empty train pulling into the station from a siding. Then the steam engine of a packed train puffed into life and bells started ringing as it pulled out of the station. I reckoned that, as part of the German transportation experiment, the trains had all been routed back to Paris. I watched as policemen shoved passengers into the cars. Conductors punched the "tickets" before they boarded.

"Where are they going? Who are these people?" I asked the Count, as I scanned the crowds, hoping to catch sight of Hannah. From time to time, I heard children's screams, followed by the murmurs of mothers silencing them in languages I didn't understand. I thought I saw Hannah and started running toward a train to stop her disappearing into it.

"Charles-Emmanuel, only I can save her!" the Count shouted. He ran out of the station to one of the booths. I saw him talking to a fat man wearing a gold-braided *képi* who I figured was in charge of operations. He saluted the Count, blew a whistle and two station masters ran up to him. At an impatient gesture from him, they handed over what looked like passenger lists. They poked at names on the list as their chief leafed through the pages.

He stopped, stabbed at a name and showed it to the Count who nodded. Immediately, the two station masters ran toward the platform where a packed train was ready to leave, as their chief waddled after them. I raced over to the Count and shouted,

"Have they found her?" He gestured to me to be patient. At a signal from the chief, the Count dashed along the platform knocking down waiting women and their children like bowling pins. He followed the head man into a wagon, with me hard on his heels. I saw the chief showing the list to a conductor, who pointed toward the last cars of the train. As whistles blew for departure and engines hissed steam, we scrambled down the steps onto the platform, dashing toward the rear of the train behind the station masters.

At the next to last carriage, one of them grabbed and questioned a conductor who held a list of passengers in one hand while he closed the carriage's door with the other. He checked the list, then blew his whistle repeatedly. Everything came to a standstill. He jumped into the carriage and we heard him inside it, shouting,

"Une nommée, Korngold, Hannah est-elle là?" When I heard her call out,

"C'est moi, Hannah Korngold." I nearly knocked over the conductor scrambling toward her and then Hannah spotted me and climbed over women and children sitting in the aisle to get to me. They looked at her blankly as she threw her arms around me, her tears on my cheeks doing my crying for me.

"Urby. I knew you'd come. I'm so scared," she said. Then she drew away from me and asked, suddenly worried, "Can we leave or are they taking you too?" I gripped Hannah's hand and we climbed down the steps and stood on the platform hugging each other. I saw the Count off in the distance, waving to us to join him. Hannah followed my eyes, spotted him and asked,

"Did your old man have anything to do with getting me off the train?"

"His driver got us here in record time."

"What's he want in return?"

"The usual. I promised him that I'd meet with him and Marshal Pétain next week for me to be crowned his son and heir. Then I pose for an oil painting for him to hang on his office walls beside my ancestors." Hannah shook her head sadly and said,

"Maybe I should've stayed on the train."

"Where was it going?"

"They never told us. They just said, 'don't worry, it's only an exercise.' Some German officers and Paris cops timed it all with stopwatches. I didn't believe this 'only an exercise' stuff they kept telling us. I talked to the women and kids and they were all foreign Jews, Urby. They were all immigrants from Poland, Germany and Austria. Their relatives who stayed behind have been shipped off to camps or disappeared."

"You think they're planning to set up camps for Jews in France and do the same thing here? The French would never stand for it."

"I'm not so sure. They'd heard rumors that a holding camp was going to be set up right here, in Pithiviers. Jews will be held in them until they're shipped East. The two things that scared the women the most was that their children would be taken away from them and that all Jews would be sent to camps in countries like Poland where they'd be worked to death or killed on the spot. And Urby, all of them believe that the French are going to knuckle under to the Germans and even help them get rid of all the Jews in France." We'd walked the length of the platform and reached the Count, who bowed deeply to Hannah, saying,

"Ah, the famous Miss Korngold, I believe. We meet formally at last. I appear to have delayed your train journey." Hannah flushed with anger.

"You'll probably put me on another train, when you've got what you want from Urby."

"Urby?" he asked, looking blank. She jerked a thumb toward me.

"Ah, you mean Count Charles-Emmanuel d'Uribé-Lebrun." I had trouble keeping Hannah from clawing his eyes out. The Count just laughed and toyed with his eyepatch. Hannah grabbed me and kissed me hard on the mouth.

"He's mine!" she protested. "He's Urby and he'll always be Urby. You stay away from him, you fascist!" His killer's eye drilled into her as his hand wandered to the Berthier holstered at his waist. Fearing the crazed look in his eye, I stood in front of her, staring him down.

"That's enough. Get us out of here!" I hollered at him. The Count quickly snapped out of his killer's rage but I knew that I'd need a miracle to keep Hannah safe from him until we escaped from France.

He changed tack and started making elaborate apologies to Hannah. Then he scolded her for having "mislaid" her passport. He took out his wallet and handed her a new *carte de séjour.* We both looked it over. It was made out in her name and valid for one month from today's date, July 16, 1940. I realized that the Count had played me for a sucker. He'd staged Hannah's departure in a Franco-German "transportation exercise" to stop me from stalling over the ceremony with Marshal Pétain in case I had qualms about renouncing my American citizenship.

His "mise en scène" had backfired because I was now determined to make a fast run for it with Hannah. The only thing keeping me off the starting blocks was the fear that the Count would retaliate by killing Stanley Bontemps. I heard him say,

"Your papers are now in order, Miss Korngold, subject to your finding your passport or having a new one issued to you. Your American citizenship doesn't authorize you to reside in France. Only the police and immigration services acting under my instructions can do that." He bowed to Hannah again, saying,

"Regretfully, I cannot accompany you back to Paris, because I must proceed to Orléans to deal with some police matters. I have arranged for my personal car to take you back to Paris in comfort, so that you can recover from the emotions of the day and profit from the beauties of our French countryside." His eye glittered with malice because the countryside looked like the Oklahoma dust bowl described in the passages that Hannah had read to me from John Steinbeck's novel "The Grapes of Wrath."

"You will have two peaceful hours to yourselves chauffeured by one of my best drivers, François Bertin, in my personal limousine. Bertin and the bodyguard don't understand a word of English, so you can whisper sweet nothings to each other in peace. You must profit from such moments, Miss Korngold. Who knows what awaits you in the coming days?"

I held onto Hannah tightly as we walked toward the Count's car. A new driver stepped forward and led us past two gendarmes who saluted us smartly. He opened the doors of a luxurious Delage limousine painted in the red and black colors of the Count's Oriflamme party with its gold lightning bolt symbol on the hood. Bertin settled us inside on the back seat. He popped open a bottle of champagne, poured each of us a glass and left the bottle in an ice bucket at our feet. He donned his chauffeur's cap and then got behind the wheel. The bodyguard gave us a quick glance and sat down beside him in the passenger seat. I tried to remember where I'd seen Bertin and the bodyguard before. Bertin revved up the motor and we roared off, the Oriflamme banners waving from their flagstaffs on the fenders.

Hannah and I toasted her narrow escape after checking that our champagne didn't smell of Mickey Finn. I didn't want to wake up to find that Hannah had been abducted again. We were silent all the way back to Paris; neither of us believed that the chauffeur and bodyguard didn't understand English.

It was late afternoon when François Bertin dropped us off at Place Pigalle. We half walked, half dragged each other through the hot, crowded streets, up the stairs to our apartment and then fell into bed, fully dressed. We tore at each other, making love like it might be the last time. Afterwards, lying naked in bed, we fanned our sweat-drenched bodies with pieces of ripped up sheet music. Hannah looked at me as if she couldn't believe she was alive and back home.

"I wonder how many times over the next months I'm going to thank you for saving my life. If we manage to stay alive that long. When your father's man Pierre and his big blonde friend took me, I thought it was all over. They told me I had to bring my residence permit and my passport with me to the Préfecture. I told them I'd lost my passport when we fled Paris in June and they ransacked the place looking for it. They went nuts when they couldn't find it and started throwing things around and smashing our furniture and records and tearing up our sheet music. I thought they were going to set fire to the place."

"Where's your passport?"

"Safely tucked away in the cellar with an extra copy of Dewey Lafontaine's report. There was no way I was going to give Pierre and his friend my passport. I knew I'd never see it again."

"We don't have to worry about Pierre anymore. The Count gunned him down in his office right in front of me." Astonished, she asked,

"How come? You've always told me he's the Count's top hit man."

"When I met up with Jean Fletcher at La Coupole, Pierre and his blonde buddy Jean-Pierre had the Nazis throw me out as a non-Aryan because the Count hadn't told Pierre that I'm white. Turns out Pierre was going to Vichy tonight to sell the Count out to Premier Laval. He was going to spill all of the Count's dirty secrets, including having a colored son he was trying to get legitimized by Pétain."

"I know it's an awful thing to say, but why didn't the Count finish both of them off? Pierre must have given his buddy the lowdown about you if they got you kicked out of La Coupole."

"I gambled that by making Pierre take the fall, the Count would lock him up somewhere and throw away the key, not blow his brains out. Tell you the truth, I thought Jean-Pierre was just a chump we could run rings around. Maybe even bribe him into helping us escape. I don't know if I pegged him right. What I know is that power's making the Count crazier and more violent." Hannah shuddered.

"The man's really off his rocker. I felt that at the train station," Hannah said.

" We've got to get out of France before the Count and I meet up with Pétain next week. Once I'm officially French and recognized as his son, I lose my American citizenship. I forgot that detail. Afterwards, he'll order Jean-Pierre to make a fatal accident happen to you and I won't be able to get help from our Embassy to stop them. We've got to run for it. Now."

"Go see Stanley," Hannah said. I got dressed and phoned him to tell him I was on my way.

⅄

Before I finished talking to Stanley about the happenings at La Coupole, Pierre's assassination, how the Count nearly shipped Hannah to oblivion at the Pithiviers train station and the loss of my American citizenship next week, he said,

"You right about makin' a run for it. I reckon you got one or two days before he close you down." He said he needed time to think up a plan. He refused again to go with us. As I was leaving his apartment, Stanley snapped his fingers and said he had a plan.

During jazz concerts in Biarritz in the thirties, he'd become friends with a French Basque classical composer, Martin Etcheverry. He was originally from Mauléon in the Soule region of the Basque country, but now lived next door in Pau in the Free Zone. Pau was some fifty miles from the Pyrenees mountains and the Spanish border. Etcheverry was worried that Stanley would fall into the hands of the Germans and the collaborationist French police if he stayed in Paris. He kept phoning him to beg him to stay with him in his Béarn hideaway in Pau, where he was convalescing from his latest electro-shock session. He wanted Stanley's jazz feeling to be reflected in a concerto he was composing. It would be his last work, he'd told Stanley. Stanley telephoned Etcheverry and passed the spare earpiece to me to listen in. Stanley asked Etcheverry if he could help Hannah and me to escape from France and leave for America from Lisbon. He agreed right away, saying that he had great admiration for my music, too. Etcheverry told Stanley that the surest escape route was to cross the Pyrenees to Canfranc in the Spanish province of Huesca in Aragon. He could call on a network of people-smuggling *passeurs* to get us to Canfranc and then to Vigo in the province of Galicia on the Atlantic coast. A fishing boat would take us from Vigo to Lisbon. Stanley handed me the telephone speaker and I told Etcheverry that Hannah and I still had our travel visas for Portugal from our failed escape attempt in June. He said that made arrangements easier. He assured me that his Portuguese agent could book a sea voyage for us from Lisbon to New York on twenty-four hours' notice. I thanked him and handed the telephone back to Stanley, who promised to visit him as soon as he could to work with him on his concerto.

"Please come quickly, Stanley," Etcheverry pleaded, a desperate note in his voice.

When I left Stanley's apartment, he was already back on the telephone, calling friends along our escape route, in case we needed to stay with them on our way to Pau.

⚔

I met up with Jean Fletcher at Les Deux Magots at three p.m. We decided to give La Coupole a miss because we might run into the same German officers who'd thrown me out the day before. We sat on the *terrasse,* which was packed with German soldiers drinking their quarter liter glasses of *demi-pression* Alsatian beer in the sun and looking like they held the keys to the city. They ogled the young Parisiennes passing by, who ignored the Germans and chattered to each other or their male companions using a lot of rapid *argot* slang words the Boches wouldn't understand. I told Jean the whole story of Pierre's murder and Jean-Pierre's sudden promotion. Jean stayed silent, thinking about what I'd said. We watched a handful of believers entering the grimy Saint-Germain-des-Prés church across the street. They were probably praying for America to enter the war soon and help the French and the English defeat the Boches. Then Jean turned to me and said,

"Have you gone nuts, Urby? Jean-Pierre's the one who got the Boches to give you the heave-ho from La Coupole. If the Count had to plug one of them, it would've been better for you and Hannah if he'd shot Jean-Pierre. It's better to deal with the enemy you know than the one you don't."

"It's beginning to look that way."

I told Jean that, to my surprise, the Oriflamme stormtroopers seemed to like and respect Pierre and hated the way Jean-Pierre treated them. They were beginning to resent his bragging about having been born a German and his looking down on the French the way the Germans did.

"They probably think Jean-Pierre/Hans-Peter's squealing on them to the Gestapo," Jean said. "If there's a revolt against the Count, Jean-Pierre will be first one to stick a knife into his back. Don't be too hard on yourself about Pierre. You can still breathe easier now with him gone."

I told Jean how I'd saved Hannah from the trains at Pithiviers by agreeing to meet Marshal Pétain for the ceremony next week, which would mean losing my American citizenship when I became French.

"That might have worked for you a few years ago, but now's not the time," Jean said. "The English and the Americans are the only hope left for freeing Europe from the Nazis." When I told her Stanley's plan for our escape, she thought it might work if we could get a head start toward Pau.

"Your biggest problem's going to be those little French bureaucrats thumbing through people's papers at checkpoints and the Demarcation Line."

" Stanley's still refusing to leave Paris."

"I'll do everything I can for him," Jean said. "If I haven't heard from you in a month, I'll get the story out to the press that Redtop's death wasn't a suicide but a murder. I've worked things out so that an English reporter friend gets credit for the scoop. I don't want the Count to think that Stanley spilled the beans. Or that I did."

"In a month, we'll either be dead or in America."

I looked at the time. Hannah and I had to get going. Jean looked into my eyes and we held hands under the table.

"The French and German big shots don't like what I've been writing about them," she said. "The French cops have put a tail on me. My driver had to make some tricky moves to get me here without being followed. I don't think we should see each other again." I pretended to wipe tears from my eyes.

"Good luck," she said, laughing. "Who knows? As soon as we go to war with Germany, I'll head to New York. We'll meet up there."

I gave her hand a squeeze and watched her as she left the Deux Magots. She waved goodbye and blew me a kiss when the driver opened the door of her Traction Avant.

⚓

The Count's personal chauffeur, François Bertin, was sitting at a table on the Café Paname's crowded terrace turning beet red in the burning sun. He was wiping his shaved head with a drenched white handkerchief. The bodyguard who'd accompanied us back from Pithiviers sat with him, seemingly unbothered by the heat. They were dressed alike in white linen suits and open-necked white cotton shirts. Their black-banded straw boaters were on the table.

Bertin rested his handkerchief on the table to cool himself down with with a Lillet publicity fan and an occasional sip of Pernod. The reptilian bodyguard with him looked like he had ice water in his veins and didn't need any further cooling. Mounds of plastic saucers with the prices of their drinks on them were piling up in front of them. They flicked their cigarette ashes into a yellow Rabarbero liqueur ashtray as I approached their table and sat down uninvited. Close up, I recognized Bertin and his companion as being among the Oriflamme stormtroopers I'd seen peering into the Count's office with stricken faces as they saw Pierre's bloody corpse sprawled on the floor.

I reckoned they were taking a break from spying on our apartment and nightclub. I'd sat down with them to feel them out on what they thought of the Count's assassination of their former leader Pierre. François Bertin nudged his icy companion who threw me a swift blank glance and then looked indifferently at a pretty blue-eyed brunette sashaying along the sidewalk with dark sweat stains covering the armpits of the tight red dress clinging to her curvy body. She flirted with the German soldiers who ogled and applauded her from their seats at the café tables. The Parisians were still giving the Germans the cold shoulder, but I figured they'd be fraternizing with them when the wintry weather set in and food, wine and other necessities ran short.

There were a lot more pedestrians and cyclists and much less motor vehicle traffic on the streets, because the Germans had commandeered cars and buses for their war effort. The lion's share of the gasoline and oil was reserved for the coming German invasion of England they kept talking about. Taxis were rare. Everyone, including the Germans, traveled by metro. To the disgust of the Parisians, the German soldiers and civilians didn't have to pay for their metro tickets. Food was already becoming scarce, because it was also reserved in priority for the Germans.

The smell of cheap eau de cologne filled the air, damping down the funky smell of sweaty, unwashed bodies. Friends had told us that the Germans had systematically disinfected the *bains publiques* before reserving them for their own exclusive use. They kept the French out of these public baths as if they carried the germs of defeat. There were rumors going around that the Germans planned to ration the water and soap the Parisians used for keeping clean and washing their clothes. The behavior of the conquerors seemed to confirm the rumors. The German soldiers strutted around in spotless uniforms with scrubbed faces, clean hair and odorless bodies. The very cleanliness of their occupiers disheartened the Parisians. I reckoned that they wouldn't even be able to count on calming themselves down with wine, beer and cheap calvados much longer because the Germans were draining away the booze.

Like their non-smoking Führer, the occupiers disapproved, officially, of cigarette smoking. However, a lot of them smoked like chimneys and they reserved most of the available cigarettes for themselves. When they'd made smoking *verboten* in the metro, another hammer blow fell on Parisian morale. People around us at the café were smoking the yellow corn paper Gauloise cigarettes the Germans disdained, or ones that they'd rolled from white cigarette paper and whatever cigarette or pipe tobacco they could scrounge up. Tough-looking, unwashed street children rootled in the gutters for cigarette butts to sell, as if they were panning for gold.

The Germans had put Paris on Berlin time instead of London time. We'd gained an hour in the summer and could now be spied on in daylight until past ten p.m. at night. Having more daylight and nothing to do with it except feel hungry and dirty and spied on for an extra hour didn't exactly boost morale.

When the frosty Oriflamme bodyguard finished his Pernod, I asked him, "May I offer you and Mr. Bertin another drink?" I smiled at him and his companion. "Pernod with a *carafe* of cold water, am I right?" Bertin relaxed and grimaced with his scaly lips and badly fitting dentures. That seemed to be as close as he could get to a smile. I figured he was pleased that "Comte Charles-Emmanuel d'Uribé-Lebrun, alias Urby Brown" had remembered his name.

Bertin and his companion weren't men who refused a free drink. We clinked glasses and slugged our Pernod down after a hearty "Tchin!" We became pals when I ordered them two more rounds up front. Bertin nodded his sweaty bald head towards his companion, saying,

"Lui c'est Emile, un des gardes du corps de notre roi bien-aimé," Bertin's friend was named Emile and Bertin had referred to him as one of their "beloved king's bodyguards." His heavy sarcasm surprised me and I planned to get them drunker to see if I was right about the Count's stormtroopers turning against him after he killed Pierre. I lifted my glass in a toast and said,

"To the late Pierre. Drink up, chers amis. Who knows, you may be next?" They slammed their glasses down so hard I thought they'd shatter.

"C'est un boucher que votre père!" Bertin burst out angrily, calling my father a butcher. "Pierre was our friend and protector. And now he's been replaced by Jean-Pierre, who is more of a Boche than a Frenchman." He hawked and spat onto the sidewalk.

"The swine!" he shouted. The patrons snuck furtive glances at him.

"Le Comte a vendu la France aux Allemands pour s'acoquiner avec ce Maréchal sénile et débile! " Emile hissed. He was telling me that the Count had sold France out to cosy up to the senile and stupid Marshal Pétain, to advance his own interests.

Bertin went on to say that he and Emile had joined the Oriflamme when they were young men, because they loved France and thought she was being destroyed by the socialo-communists and the Jews and foreigners of every stripe. They'd fought in the Great War under Marshal Pétain and his aide-de-camp and mastermind, the Count. They'd been wounded at Verdun on the *Voie Sacrée* during Pétain's victory over the Boches.

Bertin told me that he now wanted to join General de Gaulle in London, after listening to his radio appeal of June 18 calling for Frenchmen to fight on against their occupiers. When Bertin and Emile asked if I'd heard of de Gaulle, I said I knew him and I'd write letters of introduction if they wanted to join him.

I told them to come by my nightclub to speak with me and a friend about our all leaving France together. The drinks and smokes would be on the house, I promised them, as much champagne and tobacco as they could handle.

"The friend in question is perhaps Monsieur Stanley Bontemps?" Bertin asked, probing. I nodded Yes. "Nous le surveillons aussi," he confirmed.

Chapter 16

François Bertin and Emile were sitting in my office in the nightclub when the first set ended. They looked worried as they stared at me. I'd just told them Stanley's plan for getting Hannah and me to Pau in the Béarn region. They weren't overjoyed about joining us, because of the increase in control posts the Count was setting up along the Demarcation Line to limit passage into the Free Zone. Hannah and I were ready to run big risks to escape, but they were getting cold feet.

As for the possessions Hannah and I were leaving behind-the apartment building and nightclub that I'd inherited from Redtop-we were both ready to let them go without any regrets. Anyway, they'd be safe under Stanley's watchful eye for as long as he could hold out.

Stanley knocked on the door and walked into the office. He had a bottle of our finest Veuve Cliquot Ponsardin Brut 1929 champagne in each hand and he plunked them down on my desk in front of François and Emile. Their eyes lit up like fireworks on the night of Bastille Day. I got some champagne glasses from the liquor cabinet and put them on the desk. Stanley handed both bottles to François who popped their corks and handed them back to him. He poured champagne into our glasses and we toasted each other and drank the best Brut left in the wine cellar. Stanley offered François and Emile his favorite Romeo y Julieta Cuban cigars and cut their ends off with his solid gold cigar cutter. He lit their cigars and the men sat back quaffing champagne, taking contented drags and filling the office with cigar smoke. Bertin and Emile fell about laughing when Stanley grabbed Emile's straw boater, put it on and then mugged at them like Louis Armstrong.

They were looking more and more relaxed. Stanley asked me to step out of the office for a second and, as I left, I saw the men lean in closer to him. When I returned ten minutes later, they were standing up and laughing and toasting whatever deal Stanley had brokered. When he gave me a big wink, the thought came to me that they'd hatched a new escape plan. The two men left all smiles, wreathed in cigar smoke. Bertin patted me on the back, saying, "Zee tomorrow" in broken English. Even icy Emile was warming up to us. The two champagne bottles were empty.

Hannah joined Stanley and me in the office. I took a bottle of my best Domfront calvados out of the liquor cabinet and filled three brandy snifters. Stanley picked his up, took a sip and eased back into an armchair, satisfied.

"I got the feeling you came up with a new plan with those gents," I said. Stanley held his glass of calvados up to the desk lamp, studying its color.

"Sure is nice calva. Sure is." Hannah and I looked at each other and waited, knowing there was no way to rush Stanley when he had a surprise up his sleeve. I wondered whether what he'd signed up to with François and Emile would change the escape plan that he'd already arranged with Martin Etcheverry. Stanley reached into his jacket pocket and pulled out a gold-colored object and a round metal box that looked like a tin of shoe polish. He put them on the desk and Hannah picked up the gold-colored thing first. She unfolded the strings on either side of it, looking mystified. Then she said with a smile,

"It's an eyepatch. Exactly like the Count's." She read the label on the round tin and burst out laughing.

"This is makeup, for dyeing hair grey." She seemed to have figured out Stanley's new scheme and kept laughing, slapping palms with him. He made his cricket laugh, which really got Hannah hooting with laughter.

"I'm glad you're both having a ball, but I don't get it," I said.

"Urby, you gone play the role of your daddy, the Count. Those Oriflamme boys gone take him to Fontainebleau tomorrow. François told me the Count be headin' there on the q t to have lunch with some aristocrat woman got a daughter he want you to marry. Y'all gone hijack the car in the forest, hogtie the Count and hide him in one of the caves be all over the Fontainebleau forest. Then, Urby, you puts on the eyepatch and the Count's fancy duds, stick grey goo in your hair and then you be the Count. Y'all cross that De-mark line in the Count's wheels with you playin' the Count. François say they never stops his car to check his papers. When you past the line, you takes off the makeup and the eye patch and whatnot and you becomes you again. Then François and Emile gone take you to a friend of mine live by himself in his castle in that place where all them volcanoes be..."

"Auvergne?" Hannah asked.

"That be the place. My friend gone have a car waitin' for you and Hannah to swap and you hightail it for that place where Etche live. My volcano friend gone tell y'all how to hook up with him. You won't have no trouble." Hannah said,

"That wasn't the plan Urby told me about. I thought we were all going to make our way to the Béarn in the car Finn stole for us."

"Hannah," I said. "This new plan's dangerous, but it might work because the gendarmes and police never stop the Count's car when they see it in the distance through their binoculars. I don't think we can make it in the Renault without being stopped. Then they'll haul us back to Paris and the Count will sic Jean-Pierre on you." I turned to Stanley. "Go on," I said.

"Etche's friends gone guide y'all to Lisbon where you gone board you a ship to New York City. François and Emile got they own plans to escape when you changes cars in the volcano place. They gone get rid of the Count's car and head off to join up with that General de Gaulle in London. Lord knows how they gone get there, but when you wants to be free, they always be a way. What you say, Hannah?" We waited for Hannah's verdict. I didn't know if she'd be willing to go back to Spain again. She said,

"It's really risky." Then she smiled. " But the part I like is hog-tying the Count and leaving him in a cave. I like that a lot. With any luck, we'll be far away by the time he gets loose."

I thought of Jean-Pierre, the Count's new right hand man. He might reckon that, as an Alsatian who was a German again, he could grab the golden ring without the Count around. Jean-Pierre seemed to me to have enough smarts to know that the Oriflamme stormtroopers disliked him. But I figured he'd gamble that they hated the Count more than him because he'd killed their old leader, Pierre. The Alsatian would probably think that, without the Count around and with Pierre dead, he could bully the Oriflamme into submission with the help of the Gestapo.

"The Count's friends won't knock themselves out looking for him," I finally said. "If his old boss Marshal Pétain's as gaga as they say, he'll probably forget all about the Count after he hasn't heard from him or seen him for a week. I reckon Premier Laval won't break any speed records trying to find him."

"So, it's in nobody's interest to have your father around?" Hannah asked.

"Looks that way to me."

"You're a genius!" she said to Stanley. "This could work, because it suits everybody for the Count to go up in smoke. My only worry..."

"I can take care of myself," Stanley quickly said. "Y'all best take care of your own business. Your car's all ready for your trip to Fontainebleau bright and early tomorrow mornin'. That man Bertin gone tell me tonight when and where y'all gone kidnap the Count. After that, just keep sayin' 'New York, here we come', 'cause y'all gone make it."

Stanley was being tailed, he said, so it was better for him to stay away from the nightclub until we escaped. Finn would drive him to Chablis in Burgundy later tonight. He'd stay in a hotel there for a week, to set up an alibi in case he was asked about our and the Count's disappearances.

We said our goodbyes to pack for the long voyage. We knew that we might never see Stanley again. I started to speak but he stopped me and said,

"They ain't no words, Urby and Hannah, so let's not make out they is." He walked out of the office without looking back.

At 5:30 the next morning, July 20, we walked unhurriedly to the Renault coupé Finn had stolen for us. It was packed and we were ready to drive to

Fontainebleau. I drove through deserted streets, heading east to the Porte Dorée. From there we'd take minor roads to a place called the "Grotte aux Cristaux" in the Fontainebleau forest. It was there that François Bertin planned to run into engine trouble and stop to repair it, aided by Emile. On his signal, I'd suddenly appear from hiding and the three of us would capture the Count, bind and gag him and leave him in the Crystal Cave.

Hannah sat in the passenger seat, hugging a large traveling bag that she was using to carry part of our cash and valuables and our papers. She was silent, scanning every car or horse-drawn wagon that we passed, looking backward from time to time to see if we were being tailed.

Some farmers were in the fields, guarding their crops or cranking up their tractors. There was enough daylight to see clearly and Hannah said,

"Daylight's bad for us. The police and gendarmes will be out soon checking cars."

"We'll be alright. This route's slower but we should miss the cops."

Forty minutes later, we turned onto a road called the "Route Ronde" that curled through the forest like a giant fish hook. Apart from the trees, the only things we saw were huge boulders. The trail we turned onto, which was for hikers, put the car to the test as we bumped along it. We saw a hand-painted sign with an arrow pointing to the Grotte aux Cristaux. Hannah said, "Stop!" She got out of the car, wrestled the sign out of the ground and heaved it into the undergrowth.

"Why don't you hide the car behind those trees?" she said. I drove toward them, parking the car in a thicket where it couldn't be seen from the Route Ronde. I left it unlocked with the key in the ignition to make it easier for some hiker or tramp to steal it after we'd ambushed the Count.

Carrying our suitcases, I followed Hannah, who read the crude map François had drawn for us last night. We picked our way through more clumps of trees and undergrowth down a rocky pathway. The mouth of the cave was covered with so much vegetation that we almost missed it. I put our suitcases down and Hannah took a flashlight out of her traveling bag and turned it on as we entered the cave. In the flashlight's beam we could see that its floor was covered in beach sand. It was big and empty except for a few large bones strewn beneath the cave's walls. They'd been picked clean. We went deeper into it, following a bend in the sandy path which led us into a smaller cave. We kept walking for another twenty yards until we reached the end. Hannah whistled. There was no echo.

"Looks like a good place to stash the Count, Urby. With that bend in the cave he can shout all he wants and no one will hear him."

"Soundproof, just like his office."

"Let's get back to the car and wait there until 2:30," she said. We checked our watches. "If François gets it right, his car will stop near ours."

"Great place for an ambush," I said. The legionnaire in me from the Great War took over. We fought in trenches then, but the aim was the same: maximum concealment to achieve maximum surprise before an attack. I dragged our suitcases deeper into the bushes at the mouth of the Crystal Cave.

The only sound was of birds and Luftwaffe planes heading towards their new base at Villeneuve-Orly airport south of Paris. Occasionally, there was a crashing through the undergrowth and I'd pick up a big stick, ready to clobber whatever had tracked us down. The intruders turned out to be wild boar or deer running through the woods. I went to the car and opened the trunk. There was a blanket covering the jerricans of gasoline and thermoses filled with red wine and hampers of ham and gruyère cheese sandwiches which Hannah had made for the long drive ahead with François and Emile. I spread out the blanket and we sat on it, picnicking in the silent forest. Danger seemed so far away that, after finishing our sandwiches and half a thermos of red wine, Hannah and I fell asleep in each other's arms, hypnotized by the sunlight shining through the creaking pines.

I woke up suddenly and looked at my watch. It was 1:30. The pine tree branches were so thick overhead that we were already in shade. I woke Hannah up and said,

"It's 1:30. Only an hour to go, unless they're early." Hannah shook herself awake, while I put the blanket and the hamper next to our luggage and our instrument cases. We waited, listening to birdsong and to the sound of beasts crashing through the forest.

⚜

Hannah was the first to hear the car's engine. I looked at my watch: it was 2:35. Following the plan that Stanley had worked out with Bertin and Emile, the car stopped a hundred yards away from the mouth of the Crystal Cave. I stripped down to my underpants and Hannah worked on my hair, then kissed me on the cheek for good luck. As I crawled forward, I could see Emile opening the door for the Count, who walked over to some bushes, pissed into them and then stretched his legs. He talked to Emile and pointed at some birds circling in the sky.

I crept closer and could see his red and black Delage convertible limousine with "Maréchal Pétain flags" flying from the fenders. Emile lit a cigarette for the Count and the men got back into the car. The motor groaned when François started it and then went dead. He started it again with the same result. François got out of the car and opened the hood to check the motor. He fiddled around with it, took the dipstick out of its casing and pretended to check the oil. He unscrewed the radiator cap and toyed around with it too. Emile and the Count joined him to look at the motor as Bertin tapped on it with a monkey wrench. Then he closed the hood and banged on it twice which was the signal for the operation to begin.

Emile drew his pistol and pointed it at the Count who stuck up his hands, watching astonished as his bodyguard removed the gold-plated pistol from its holster matching the Count's white Oriflamme dress uniform and pocketed it. The Count was shouting at François and Emile and turning purple with fury, when I suddenly appeared before him. The Count stared at me dumbfounded as he saw me wearing only my underpants and with my hair gone grey, thanks to Hannah's work with the tin of stage makeup. When I reached into my underpants for the gold colored eyepatch and tied it over my right eye, the Count burst out laughing.

"Mon Dieu!" François called out, staring at the identical twins before him. He threw the Count to the ground and pinned him down while Emile stripped off the Count's uniform, handing each piece of clothing to me. When I was fully dressed and François released the Count, he stood up covered in dirt, wearing only a pair of blue silk underpants with the d'Uribé-Lebrun coat of arms embroidered on them. He shook his head approvingly and said,

"Looking at you, I realize how handsome and impressive I look in my dress uniform. But, my son, you are making the biggest mistake of your life. I have offered you everything, my name and my fortune. I hired a private eye to give you the greatest treasure that you will ever possess, the knowledge of who you are. And now you turn against me. Why?" Hannah parted the bushes hiding her. When he saw her walking toward us he spat out his own answer,

"For a Jew! The daughter of a rag-and-bone man? " I said,

"You know, Hannah's father was the first person ever gave me something. A clarinet for my eighteenth birthday."

"It's all about a clarinet?" He looked at Hannah with disgust and was about to yell at her when François took a sap out of his pocket and brought it down hard on the Count's head. He toppled forward and sprawled on the ground. François and Emile kicked him and pummeled him with their fists.

"Salaud! Sac de Merde! " François shouted and Emile screamed "Traître!" at the Count, as they rained blows down on him. The Count suddenly sprang to his feet, crouched like a boxer and unleashed a vicious right uppercut which landed on the point of Emile's chin, knocking him to the ground. He fumbled his pistol out of Emile's pocket and stomped on the defenseless man who lay rubbing his chin. The Count stood up straight and carefully aimed his gold plated Berthier at Hannah's heart with a maniac's grin on his face. I saw him start to squeeze the trigger and stepped in front of her, shielding Hannah with my body. She wrapped her arms around me. The Count, his finger still on the trigger smiled, plainly enjoying himself now. He aimed at my right hand and said,

"How convenient, Charles-Emmanuel. With only two bullets, I can make sure you never play that decadent music again and also kill the woman. Killing two birds with two stones, quoi? Prepare yourself…"

He was squeezing the trigger when François, who'd snuck up behind him and flicked open his switchblade, calmly slit his throat. The Count dropped the pistol and fell to his knees looking amazed at the blood pumping out of his jugular vein and over his upper body. He stared at me, his blue eye already clouding over, then screamed "Vive la France!" and pitched forward dead onto the ground. Standing behind me, Hannah had missed it all. She cried out, terrified,

"Urby. Are you hurt?" I steered her away and said,

" No. The Count's dead. I don't want you to look at him again. Ever. Go get the picnic blanket, but don't look at him when you come back." Emile, still groggy, got to his feet, picked up the Count's pistol, wiped it clean with his shirt and handed it to me.

François, Emile and I stood looking at the bloody, near-naked corpse of the man whose identity I'd now taken. Images of him from all of our face-to-face meetings over the years flashed before my eyes like a crazily sped up newsreel. At the end of it, I felt nothing for my father, the monster now lying dead at my feet. His role in the "Joke of God" had ended. He'd destroyed many lives before dying, but Hannah and I were still together. I hoped that he would be tortured by that knowledge forever in whatever Hell he was now residing.

"Qu'est ce qu'on fait du macchabée?" Emile asked.

I answered that we'd carry out the plan as before with the "stiff."

Emile took the picnic blanket from Hannah who held a hand over her eyes. The two men wrapped the Count's body in it and we followed them as they dragged it deep into the cave. We packed our things in the Count's car and then left our stolen car in the forest.

François and Emile drove us in the Count's limousine, with Hannah sitting beside me on the back seat, to the town of Valençay in the Indre department where we crossed the Demarcation Line into the Free Zone. I saluted the gendarmes and border guards as we sailed past one checkpoint after another. We weren't stopped.

Once we were in the Free Zone, I changed into my own clothes and turned the Count's uniform and papers over to François and Emile. Stanley had phoned us with a change in our plan before we left. We wouldn't all go to see the "volcano man" in Auvergne, but they'd drop Hannah and me off at the castle of one of Stanley's friends. The friend would drive us by back roads to Martin Etcheverry's house on the outskirts of Pau. Etcheverry would turn us over to *passeurs* who would guide us across the Pyrenees and on the long journey through

Spain to get to Portugal. Members of their network would transport us to Lisbon in a fishing boat, pick up our steamship tickets and get us aboard a ship bound for New York.

François and Emile would continue toward the Auvergne region in the Count's Oriflamme car. They planned to ditch it and the Count's uniform and papers in a gorge and blow everything up. Using forged papers, they'd make their way south to the town of Sète where they planned to bribe a fishing boat to ferry them to Tangier, which Franco's forces had occupied on the day the Germans marched into Paris. They both had connections in the Spanish legion who'd help smuggle them from Morocco to Gibraltar. From there, they planned to hook up with the English and volunteer to sign up with de Gaulle and his Free French outfit in London. They'd carry my letter of introduction singing their praises and reminding the General that Hannah and I had tried to help him escape to London.

Everything went according to Stanley's plan. The friend greeted us at his castle and we said our goodbyes to François and Emile. They saluted me as if I were there now dead leader and drove off in the Count's Oriflamme car, heading for Auvergne.

⚶

Hannah, Martin Etcheverry and I rolled into Pau late the next afternoon. We had time to have a quick dinner with him and two members of his *passeur* network who had disguised themselves as farmers. They hid us in their truck and we crossed the Spanish frontier under cover of darkness and made it to Canfranc without being stopped. Two other members of the network took turns driving us all day to the port of Vigo in Galicia on Spain's Atlantic coast. From there we embarked at night on a fishing boat, which ferried us to Lisbon. Hannah and I waited in Lisbon for two days while Etcheverry's agents made all the arrangements for our voyage. We finally embarked for New York on July 27, aboard the S.S.Excalibur.

In the afternoon sun, Hannah and I stood at the railing with fellow refugees from every corner of Europe, watching its receding shoreline. Seagulls soared and swooped overhead and then wheeled and headed back toward

Europe as its land mass dipped below the horizon. Once it had disappeared, we stood at the bow, looking at the S.S. Excalibur's churning green wake. I took the Count's pistol out of my pocket and heaved it as far as I could. We saw a flash of gold as it made a splash and sank.

Hannah and I finally turned our backs on the view and sat down in deckchairs watching the passengers who still peered toward the now invisible continent. Europe was drowning in another bloodbath, just over twenty years after the last one. We weren't going to be there for the second carnage.

"What's on your mind?" Hannah asked.

"Just wondering where we should go first after we arrive in New York. New Orleans or New England?"

"Seems to me New Orleans should be our first stop. But we've got ten days to think about it."

"You going to look up your folks?" I asked. Her face clouded over and she said,

"No. When they told me I was dead for them, they died for me too. It's just you and me, Urby. Sure you can handle that?" She looked into my eyes and squeezed my hand.

"Yes," I said. "It's only ever been you and Stanley and me, the Three Musketeers."

"Maybe Mary Goodyear will turn out to be the Fourth, if she's still alive."

"I don't want to think about it. Let's just rest up." Hannah eased back into her deck chair as we faced our new destination. The sun was shining in her dark eyes and later her face glowed in the setting sun. She pulled me to her and we kissed.

"For the first time since we've been together, we have nobody and nothing to run away from. Ten days on the S.S. Excalibur with just us and the Ocean. When we arrive in America, whatever happens, promise me not to change from the man I fell in love with when we had to fight to stay together."

"Nothing will make me change now," I said. "The only thing that was standing between us is dead and rotting in a cave."

PART III

PART III

CHAPTER 17

W hile we got used to being on land after ten days at sea, Hannah and I stayed in a rundown hotel on one hundred and fifth street and Broadway, called the Hotel Mogador. We'd headed there because lodgings and diners were cheap and I knew the area from my time in New York before I left for France in July 1914. It hadn't changed much in twenty-six years. Shady characters leaned against its brick walls smoking and spitting at passersby in the stifling August heat. They reminded us of the small-time pickpockets and pimps who buzzed like gnats around the Place Pigalle. But here we were outsiders and they stared at our foreign-looking clothes, sizing us up for a fast mugging. Once, four of them split from the pack and started closing in on us and I braced myself for their attack. When a cop suddenly appeared, twirling his billy club, they scattered like sharks, searching for new prey.

We were getting stared at so much that we finally ducked into the subway and headed to thirty-fourth street to go shopping for clothes and shoes at Macy's Herald Square. We changed in the store and gave our used stuff to the sales clerks. They ooohed and ahhed when we told them our clothes and shoes and hats came from Paris, France and we left them fighting for our leftovers.

We road tested our new duds by walking from Macy's east along thirty-fourth street towards the Empire State building which was blocking out a large patch of blue sky. No one gave us a second look. We'd blended into the lunchtime crowds jostling each other to get out of the humid oven of the steets and into a building with fans whirring.

I remembered the August heat from my year of living in Manhattan following my escape from New Orleans the day after the Count's late hit man, Pierre, put the torch to the Saint Vincent Colored Waifs' Home.

The Manhattan August made my head spin more than the New Orleans summers that I remembered from my boyhood.

We craned our necks to look up at the Empire State Building. It hadn't been there when I left Manhattan for France. It made me dizzy so I turned my back to it and Hannah laughed.

"The Eiffel Tower doesn't bother you and it's not all that much shorter than the Empire State, so what's your problem?"

"What if it falls down with all those people inside?"

"Never happen. It used to be like a ghost town inside. We called it the 'Empty State Building' when I worked there as a tourist guide a year after it opened in 1931." I knew that soon she'd be remembering 1932, the year we broke up in Paris and Hannah returned to New York. She had a pained look whenever she talked about the four years she lived in the city before returning to Paris to give me another try.

"Working one hundred stories up was how I kept body and soul together for six months before I landed a job as second violin in the New York Philharmonic," she said. "You want to take an elevator up there to see if any of my old girlfriends are still working as tourist guides?"

"No thanks. What I'd like right now is something to drink and eat."

Hannah asked me if I'd ever heard of a Horn & and Hardart Automat and I said,

"Sounds like a place with robots running around in it. Like in that film we saw at the Cinéma Max Linder..."

"Metropolis?" she asked. I nodded Yes and she explained that there were no robots but it was a restaurant where you walked around with coins and a tray looking at a wall of food displayed behind glass in little cubbyholes. When you found something you wanted, you put your coins in the slot, turned a knob and took your sandwich or pie out, put it on your tray and found a table. Hot dishes were a little more complicated.

"You buy your wine the same way?" I asked.

"Welcome back to America," Hannah said, laughing. "No wine, my love. You're going to drink milk, water or coffee with your meals. Unless we go to a swanky restaurant like Delmonico's near Wall Street. It costs an arm and a leg and we're not exactly rolling in money right now." Without thinking I said,

"They probably don't serve colored folks there anyway, let's skip it."

Hannah looked at me, suddenly sad. She knew, as I did, that it would take me a long time to realize that I was white after the shock of learning it less than a month before.

I thought of the Count. His corpse was rotting away inside the Crystal Cave, unless it had been discovered by hikers or tramps or devoured by some animal. I wondered if his final revenge on me was that, once I knew the punch line to what he called "The Joke of God" the knowledge wouldn't set me free.

Hannah said, "Let's never to go to a restaurant or bar where they refuse to serve colored people." Remembering how segregated restaurants and bars were all over America when I left for France, I reckoned we'd either starve or be patronizing a lot of colored establishments from now on-if they'd serve us. Hannah added,

"We'd better stick to bars and liquor stores for beer or booze." Seeing the surprise on my face, she stuck the knife in. "Cheer up," she smiled. "On Sunday, liquor stores are closed. Some bars open after church hours."

"Maybe Stanley was right to stay in Paris," I said. Hannah went on,

"It was a shock for me too, when I came back. I still don't know how I stuck it out here for four years, thinking of you every minute. And you kept sending me letters and beautiful songs I didn't know about, begging me to forgive you and come back to Paris. I gave in when I finally believed you regretted all the craziness and the drugs and women and that you weren't about to start that stuff again."

I hugged her tight, as people flowed around us. I was hoping that she wouldn't start thinking about my last real case as a private eye, tracking down Daphne Robinson, "New Jersey's Runaway Heiress." When Hannah returned to Paris in 1936 and I told her the whole story about how I'd become richer by one hundred grand for tracking Daphne down and how close I'd come to falling for her, she nearly got back on the next ship leaving Le Havre for New York.

I never let on to Hannah, but when she mentioned Delmonico's Restaurant and Wall Street, she'd set me thinking about Daphne again. Despite having tried to forget her, I knew that she was only a few miles away now, instead of us being an ocean apart. I knew that all I had to do to see her again was to take a subway to Wall Street, walk into the Robinson Building, which belonged to her now, make my way to her office and give my name to the receptionist. I flattered myself in thinking that one of the most beautiful young women on the planet, and one of the richest, would rush out of her office, throw herself into my arms and beg me to start again where we'd left off in France six years ago.

But I was pushing thoughts like that out of my mind, because there was no way I could live without Hannah again. Still, knowing myself all too well, I reckoned that it would be best for us to cut out of Manhattan fast, to silence Daphne's voice sounding in my head, a voice as dangerous as Billy Holiday's when it came to a siren song.

We walked by a newsstand and Hannah stopped and ran over to it. She picked up a copy of the "New York World-Telegram" which had a banner headline reading "Murder in Nazi-Run Paris." There was an old photograph of a smiling Marshal Pétain and the Count standing arm-in-arm. It must have been taken after the Marshal's great victory at the Battle of Verdun.

The accompanying story was one of murder and villainy in Vichy France. The newspaper came straight out and accused the Count of being implicated in the murder of "...the nightclub owner, Redtop, one of the most famous and well-loved Americans in Paris and a pioneer in bringing jazz to The City of Light. Up to now, the lying Nazi-led Vichy government of the disgraced Marshal Pétain has claimed that Redtop took her own life back in March 1938. The New York World-Telegram can now reveal in an exclusive that Redtop didn't commit suicide, but was murdered on the orders of a top Minister in the Vichy government, Count d'Urby-Lebrown, whose sudden disappearance weeks ago remains a mystery to this day. How long does FDR have to wait to declare war on Germany and wipe Hitler and his dirty French collaborators like Marshal Pétain and Count d'Urby-Lebrown from the face of the earth?"

"Jean Fletcher got the story published!" Hannah whistled the opening notes of the Marseillaise, then hugged me. We laughed like maniacs and kissed as the crowds passed giving us a wide berth.

There was a real bounce in our strides as we strolled up Fifth Avenue and turned east at forty-second street opposite the New York Public Library. I remembered that we could walk along it towards Grand Central Station, if it hadn't been torn down since I left.

We entered the automat, which looked like an eating factory, its walls covered with white tiles before which stood lines of people waiting in front of chrome rimmed windows to put their coins in slots. They took food out of the windows then searched for a place to sit and eat.

"Grab a table and I'll get the food." Hannah went off to change dollar bills. I found a table next to a young colored couple who nodded Hello and I nodded back. The tables around them were empty although the rest of the automat was crowded.

Hannah brought a tray to the table with our food and some milk to wash it down. I looked at the tuna fish salad sandwiches on doughy white bread, the small bottles of milk and the shiny slices of apple pie and said,

"Let's get out of here and find a bar and drink to Jean Fletcher getting Redtop's story out." Hannah, reading my mood, stood up to go.

The man in the colored couple looked a lot like a young version of Lonny Jones, the hit man, drummer and ex-preacher in my quartet at Urby's Masked Ball. Lonny, who'd admired Adolf Hitler and spied on us for the Count, had been punished for his betrayals by Stanley and his Corsican friends. The past came flooding back again. Lost in my own thoughts, I must have stared at the man for too long. He and the pretty young woman with him were nervous, as if expecting me to dump our tray of food over their heads and to start spouting bigotry at them. Instead, I offered them our food, saying,

"It's crazy, but we've lost our appetites. It's a shame to let all this good food go to waste. We haven't touched it, so you're welcome to it." Suddenly, I worried that they might think we were leaving because we didn't want to sit next to them. Instead, they both smiled and the man said,

"That's mighty kind of you, sir. We sure could do with some more food. We're a bit low on cash now and this automat's kinda pricey for us." I put our tray on their table.

"You from around here?" his pretty girl companion asked. I got her message. She thought we were white tourists from abroad, because they didn't expect any generosity or respect from white Americans.

"We're both from New Orleans," I said, bringing Hannah in. "But we've been living in France for a long time." The man's face lit up.

"Paris?" he asked and I nodded Yes. Then he went on, "My father was in the 369th infantry regiment during the last war in Europe. He had a leave in Paris and told me stories about how kind the French were to my people."

"I fought that war in the French Foreign Legion. If there was an American army unit I wished I'd served in, it was the 'Harlem Hell Fighters.' I'm a jazz musician." The couple looked at me open-mouthed.

"Hold on a minute," the man whispered. "Are you telling me that you're one of the people? You passing for white, sir?"

"No, I'm white. It's a long story, but I know what you're going through." They looked at each other like I was crazy. I held out my palm and the man hesitated and then we gave each other skin. He and the woman stared at me, amazed.

The man said,

"You sure look white but you got the hand slap down. You got the groove. Would you mind telling me your name, sir?"

"I'm Urby Brown." He shook his head in disbelief.

"You sure got me confused now sir. My daddy used to play Stanley Bontemps and Urby Brown records all the time. He'd tell me that if I kept working hard on my drumming, I might end up playing in your quartet one day. He never said you were white. I remember how proud he was that you and Stanley were **colored** Creoles from New Orleans. He was from Baton Rouge."

I wondered how often I'd meet with the same surprise and confusion from now on. Hannah was listening to us; she turned to go.

"Take care of yourselves folks," I said as we left. Hostility flared from the white diners as we passed their tables on the way out. We stared them down and they ducked their heads back toward their plates.

"This isn't going to be easy," Hannah said.

We walked to Second Avenue, heading to a bar Hannah knew called "Paddy Hanrahan's." She said it served good bar food and stayed open all afternoon. We entered it and saw that it was nearly empty, the lunchtime crowd having gone back to work. That left the serious drinkers sitting at the bar, with only a big overhead fan to cool them down. They were talking about whether America should get into the war in Europe. Most of them favored staying way out of it. One tough looking customer with a mashed-in nose said,

"It's the kikes want to get us into it. Just like the last time. We should be fighting with Hitler on the same side. Then we can kick the kikes and the niggers and the chinks and the spics out of New York." The other men brayed their approval, one shouting,

"To hell with FDR and Eleanor!" Another said,

"I won't vote for that Wendell Wilkie though. He wants us to get into the war to save the limeys again. I wish Lindbergh was running. I'd vote for Hitler for President-anybody but that Jew-lover FDR and his nigger-loving wife." I was about to get into a brawl with the men, when Hannah said,

"Easy Urby. Let's get some drinks and find a booth where we can't hear them."

We ordered double whiskies and sat down in a dimly lit corner, where the voices of the men droned on in a low, angry murmur. There were dozens of cigarette butts and some gummy stuff underfoot. We clinked glasses and Hannah said,

"To Jean Fletcher. Here's hoping she and Stanley are safe."

"Tchin," I said. Hannah looked toward the bar where the men's voices were growing louder.

"Welcome to America," she said. "Those guys would have been right at home in the Count's Oriflamme stormtroopers."

"Maybe they're worse. Let's get out of here."

We left Paddy Hanrahan's and found a quieter bar a few blocks further north on Second Avenue. We spent a few hours reminiscing about Paris, then took a taxi to Penn Station to buy train tickets.

⚔

Hannah and I left for New Orleans the next day to search for the survivors among the witnesses mentioned in Dewey Lafontaine's report. We figured they'd probably be in their sixties now. We wanted to find out what they knew about Josephine Dubois and Mary Goodyear and two of their boys, one of them an unidentified octoroon who shared a father, the Count, with his white half brother, namely me. I still had trouble believing that the report could be true, because it fitted too neatly into the future that the Count had destined for me as the heir to his d'Uribé-Lebrun lineage.

Once Hannah and I did our digging in New Orleans and satisfied ourselves that Lafontaine's report wasn't a hoax, we'd head for Wellfleet, Massachusetts. We'd look for my mother, Mary Goodyear, and try to locate my half brother, if they were still alive.

Our first stop in New Orleans was at the Central New Orleans Police Department. We gave a desk cop a cock and bull story about me being Dewey Lafontaine's nephew and we were trying to locate him about inheritance matters. We said that my father, Dewey's only sibling, had told us that he'd served in the police department around 1900. We'd heard through the grapevine that Dewey had died in a fire in New Orleans about a month ago. Hannah and I both knew that the magic word "inheritance" would make a New Orleans cop pay attention, because it meant "money" and a possible tip if they cooperated. When the desk cop had listened to our story, he spent some time looking us over before asking,

"You folks from out of town?"

"Sure are," I said. "We're Americans who lived in Paris, France until the Germans marched in. Then we decided it was time to leave."

"Gay Paree," he said, nostalgically. "I spent a night there on leave during the last war. What outfit were you in?"

"French Foreign Legion."

"French Foreign Legion? But you said you're an American, didn't you?" I nodded Yes.

"How come you fought for the French? Wasn't the American army good enough for you?" he asked, suddenly hostile.

"I wanted to start fighting the Germans in 1914, because I reckoned that they were fixing to take over the world. So I signed up with the Legion. America only came into the war in '17. I stayed with the Legion, because we were fighting the same enemy," I lied. The cop thought it over, chomping on the wad of tobacco in his cheek. Finally, he decided I hadn't done anything he could lock me up for. He calmed down and stopped chewing long enough to say,

"Well, I wouldn't have done that myself, sir. It's us Americans who saved those frogs and limeys and won the war for them. Now, y'all please wait here while I find out what I can about your Uncle Dewey." The officer left us and went down a long corridor and disappeared into a room giving off it.

"What if they end up arresting you because you fought for the French? That may be against the law in Louisiana nowadays," Hannah asked.

"Let's wait and see," I said. After a half hour, the officer returned with a file. He was cooling himself with a fan bearing a garish picture of a brown-haired Jesus with a well-trimmed beard and a firm jaw. Jesus looked like a younger version of the Confederate General, Stonewall Jackson, whose picture I'd seen in one of Father Gohegan's history books.

"Well folks," he said to me. "I'm sorry to have to tell you, but it looks like your Uncle Dewey was kicked off the police force in '09 on corruption charges." I thought to myself that Dewey must have done something seriously corrupt to be kicked off the New Orleans police force back then. I read somewhere that it was near the top of the list of most corrupt police forces in America when I left for France in 1914. Dewey must have refused to dish out bribes to fellow cops to shield his rackets.

"Says here that old Dewey set himself up as a private eye down by Rampart Street and the Congo after he left the force," the officer said, scanning the papers in the file. "Some officers testified that Dewey did mostly keyhole peepin' stuff for his customers. Then he'd bribe them, a kind of double play deal old Dewey was cuttin' for himself. I know he's your kin and all but old Dewey weren't no square shooter."

"Can you tell me anything about the hotel fire he burned to death in about a month ago?" The cop scratched his head and said,

"There **was** a hotel fire near his place about that time killed somebody. But we heard the coroner couldn't rightly tell if the deceased was man or beast." Hannah asked,

"So, Dewey Lafontaine could still be alive?"

"Ain't nothin' points to the contrary, m'am."

"Would you have the address of his private detective agency?" The officer opened up a register on his desk and skimmed through it until he stopped and said,

"I've got an address. But it says here we closed his business down in 1922 'cause there was so many complaints from folks he was trying to blackmail. He went too far and pulled his tricks on a councilman." He chuckled. "Fellows like him sail so close to the wind, they likely to end up in jail. We'd have locked his ass up and thrown away the key, but old Dewey had taken out an insurance policy, you see. He'd locked away some dirty stuff he had on the Police Commissioner so we let him slide." The cop slapped his thigh, laughing and coughing up tobacco juice.

I knew what kind of private eye Dewey was. The same animals existed in Paris. I was thinking of becoming one when I was down to my last few sous and facing a long, cold winter in February of 1934. The electricity had been cut off after I stopped taking the money Stanley had anteed up to make me a shamus and keep me working. But, thanks to Father Gohegan of the Saint Vincent's Colored Waifs' Home, I'd grown a conscience and it kept me from becoming a Dewey Lafontaine.

I asked the desk cop to give me Dewey's old address. When he hesitated, I put a five spot on his desk and he wrote on a slip of paper and handed it over.

"Thanks for your time," I said. I shook his proffered hand, a hand which had probably gripped a police baton a bunch of times to slam it upside the head of some colored kid in the Battlefield. He might have even ended up using one on me, if I hadn't left New Orleans for Harlem.

"Welcome to New Orleans, folks," he drawled as he pocketed the dough.

▲

Colored musicians were playing jazz at Jackson Square, busking for the tourists. Men sat on benches in the plaza surrounding the statue of old Andrew Jackson on horseback. They fanned themselves with their straw hats, while the women cooled themselves with fans touting Baptist churches eager to convert local Catholics.

It was so hot, that we decided to take a taxi to the address of Dewey Lafontaine's old private detective agency on Rampart Street, just south of Congo Square where slaves used to be auctioned off like the bales of cotton they picked.

A store stood at Dewey's old address. It specialized in selling charms and hoodoo and voodoo knickknacks to locals and tourists. A wizened old white man whose shop had a sign over the door with the words "Freelys White Magic" on it sat behind the counter fanning himself with a straw church fan. There was a sweaty Jesus wearing a crown of thorns crudely painted on it. We could hear the buzzing of a swarm of flies, attracted to a chunk of watermelon on the counter in front of him. He swatted feebly at them and lifted a weary toothless grin toward us. We asked him if he knew someone named Dewey Lafontaine.

"Don't reckon I knows anybody by that name, me," he said, spitting out watermelon seeds like machine gun bullets. He swatted more flies away from the watermelon, which smelled like it was fermenting in the heat. He tore off a chunk of it and worked his gums on it warily, like a baby teething on a crust of zwieback toast. I took out a five dollar bill and he sat up and dried his hands on his faded denim overalls. He held Abe Lincoln up to his rheumy blue eyes tut-tutting as if he wished Jefferson Davis's mug was on the five spot instead. Resigned to Lincoln, the old cracker folded the bill carefully and slipped it into his bib pocket.

"Old Dewey. Yesiree, I known him good as anybody hereabouts."

"We heard he died in a hotel fire about a month ago," I said. He wheezed with laughter and then coughed his lungs back into place.

"Cops must have told you that, 'cause they was in on his rackets. No, old Dewey was gunned down by dagoes, Sicilians what call themselves the New Orleans Mafia."

The old man told us that Dewey had been pulled out of the Mississippi with a slug in the back of his head nigh on to a month ago. Dewey's good buddies figured that it was the work of a professional hit man and bore all the hallmarks of the Sicilians who'd "infected" the city since the turn of the century. The old man spat out more watermelon seeds with venom as he ranted on about the Sicilians being even worse than the niggers and said he didn't believe their claims they were white.

He and his friends had done everything they could to stop the "dagoes" from invading New Orleans, even lynching eleven of them back in March of 1891 after they killed Chief of Police Hennessy, he said. But the Sicilians had got a toehold and now they were gunning down real white men at will. The man was too old and set in his hatreds to believe that Dewey Lafontaine's death bore all the hallmarks of French, not Sicilian, handiwork: of Pierre Lestage carrying out the orders of a French Count who was my father.

We asked the old man if he knew anyone who could tell us more about Dewey, but he clammed up. Even the offer of five bucks more didn't prise open his toothless mouth. He finally fled into the back of the shop to seek comfort with his fake voodoo dolls and jujus.

We made our way toward the area where Storyville was located until the military closed it down during the Great War. We wanted to get a lead on the fate of Madame Lala, her brother Bartholomew Lincoln Thigpen the Elder or of any of her prostitutes who might still be alive to help us nail down what happened to Josephine Dubois, Mary "Claudette" Goodyear and my octoroon half brother by the Count and Josephine.

CHAPTER 18

It was still too hot to stand in the sun waiting for a streetcar, so we decided to take a cab again to go to the church near the Mahogany House. When we told the driver our destination, he said,

"Whoaaa! I ain't goin' to those parts, folks. You'd best not go there."

"I'll double your fare if you take us to the Heavenly Peace Abyssinian Baptist Church. Do you know where it is?"

"I know where it's at, but I ain't packin' my pistol today." I held out a ten dollar bill and he eyed it as he fanned himself. Finally, he took it and said,

"I'll take you, but you got to step down quick when we get there."

⚐

I recognized the colored preacher watching us from the sidewalk in front of the church. The last time I'd seen Reverend Potts he was in his mid-forties, having taken over the pulpit twenty years earlier with the ink hardly dry on his preaching diploma, people said. I used to play gospel music in the church on Sundays with the Saint Vincent's Colored Waifs' Home band and remembered thinking he would make a good drummer. He was always right on the beat as he slapped his hymn book in time to our music. Now, he looked as old as Methuselah, bent over at the waist like an upside down L. He swayed tensely on his cane and squinted at us through the cracked lenses of his eyeglasses.

When we asked him if he could give us some directions, he relaxed, probably thinking that we were just two foolhardy white tourists gone astray who could use his help. Concerned for our safety, he offered to accompany us to wherever we wanted to go, but I refused as politely as I could. I told him we both knew the city, having been born in New Orleans. We'd left a long time ago to live in Paris. He beamed at us then, saying that he'd wanted to be a chaplain to the Negro soldiers sent to France during the Great War, but they'd turned him down because of his gimpy leg. I was surprised that he said "Negro." "Colored" was the polite word when I'd left for France in 1914. He asked how come we'd left New Orleans for Paris.

"We both hate Jim Crow so we didn't want to stay in New Orleans. Or America," Hannah said. The preacher's jaw dropped. He looked at us as if we'd landed in New Orleans from Mars.

"I been on this piece of the planet for seventy years and I ain't never heard no white folk say that. There may be hope for the Negro race if there be more white folk like you. If you know any, please tell 'em to send letters to Reverend Frederick Douglass Potts. I'll read 'em out on Sunday to cheer up my flock, I surely will."

"The Mahogany House used to be around here, didn't it?" I asked.

He looked surprised that I knew about it.

"I hope y'all didn't come all the way from Paris to see it, 'cause it ain't here no more. The Navy shut Storyville down in '17 to keep them soldiers' minds locked into righteousness when they was fixin' to go off to war."

"Did you ever meet Madame Lala? Or her brother, Bartholomew?" Reverend Potts wobbled so much that I had to steady him.

"Are y'all from the police? Or that J. Edgar Hoover bunch?"

"No, we're not cops and we're not F.B.I. We have a good friend in Paris named Stanley Bontemps who wanted to find out if they were still alive," Hannah lied. At the mention of Stanley's name, the Reverend dropped his formal ways.

"You **friends** of Stanley's? Lord, he and Louis Armstrong and a man name of Urby Brown be **the** most famous folks ever come from these parts.

All three of them was Negro Waifs from the Saint Vincent's Colored...I mean 'Negro'... Waifs' Home burned down in July of '13." My curiosity about his use of "Negro" finally got the better of me and I asked him,

"How come you say 'Negro' Reverend Potts? Colored folks used to avoid that word as a holdover from slavery days." He paused and smiled,

"Sure did. Tell you the truth, I have to think to say 'Negro' because a lot of folks don't like 'Colored' no more. Lord knows what we'll be callin' ourselves next. 'Nigger' is the word I hates."

Now animated, he reeled off names and dates like a tourist guide reciting travel tips. Then he said,

"When the Waifs' Home burned down, we lost a good white man name of Father Gohegan. I remember watchin' the Home burn to the ground with him inside. Sure was a tragedy, sure was."

"I'm Urby Brown." The preacher looked at me and then at Hannah and then hobbled away from us, his eyes wide with fear.

"You a Negro passin' for white then, Mr. Brown. Any police recognizes you, y'all gone be lynched. I don't want no trouble. The police hear I even spoke to you, brother, they gone don them Klan robes and burn my church down the way they done the Waifs' Home. I be much obliged y'all didn't tell nobody you been here."

"He's white," Hannah finally said, clutching my arm. "A New Orleans policeman looked into his birth records. His mother was a white prostitute from Madame Lala's and his father was a Frenchman, a white Count from Paris." He looked even more amazed.

"You tellin' me Urby Brown's white? That ain't possible. I heard him play jazz with Stanley Bontemps at Lake Pon..." He stopped suddenly and shuffled right up to me and pushed him wizened ebony face so close to mine that I thought he was going to kiss me.

"Lord have mercy!" he shouted. You **are** Urby Brown. People used to joke you was a white man passin' for Negro until they heard you play the clarinet. You played it better than Stanley. You used to play in my church with the Waifs' Home band when you was still in short pants." He laughed then, snapping his fingers and swaying his bent up body. "So folks **was** right, you **was** passin' for Negro."

"I wasn't passing," I said. "Father Gohegan told me that my mother was a quadroon prostitute named Josephine Dubois and I learned only a month ago that my real mother was a white prostitute named Mary Goodyear." His shifty expression told me that he knew those names.

It looked like Reverend Potts was at ease again, now that he knew he was dealing with two white people who were friends of Stanley's. He still couldn't believe that I used to be a boy named Urby Brown who played clarinet in his church on Sundays with the Colored Waifs' Home band.

"How's Stanley holdin' up?" he asked. "He send us silent money to keep this church goin', no nickel and dimin' from Stanley. He keep us from goin' under during the baddest days of the Depression. If I had my way, I'd rename this church 'The Stanley Bontemps Baptist Church,' instead of the 'Heavenly Peace Abyssinian Baptist Church.' I be glad to answer any questions you got, Mr. and Mrs. Brown." Hannah smiled at that and Reverend Potts went on,

"Now you asked me about Madame Lala and Bartholomew Thigpen, who we called Big Buster? He was shot dead in the Battlefield, way back in June of '30. His sister Laurence called herself Madame Lala, had her throat sliced open with a straight razor a few months later. Nobody never found out who killed them. Those be the wages of sin."

"The cop who looked into my birth history didn't mention their deaths in his report," I said.

"Did you ever hear of a woman named Josephine Dubois? Or one called Claudette?" Hannah asked him. This time, he smiled and then said,

"Stanley Bontemps sure educated you folks about the goin's on at the Mahogany House, because he used to music for the powerful white men goin' there, and I mean powerful. Claudette's real name be Mary Goodyear."

"She's my mother," I interrupted him.

"My, my," he said, clearly surprised. "She used to come by here to play the piano until the police heard tell of it and warned her never to go inside a Negro church again. She was one stubborn Yankee woman though, so she didn't pay the police no mind. Then one day, she walk in here cryin' and all and say she be in trouble 'cause she be pregnant with a baby by..." he looked at me..."a French count." Puzzled, he asked me,

"How come Mary put you in the...Negro Waifs' Home instead of a White Waifs' Home?"

"It was Josephine Dubois who took me to the Waifs' Home. She had a baby boy by the French count at the same time as Mary and Josephine switched babies with her so that Mary would raise Josephine's son as white and I'd be raised as colored." Reverend Potts looked shocked and said, angrily snapping his fingers,

"That be Josephine Dubois, alright! She got the face of an angel and the heart of Beelzebub. Thinkin' of her make me sad to this day. First she go and have a baby with Big Buster Thigpen we calls Little Buster. But Little Buster be wild and mean like his mama and daddy and run away North to be a drummer in Harlem."

"I was at the Waifs' Home with him and we played jazz together in Harlem," I said. I didn't want to tell him more about my later doings with Little Buster. Reverend Potts was still indignant at what Josephine had done. He said,

"I hear tell that wicked girl have her a baby boy by the French count same time as Mary's but that she done drown it in the Mississippi. You say she switch babies so that Mary be raisin' Josephine's, while you, Mary's baby and a white man, be raised in the Negro Waifs' Home?" I nodded Yes. He went on,

"Father Gohegan never talk to me much about you. I hardly known the man. Matter of fact, word was that he don't like Negro folk and I don't take kindly to no Catholics snatchin' our people away from the Baptist Church." Reverend Potts bowed his head and said,

"Everybody known she suicide herself by hangin' from a tree. At the time, I reckon she do it out of shame over drownin' her baby in the Mississippi. Now I reckon it be out of shame for switchin' the babies. The Lord sure punish her for her wickedness, He surely did." I looked at him and waited. My gut told me that Reverend Potts knew more than he was letting on. I asked,

"Are you sure she committed suicide? Is Josephine Dubois still alive, Reverend Potts?" As if a great weight was being lifted from him, he finally confessed,

"I don't rightly know. You the first people I ever tell what I'm gone tell you now, 'cause you be friends of Stanley. Never repeat what I say, 'specially to nobody white." We gave him our word and he went on,

"Right after they cuts her down from that tree and be fixin' to bury her, Big Buster come by here to ask me to say some words over her. He say that Father Gohegan won't 'cause she a Catholic done suicide herself. So I goes to the funeral parlor with Big Buster and Laurence and looks inside that coffin and ain't seen nothin' but a thing so burnt up you can't tell if it be a man a woman or a hound dog. A few nights later, I be readin' my bible at home when I hear a tap-tappin' on the door. It be Josephine on the run. She know she in big trouble and she ask me to help her, so I done give her a letter to take to a young preacher friend of mine live in Natchez, Mississippi."

So far, I thought to myself, Reverend Potts's version of Josephine's story was close to Stanley's and Dewey Lafontaine's. Reverend Potts went on,

"My friend say he take care of her, though she be a sinner. I'm talkin' 1895 or so, so we still be close to slavery days and a lot of colored...Negro folk be on the move. I promise Josephine I keep her secret if she mend her ways. She give me her word on the Holy Bible and head out into the night. I swear, Mister Urby, nobody never said nothin' to me about her switchin' babies with Mary to land you in no Negro Waifs' Home instead of a White Waifs' Home where you belongs." I looked at Hannah. Her expression told me she didn't like or believe Reverend Potts.

"I'm glad I ended up in the Colored Waifs' Home," I said, still unable to say "Negro Waifs' Home."

"God bless you, sir. You got forgiveness deep in your soul. A year or so after I send Josephine off to Natchez, my friend write to tell me she be up to her wicked ways again. She be goin' from bordello to bordello, livin' a life of sin and abusin' her body with drugs and liquor. I reckon the shame of runnin' away from Little Buster and what she done switchin' her own baby with Mary's baby, yourself sir, be eatin' away at her soul."

"Have you seen Josephine since the '90s?" Hannah asked.

"Yes'm. In August of '31, she come gallivantin' into my church, bold as brass. She be well past fifty, I reckon, but she still look fine. I catch her up on the happenin's while she away. That Laurence and Big Buster be killed. Her son Little Buster Thigpen done left town. She never ask about no child of hers be gone up North with Mary. She ask if a French count done come lookin' for her. I tell her nobody come lookin' for her 'cause she 'spose to be dead. She want to know about the Saint Vincent's Negro Waifs' Home and I tell her it done burned to the ground with Father Gohegan inside. She act all shook up and go off again." He hesitated an instant, then said, "Maybe she be playactin' sayin' she don't know the Home done burn down."

"You ever see her again, Reverend Potts?" Hannah asked. He smiled gratefully, hearing her use his title with respect in her voice.

"She come back two years later and tell me she be livin' in Faubourg Tremé with a railroad porter. She seem clear in her head again. Since then, I ain't seen hide nor hair of her. Nobody I know in Tremé never hear of her nor no railroad man. I reckon she done lie to me to hide her tracks from anybody come lookin' for her. She sure was right to do that, 'cause some white man come around askin' questions about her a few years back."

"Did he say he was a policeman? Or a private investigator?" He looked shifty. Feeling that a puzzle was falling into place, I asked him,

"Did he offer you money for information, Reverend Potts? Was his name Lafontaine?"

"He didn't tell me his name. He offered me a heap of money, but I didn't like the look of him. Nor his tone. I didn't tell him nothin' so I didn't take no money from the man. Truth is I don't know if she be dead or alive." When we left him, Hannah said,

"That man was doing a lot of lying. I don't see him as someone who'd turn down money, even from the devil."

I felt the same way Hannah did about Reverend Potts. I remembered that, in his report, Dewey Lafontaine said his investigation had revealed that

Josephine Dubois was still alive as of August 1931. I reckoned that the good Reverend had been paid "a heap of money" for that information.

⋏

Hannah and I spent another two days in New Orleans, most of the time being driven through angry neighborhoods by nervous colored guides. In Tremé we asked if anybody knew a quadroon woman named Josephine Dubois living with a railroad porter, but nobody wanted to give us any information. To them, we were just "white folks" who had nothing to give a colored person except trouble. Josephine Dubois had vanished into thin air. I said,

"We're finished here, Hannah. Let's head to Wellfleet, Massachusetts.

We'll try to track Mary Goodyear down. If she's still alive, maybe she can tell us what happened."

The next day, we took the train back to New York City. We spent weeks sweltering in Manhattan and reading any news about France that we could get our hands on. There were more stories denouncing the Count for murdering Redtop, as well more revised obituaries about her.

Chapter 19

It was a sunny early October day and the leaves were blazing with color as Hannah drove us through New England in the secondhand Dodge we'd bought. All around us, the trees shone with shades of gold and a flame-like red that I'd never seen before. To our right, the Atlantic Ocean stretched towards the hell on the other side, in Europe, over three thousand miles away. The fairy tale world we were driving through seemed asleep, its inhabitants under a spell. I reckoned that the nightmares ruining people's lives on the other side would soon become theirs.

We stopped for the night at an inn in New Bedford, Massachusetts which Hannah told me was an old whaling town. She said that the opening chapter of a book called "Moby Dick," by Herman Melville, took place in the Seamen's Bethel around the corner from us. When I told her that I hadn't read it, she said I should read something besides Victor Hugo's *"Les Misérables."* I could start by reading "Benito Cereno," a short novel by Melville. It was about a revolt aboard a ship transporting slaves to America from Africa. The slaves captured the ship at first, but ended up losing it because of betrayals. When Hannah saw from my expression that I wasn't in the mood for talking about books, she changed the subject and asked,

"Do you think Mary Goodyear's still living in Wellfleet?"

"We'll get an early start tomorrow morning. If she's there, we'll track her down."

We stayed up talking about what we'd been through over the last year since the new war started in Europe. We both had the feeling that we were coming to the end of our long road from Paris. I hoped that Mary Goodyear was alive and could fill us in on the details missing in Dewey Lafontaine's report. We were looking forward to finding out where my half brother was, if he was still alive. Hannah and I couldn't get to sleep, both of us too excited by what tomorrow might bring.

When we arrived in Wellfleet just before noon, we drove to the Post Office and asked a clerk if she could direct us to Mary Goodyear's house. Hannah told her that we wanted to stop by to say Hello on our way to Provincetown. The last letter we'd received from her a few years ago was postmarked Wellfleet, but we didn't know her address.

"Where are you folks from?" the clerk asked, clearly interested.

"New York City," Hannah answered.

"New York City?" she repeated dreamily. "You've sure come a long way."

"Sure have," I said. The woman turned to the clerk at the adjoining counter, asking,

"Do you know Mary Goodyear's address? These folks are from New York City and they want to say hello to her before moving up the Cape to Provincetown."

"You betcha Sue, she's at...hold on a minute." He took down a sheaf of papers and rustled through them, then stopped and slapped his forehead. "She lives at 1400 Commercial Street, of course. That's where the Goodyears have always lived. Facing Wellfleet Harbor, close to the road to the pier. Goodyear is Mary's maiden name and she's gone back to using it since she was widowed." I was excited to learn that my mother was still alive but, having lived in Paris for so long, I was surprised that so much of her personal information was being bandied about out loud. We looked at the people in the Post Office, who were all nodding their heads as if they knew every detail of Mary Goodyear's family and her life.

"You know where 1400 Commercial Street is?" a young man behind us asked. We said we didn't and he told us he was going that way. He'd show us where it was, if he could hitch a ride with us.

The youngster got into the back seat and he wouldn't stop asking questions about New York City. Hannah gave him a rundown on the Statue of Liberty and the Empire State Building and Central Park. He wanted to know about Greenwich Village and all the writers and artists who lived there. Hannah was keeping Paris out of it, I reckoned, because she knew we'd never get him out of the car if she mentioned it.

"There she is," he called out, pointing to a pretty, clapboard house perched on a rise overlooking Wellfleet Harbor. We parked the car, thanked the youngster and he jogged off, heading toward some houses in the direction that we'd just come from. It was about a mile from the Post Office.

We knocked on the door. Hannah kept her eyes on the man, who was headed back the way we came.

"I wonder if he really was coming this way, or if he just rode with us to find out about New York City. He's probably going back to the Post Office."

The door opened and we heard a gasp. A white-haired lady with piercing blue eyes was standing in the doorway looking at me. Her hand was clamped over her mouth as if she'd seen a ghost.

"It can't be," she said, her voice trembling. "You can't have stayed so young, Mister René. The devil must have..." She seemed caught up in a nightmare.

"I'm René d'Uribé-Lebrun's son," I said. She started crying.

"That means you're my son's half brother. I never believed that even Josephine Dubois could have drowned her own son." She looked anxiously at the neighboring houses. I guessed she wanted us to go before anyone saw us. Remembering the people in the Post Office, though, I reckoned she'd have a lot of questions coming her way about our visit. I wondered what new lies she'd come up with to cover her tracks.

"I'm sorry to be inhospitable, but no one here knows anything about my past sins. My son doesn't know that he's illegitimate. Everyone thinks that his father died far from here when he was just a little boy. From Yellow Fever while he was working on the Panama Canal. Please forgive me for not inviting you in, but my son's gone out for groceries and is due back any minute." Hannah squeezed my hand for us to leave. I said,

"This is Hannah Korngold. She's my...fiancée." Mary Goodyear gave Hannah a peck on the cheek. She stood holding the door open and then looked at the old grandfather's clock in her parlor that tick-tocked loudly as its pendulum swung back and forth.

"You look nice," she said to Hannah. "It's a shame so many places don't allow mixed-race marriages." She turned to me and said,

"Unless you're passing for white. You certainly look as fair as your father. There's nothing wrong with passing, as far as I'm concerned. Whatever you're doing, good luck to you. Have a happy life. But please don't try to get in touch again. The past has to stay the past, I'm afraid."

"I just wanted you to know that my and your son's father passed away four months ago, when the Germans defeated France," I lied. "He talked about you. When my fiancée and I came to America from Paris to escape the Nazi occupation, we wanted to look you up and let you know that he'd passed away." She looked sad for a moment and then furtive again.

"My condolences. I'm glad that France is a tolerant country so that he could take you in although you're a..." She bit her tongue and then asked, "How's your mother Josephine taking it?" There was still a hot anger in her voice when she said "Josephine" which the passage of time hadn't cooled down. I could see that my mother was getting more and more frightened that we would still be there when Josephine's son returned.

"She's dead too," I said, to put an end to her heart's forty-five year long war with Josephine over which of them was my father's favorite.

"I'm so sorry to hear it." She cooed her sympathy, but there was a harsh glint of triumph in her eyes.

"Thank you. We'll be going now. Don't worry, we won't be back."

"I'm truly sorry that I can't be more hospitable, you've come so far."

"We understand," Hannah said. We waved goodbye and walked to the car. We drove it away from her front door and parked it around the corner where we had a clear view of the front of her house. Hannah held my hand.

"Maybe we should just go," she said.

"I can't," I said. "I want to see what my brother looks like."

Just then, a battered old Ford passed us and stopped in front of my mother's house. We both recognized the man who got out of the car. I laughed.

"The Joke of God? That's what you're laughing at?" Hannah asked.

"Yes," I said.

It was hard to drive away, knowing that I'd never see my mother again. But as I saw my brother, Evan Shipman, rest his bag of groceries on the ground and unlock the door to 1400 Commercial Street, I was filled with hope that we'd cross paths with him again somewhere down the road. I remembered how he'd put his life on the line to help rescue Hannah's friends Jascha Cohen and Elam Rosenthal from Germany, only for the two men to be betrayed to my father and the Paris police by my late drummer Lonny Jones, the grizzled old hit man and ex-Baptist preacher from Natchez, Mississippi.

The last time we saw Evan Shipman he'd mentioned his plans to return to the South to join protests against Jim Crow laws. I knew that Hannah would want to get involved in a fight like that and I felt ready to join them and go into battle again after spending so long on the sidelines.

"Let's get going," I said to Hannah as we watched my mother hug and kiss Josephine's son. Then he picked up the groceries and they went inside and shut the door.

CHAPTER 20

On August 25, 1944, as the allied armies closed in on the city, the Parisians finally rose up against their German occupiers. The American, British and Canadian allied armies, who'd landed in Normandy on June 6, 1944, D-Day, allowed de Gaulle's ever-increasing Free French forces to enter Paris first.

In July 1946, over a year after Germany's unconditional surrender to the Western allies on May 8, 1945, the State Department and the Department of Defense contacted the National Broadcasting Company. They wanted to arrange a series of Paris concerts by my integrated NBC Jazz Band to entertain the white and colored troops still stationed there in the segregated American army. Hannah and I both wanted to return, so I accepted on the condition that the concerts had to have integrated audiences. When the Army agreed, I talked Hannah into overcoming her fear of flying so that we could return together.

We'd both passed fifty and had reached a point in our lives where we wanted to spend more time together, after living in separate worlds, with Hannah in great demand as a concert violinist and me touring nonstop all over America with my Urby Brown's Jazz Quartet and the NBC Jazz Band.

My NBC Jazz Band and Hannah and I flew to London on a US Army Air Forces plane. We were whisked from there to Le Bourget airport and then bussed into Paris. As we approached the city, Hannah squeezed my hand and showed me her crossed fingers. I crossed mine too for good luck. We were hoping that Stanley had made it through the war. We saw Sacré Coeur through the window and knew that Place Pigalle was nearby.

Apart from the bullet impacts on some buildings we passed, they looked as grimy and beautiful as when we escaped. We settled the band in at the Hôtel de Crillon then took the metro at Concorde, direction Pigalle.

⚓

Urby's Masked Ball had made it through the war by a whisker. It was boarded up and the old sign above its door, with the name of the club surrounded by New Orleans carnival masks, was covered with racist graffiti, "Nègres et Juifs Dehors"- "Niggers and Jews Out," probably scrawled there by the fascist followers of my father's Oriflamme du Roi movement. Inside, the nightclub had been gutted by fire and every bottle in the wine cellar had been looted or smashed to pieces. We climbed the steps to our apartment to find that the door had been removed and it had been stripped bare. That's when we started panicking about Stanley. We ran to his apartment building. His private elevator wasn't working so we had to run up four flights of stairs to get to his penthouse. The buzzer was dead so we hammered on the door; there was nobody at home.

We met Jean Fletcher at La Coupole. Honoré, my old waiter, recognized me at once and led Hannah and me to my usual table. He'd aged during the occupation, but had managed to survive as had La Coupole. It was packed again and the air was filled with loud conversation and laughter, as if four years of occupation and deprivation had never happened. Paris had bounced back from defeat, again. Jean stood up as we approached and we all hugged each other. She'd brought a bottle of champagne. She told us she'd kept it with her during the war, vowing not to pop it open it until we were all together again.

She'd escaped to Switzerland with the champagne, her typewriter and a suitcase of her necessaries when America finally declared war on Germany, Italy and Japan, after the Japanese attack on Pearl Harbor on December 7, 1941. Right away, Americans in Paris had been declared enemy aliens and when caught had been interned by the French and their German masters. Jean told us that some German bigwigs wanted to send her to the Ravensbrück female concentration camp north of Berlin because of her articles in the New York Knickerbocker Magazine giving Americans the lowdown on France under German occupation. They also suspected that she'd been the source of the leaking of the lurid story of my father's role in murdering Redtop that made headlines in newspapers in America and England. She said she'd escaped capture thanks to an anonymous tipoff from a telephone caller minutes before the Gestapo and the French police raided her apartment.

Honoré popped open the champagne for us and Hannah and I clinked glasses with Jean as she said, solemnly,

"To Victory."

We caught each other up on what had been happening since our escape from France. We told her how the Count had died and she told us that, after his disappearance, his right hand man, Jean-Pierre/ Hans-Peter Kaltenborn, had taken over my father's Oriflamme du Roi movement. Two months later, his own Oriflamme stormtroopers assassinated Kaltenborn and blew up the Count's headquarters. Most of them had disappeared into thin air. There were rumors that many of them had joined the French Resistance or made their way to London to sign up with General de Gaulle.

"By the way Urby, your family castle in Bagnoles-de-l'Orne was bombed to smithereens by the U.S. Air Force. Hans-Peter had handed it over to the Germans and the top Boches were using its airfield to ferry art works stolen from French museums and Jews to their private collections in Germany. It's nothing but a pile of rubble now." We finally came to the question we'd wanted to ask her first of all.

"What about Stanley?" Hannah asked. "We went by his place but nobody was home." Jean looked at us for a long time without speaking. She finally said,

"I'm sorry to have to be the one to tell you, but he's dead. When I returned to Paris nearly two years ago just after the insurrection against the Nazis began, I slipped into Pigalle and went by his place. His man Finn O'Sullivan was there, drinking himself to death from grief. He told me the

French fascist militia and the Germans had raided them right after America declared war on Germany. They took Stanley off to a concentration camp near Hamburg called Neuengamme. From what I've been able to find out from your old friend Colonel Schulz-Horn-he's working with the American Occupation forces in Berlin now-the Boches segregated the colored prisoners away from the others in a Jim Crow section and treated them the worst of all the prisoners except for the ones they exterminated. Stanley wasn't worked to death on low food rations like some of the others because the Prison Director was a secret fan of his. But when his fingers gave out on him and he couldn't play his soprano sax for him anymore, they put a shovel in his hands and he went crazy and attacked a prison guard with it. He was executed by a German firing squad. The Prison Director decided to cremate him, put his ashes in an urn and turn it over to the colored prisoners. Finn told me that a colored army detail will bring his ashes to Paris tomorrow."

I felt like a dagger had been plunged into my heart. Hannah and Jean broke down and we all held each other. It was too much to bear. Stanley had come to France to escape from Jim Crow in America, only to be murdered in a Jim Crow Nazi concentration camp. I wanted to cry but no tears came.

"He went down fighting," Hannah said, crying even more. "At least he went down fighting." Jean dried her tears and then said,

"Stanley wouldn't want to see us like this. Let's order some rye. It doesn't go down well with champagne and we'll regret it later, but that's what Stanley would be drinking if he were with us now." Honoré took a while to find some in La Coupole's "American Bar" but he finally brought us three whiskey glasses and filled them with Hiram Walker straight rye.

"To Stanley," I said, proposing a toast. "He was a father to me, I'll never forget him."

"He was a father to all of us," Hannah said. We drank to that and then Hannah and I left Jean and returned to the Hôtel de Crillon. I had to give an outdoor evening jazz concert, which was to take place on the Champs de Mars between the Eiffel Tower and the Ecole Militaire.

The next morning, Hannah and I took the metro to Pigalle and walked to the rue Caulaincourt. Since yesterday, the electricity had come back on in Stanley's building. We took the private elevator up to his apartment and walked through the now open door into his living room. His butler, Finn, was sitting in a bistrot chair. It was the only piece of furniture in Stanley's apartment. The place had been stripped bare and racist graffiti covered its walls.

"Finn," I called out and he looked up and limped over to shake hands.

"Hello sir. Madam." he said. "A detail of colored American soldiers just dropped off Mr. Bontemps's ashes. They're in that urn on the mantelpiece." The shabby giant looked like he was nearing his end, broken by grieving over Stanley. He led Hannah and me to the urn, which was a simple grey ceramic one without any ornamentation. It was a far cry from Stanley's flamboyance.

"What should we do to honor him properly?" Finn asked.

"We're not taking him back to America," Hannah said. "He kept saying the only way he'd leave Paris was in a pine box and he should stay in Paris. I say we scatter his ashes in Montmartre. No ceremony, just the three of us."

"That's the way he'd want to go," Finn said, finally brightening up.

"Let's head for the vineyard," I said.

The three of us walked to the Montmartre vineyard, me carrying the urn wrapped up in a poster from a concert that Stanley, Louis Armstrong and I had given at Urby's Masked Ball a year after its reopening in 1938.

The vineyard was about a third of an acre in size and had been replanted. The grapes were ripening on the vine as we unlatched the gate and went inside. I unwrapped the urn and Hannah, Finn and I took turns scattering Stanley's ashes. Then we said our goodbyes to Finn. I gave him all the money I had on me and he said, "Ta" and then walked away without looking back, just as Stanley would have done.

By the time we returned to America, the American Army's public information bureau had released a series of press releases about Stanley's tragic death in the Neuengamme concentration camp, referring to him as one of the founding fathers of American jazz and one of the greatest American jazz musicians of the twentieth century. The press releases were taken up by the national press and The New York Times ran a front page story about Stanley's death and the forthcoming "remembrance celebration" to be held in New Orleans. I was told that the newspapers there, unusually for Southern ones when covering the death of a "Negro," had run banner headlines proclaiming Stanley Bontemps as one of New Orleans' greatest Colored Creole musicians. The newspaper even used the courtesy title "**Mr**. Stanley Bontemps." Usually, Southern newspapers only gave a colored person's first and last names. Articles on the arrangements mentioned that Louis Armstrong, Sidney Bechet and I would be leading the funeral cortège through the French Quarter street by street.

The Mayor of New Orleans proclaimed the day "Stanley Bontemps Day" and provided a black funeral carriage drawn by six black horses, with Stanley's soprano saxophone on view inside its glass windows on a black velvet cushion.

Colored and white people crowded the sidewalks to cheer the passage of Stanley's funeral wagon, and the musicians following behind it. I walked arm in arm with Hannah, beside Louis Armstrong and Sidney Bechet, in the front row of the mourners. Benny Goodman, Duke Ellington, Billy Holiday and scores of famous jazz musicians and singers walked behind us. When we promenaded beside the Mississippi River, I remembered the crystalline sound of Stanley's horn cutting through the air from the paddle boat steamers plying up and down its waters a lifetime ago. The roars and applause from the crowd swelled when Louis Armstrong improvised an up-tempo funeral march on his trumpet and Sidney Bechet and I joined in.

I looked into the crowd and stopped playing when I saw Evan Shipman waving at us.

"There's Evan Shipman," I said to Hannah. "Why don't you go say hello?" She ran ahead and I saw them hug and Hannah kissed him on the cheek. Kindred souls, I thought with a twinge of jealousy and then wondered what I'd say to comfort Hannah after the remembrance celebration was over, other than to tell her how much I loved her. I didn't know what I'd say to Evan Shipman.

I was waving at them as we marched past, getting ready to join in the music again. I didn't see the old woman in the black veil until she was standing right in front of me. I started to walk around her and she lifted her veil. She was a light-skinned, yellow-green-eyed woman, a quadroon I reckoned. She looked to be well into her sixties but was still beautiful. The thought flashed through my mind that she had Buster Thigpen's eyes, just before she said to me in a calm voice,

"Lonny Johnson done told me you killed my boy Buster Thigpen. Ain't no white man gone kill my baby boy." I heard an explosion and then felt as if I'd been kicked in the stomach by Goliath. I was propelled backwards and slammed onto the street by the bullet Josephine Dubois had fired into me. I felt myself being swallowed faster and faster down the gullet of a giant whale as I sank deep into its warm, soft belly.

I could hear distant screams and the sound of footsteps running away. A voice inside my head whispered to me that I'd never hold Hannah in my arms again. As my eyes closed, I felt tears seeping out of them and rolling down my cheeks. I saw Evan Shipman disarm Josephine Dubois. They don't even know each other I thought as the police dragged her away.

Josephine Dubois's long grey hair fell down her back, twisted into a thick plait like a hangman's rope. Hannah was holding my hand and screaming "No, Urby, No!" She stood up to call Evan to my side.

As I lay dying, I thought: Josephine killed me with a perfect gut shot. I wanted to laugh, but stopped myself, knowing I'd end up screaming. My eyelids felt heavier and heavier. When I awoke, I saw Evan mopping his brow. His hand was covered with my blood, making us blood brothers now. They'll take good care of each other, I thought. He put his hand on my forehead as if giving me a blessing and stood up. Hannah knelt and covered my face in kisses, her tears mingling with my own at last. Evan pulled her to her feet and took her away.

The music stopped and the light dimmed again. I heard Hannah's sobs retreating and then Louis Armstrong started playing "Oh! Didn't he Ramble?" I wondered if he was playing it for Stanley or me or both of us. Then the music floated away like a feather blown by the wind.

THE END